A LONG ROAD
HOME

Karl D. Keen

Author's Tranquility Press
COLLEGE PARK, GEORGIA

Karl D. Keen/Author's Tranquility Press
2300 Camp Creek Parkway Ste 120 #1255,
College Park GA 30337, USA
www.authorstranquilitypress.com

Ordering Information:
Quantity sales. Special discounts are available on quantity purchases by corporations, associations, and others. For details, contact the "Special Sales Department" at the address above.

A Long Road Home/Karl D. Keen
Hardback: 978-1-966088-50-9
Paperback: 978-1-966088-51-6
eBook: 978-1-966088-52-3

Contents

A LONG ROAD HOME

Battle Fatigue, Shell Shock, Post-Traumatic Stress Disorder. They all have plagued soldiers since the first battles were ever fought. Men and women react differently to stressful events in their lives. Mike Malloy was like any other American teenager trying to find his place in society until he was drafted and sent to Vietnam. Arriving in a humid war-torn country, he was thrown into battle and forced to kill or be killed. Seeing and caring for men who were severely wounded forced him to grow up long before he was ready.

The brotherhood he developed with Tex Johnson, a black sergeant, helped him through moments of sheer terror followed by days of boredom, which gave him too much time to think about what he was doing and what had happened to him. The accidental killing of civilians bore strongly on his mind. Plagued with horrible nightmares about the war, Mike fought to retain his sanity. This is his story and the events that led him to live on the streets--and to make his journey back via "A Long Road Home."

This book is based on a true story. Names and locations have been changed, and some events have been dramatized for reading enhancement.

Dedicated to

All my great friends at the coffee club who put up with me each morning.

Chapter One

The Vietnam War was in full swing the summer I graduated high school. I'd just turned nineteen and didn't want to be drafted, so I enrolled in college. I only wanted to raise hell and have a good time. I had discovered girls, booze and pot. Like most of the other boys I knew, I wanted to be free for awhile and have some fun.

I had been raised on a small farm just outside Springfield, Missouri, where my father and I milked about thirty head of cows and put up enough hay and feed to get them through the winter. I was a fair athlete in high school, lettering in football, basketball and track. My mother saw to it that I attended church each Sunday.

Why I ever entered ROTC is beyond me. I never wanted to be a soldier; it was just a way to get my college paid for. Now I had screwed that up. I wasn't officer material; hell, I wasn't sergeant material either. But here I am with stripes on my sleeve and an M-16 slung over my shoulder, headed to some damn place I sure don't want to go.

I had been kicked out of college and the ROTC program after two years for smoking pot. So now, with three years left to serve, I'm headed for Da Nang Air Base in wonderful Vietnam. My stomach churned as we circled the base to land. All I could see were hills, jungle, and rice fields full of water.

We got off the plane and fell into formation. The ground was still wet from the last rain and the fog hung around the hilltops like some misty grey curtain. The humidity made me gasp for air, and the pungent smell of jet fuel and burning garbage stung my nostrils. My fatigues instantly were soaked in sweat. I thought to myself, What a lovely place this is going to be.

Some cigar-chomping Colonel came out to inspect us. He took one look at me and took an instant dislike at what he saw. It looked the same from my position; I sure didn't like the looks of that stuffed-shirt SOB. Only thing was, he could do something about his dislike.

He soon called a meeting of all non-coms. After a brief look at our records he started assigning us to duty. Guess who got put in charge of garbage, latrine and base clean-up? Just the thought of burning half barrels of human shit soured my mind and stomach on this fucking place. And to make it worse, my help was every screwed-up misfit who had ever come to Da Nang. Only good thing about it was all the cold beer we could drink, that is if you knew the right people. I soon learned who they were.

I didn't push my men as long as they went through the motions of working and got the main places cleaned up each day. After awhile it was like heaven! No one bothered me; I stayed out of the main flow of things, and kept as low a profile as possible.

Except heaven didn't last very long.

One rainy morning I was told to get my battle gear, check my weapons and meet at the helicopter pad in one hour. We were flown to a dugout base called Ben Wa. It was little more than a bunch of pits covered with logs and sandbags with plastic over them to keep out the rain. The damn mud clung to your boots, almost sucking them off your feet. We weren't given time to get settled. On the first day there, we were sent out on patrol. The fog hung down over the rice patties and hovered about three feet off the ground, making it damn hard to see. There were twelve of us scattered out along the dikes that kept the water in the rice paddies. I sure hoped to hell someone knew where we were going and what we were looking for.

Trudging along, thinking about the girls back home as I followed the guy in front of me, we were spaced about ten yards apart, me being the second man back on the right side. We had gone only about a mile from the base when the stillness was shattered by a loud crack. The man in front of me let out a half-moaning sound as he went down. I dove in behind the dike, losing my helmet on the way. Like a damn fool I reached for it as several rounds splashed mud and water in my face, striking inches from my head.

Over the yelling and screaming of the men, I could hear the crack- crack sound of AK-47s mixed with the pop-pop-popping sounds from our M-16s. Pulling my helmet down tight as fear engulfed my whole body, I tried to crawl inside of it. I lay there afraid to look up. Raising the 16 up over the dike without looking, I emptied a clip as fast as I could. Ducking back down, I lay there with the sick bile taste of fear in my throat. I could hear my heart pounding against my chest as I lay there trying to bury myself in the water while listening to the firefight and the constant yelling and moaning of the men mixed with rifle fire and grenade explosions. Our medic was busy everywhere trying to help the wounded.

I shoved another full clip of ammo into the 16 and with trembling fingers pulled a grenade from my vest, yanked the pin and threw it out as far as I could. It made a whooshing sound as it exploded in the water. Slowly I rose up and fired. This time I had a target--two North Vietnamese Army regulars were just getting up from the grenade blast. I could see rice stems and vegetation stuffed into their pit helmets and tied to their clothing. They looked small and childish as their bodies were hurled backwards in slow motion from the 223 rounds striking them high in the chest. I took a quick look both left and right, praying for God to save me as I sprayed the rest of the clip. Ducking back down behind the dike, I kept praying as I fumbled and shook. Jamming another clip into the 16, I looked around for the other men.

My mouth was so dry I couldn't swallow and my hands were shaking so badly I could hardly hold onto my weapon. I could see the medic working on someone and another lying close by. My mind was going in circles. Who got hit? Were they killed? How many are out there? Everything happened so fast I even wondered if we had fired on our own troops. The damn fog was thick and the acrid smell of gun powder still hung in the air.

Things were quiet now except for the moaning of the wounded. Off in the distance I could hear the lonesome popping sound of a helicopter and the muted bawling of a water buffalo. There was a stale, moldy death smell about this place, an odor different from any I had ever encountered. It was another world, like a bad dream late at night. I was lost in silence as I listened to my own heart beating. I swallowed the bile that kept building in my throat.

Someone rose up along the dike. I lay there watching him as another man stood up. I expected to see them blown down but nothing came. I was still too afraid to even look up. What if a soldier was lying out there with his weapon trained on the spot I was last seen. I crawled about ten yards through the muddy leech-infested water until I came to the corner of the dike. Slowly I rose up, took a quick look, then ducked back. Crawling about halfway back to where I had been before, I stood up ready to fire but everything was quiet.

We slowly worked our way around the banks to where the attack had come from. We found seven enemy soldiers lying in the rice paddy; the water was turning red all around them. No one checked to see if they were alive, we just made sure they were dead.

Three of our men were down, one with a bad head wound. I had the radio man call a medivac. Within minutes a rescue chopper was hovering overhead. The pilot was damn good. He set the chopper down on a dike that wasn't four feet wide, with the skids sticking out over each pond. We half drug, half carried the limp, wet bodies of the three wounded men and loaded them aboard the chopper along with our medic.

I fought the sickness that was building up inside me as I stood there cold, scared and wet, not wanting to make eye contact with those around me. I knew I'd had enough of this damn war for one day; hell, I'd had enough for a lifetime. I felt tired and old as we walked the mile or so back to the base, each of us lost in his own thoughts, thanking our maker that we were still alive.

I knew I would have to spend the next four hours making out reports. I wish someone had these damn sergeant stripes shoved up their ass. I don't want to be in charge of anything; I just want to go home and forget this place ever existed.

I never knew the real names of two of the men who were wounded. One they just called "Cherry," a name that was always hung on the new kid; the other soldier was called "Arkie." Thompson was the most seriously wounded of the three; we had shipped over on the same plane. He was from someplace on the northwest coast, either Washington or Oregon, one of those places where it rains a lot and all those damn big trees grow.

I was mentally exhausted when we got back to the base, my nerves were shot, and I wanted a good stiff shot of booze or a long tote on a joint. Walking over to the mess tent, I wasn't hungry but I did want a cup of coffee, even as bad as the damn army stuff tasted. I sat down and started to shake. It wasn't cold out, so it must have been my nerves. The coffee tasted like it had been boiled in an old rusty bucket. Cookie took one look at me and brought over a glass of orange juice and set it down. I took a sip trying to get rid of the coffee taste. Hell, it was half booze! Where he got it I didn't know and didn't ask.

The shot of booze was just what I needed. I drank the terrible-tasting coffee and walked over to HQ. I got a sheet of paper, sat in a corner and wrote out a brief report. They had sent another chopper out to retrieve the bodies. I don't think this was a planned ambush; we just happened to walk upon those men before they could hide. One of them panicked and the fight was on. It cost seven men their lives and aged me a few years.

That was my first time in combat. I had killed at least two of those men, reacting out of fear and training. I would get a medal for it. Shutting my eyes I could see their bullet-riddled bloody bodies lying there half- submerged in the muddy waters of the rice paddy, their glazed eyes fixed on nothing. I tried to shake it off and not let it bother me, but I kept wondering, who were they and did they have families? Who would notify their next of kin? Thinking about this kind of shit will drive you bonkers. We would give their bodies back through some diplomatic channels. Hell, if we can do it with the dead, why can't we just stop all of this madness and send the living back home? I soon realized that you don't want to think about this stuff or they will ship you back in a straight jacket. I was having a hard time sleeping in this humid bug-infested place so I just walked around the base in the dark. One evening I met a black sergeant from our outfit by the name of Tex Johnson from Austin, Texas. This was Tex's third tour in Nam. Said he loves this damn army life. Hell, he said it was safer here than it was on the streets where he lived.

It wasn't long before Tex introduced me to some buddies of his from another outfit. We sat and smoked all night; that Nam pot really had a kick to it. We were all so stoned by morning it was a wonder we even found the mess tent. I can't recall what we ate, but we put a lot of it away. That damn Asian weed really stimulates your appetite.

After a couple weeks of beer and smoking we were sent out on another patrol. Search and destroy were the orders. We took enough rations for three days. I sure didn't feel like eating those damn field rats, but guessed I'd get hungry enough before we got back.

The Huey dropped us off near some godforsaken jungle with rice paddies in front and no cover behind. We jumped from the chopper into the water. It wasn't raining but the damn army always finds some way to get your ass wet. We hid in the short rice until we knew we weren't going to get our balls shot off. I hated this damn wet place. To make matters worse, the rain came down in sheets blown by the wind and then turned into a steady downpour.

There were twenty-four of us with some hot-shot lieutenant in charge. I was the second in command, followed by Tex and one other sergeant who was a medic. I believe his name was Clayton, but we just called him "Doc." We lined up about ten yards apart and started into the bush one man behind the next. Tex Johnson and I were on point. I was so damn scared that my teeth were chattering, but Tex was into this shit. I just followed him hoping to move farther back when the going got tough. No one ever wants to be up front, not in this thick, brushy, booby-trapped, leech-infested damn jungle.

We had gone about five miles into the brush when we came to a hacked-out trail. The lieutenant called a halt and told us we would stay here for the night to build some fortification and make ourselves comfortable. We were to stay spread out with no fires or smoking and keep all talking to a minimum. He figured the VC would come through here after dark. We were to let them pass, then ambush their patrol from behind.

Tex and I sat together under a large leaf plant of some kind with our ponchos pulled tightly around us trying to keep out the rain. Most of the men put on condoms to keep the leeches out of places you don't want them. The blood-sucking little bastards will get into any place that is moist-- especially your mouth, nose and eyes. But they are a real problem if one goes down the end of your dick. You can't piss the little bastards out and it is a real pleasure when Doc tries to get one out with a pair of long, sharp- bladed tweezers or has to flush one out with alcohol and a catheter. The rain seemed to hold them at bay, but you always had a few find you.

We ate from the field rations. I wanted a smoke something awful only I wasn't stupid enough to light one up. You can smell tobacco smoke out here a mile away.

As darkness crept in Tex moved over and we pulled a couple of small logs up in front of us so we could both rest our backs on the same tree. He looked at me and said, "Don't you just love this?"

"Yeah, you bet, especially when I am sitting on a riverbank holding a pole trying to catch a big catfish. Only you can have this damn leech- infested place. I hope one crawls up your ass tonight and Doc has to dig it out with a hooked wire."

He laughed as we checked our weapons and made sure we could reach the grenades that were hanging on our vest. I tightened the neck string on my poncho and pulled my knees up, resting my chin on them. As little rivulets of water trickled down my back, I soon dozed off into a light sleep. I have no idea what woke me but whatever it was, it brought me to full alert.

With my heart beating hard, I sat there frozen, staring into the darkness. All I could hear was the rain hitting my poncho. I could barely hear Tex's heavy breathing and knew he was asleep.

I sat there listening and staring as something moved in front of me--not more than ten feet away stood a dark-clad figure blacker than the surrounding jungle. My heart was pounding so loudly in my chest that I was sure everyone could hear it. I slowly slid the 16 from under my poncho as I stared into the night. Straining my eyes, I could make out the form of a man blended in with the jungle. It was a VC soldier just standing there. Was he looking at me? I used my whole hand to ease the safety off my weapon hoping he wouldn't hear the click, which sounded damn loud from where I sat. The figure just stood there like he was frozen. Did he see or hear something? The rain hitting my poncho sounded like a thousand drummers playing--surely he could hear that.

Was Tex awake? I hoped to God he doesn't move or snore. I plucked a grenade from my vest, pulled the pin and held the hammer down. Still the figure just stood there motionless. Then I realized how damn stupid I was. Hell, I couldn't throw a grenade in this brush--it wouldn't go ten feet before bouncing back into my lap. Laying the 16 against my leg, I tried not to move as I fumbled with the pin until I got it back in place. Sticking the grenade under my leg I moved the 16 up to fire. By then the figure was gone.

Reaching around, I nudged Tex. He tapped me back three times telling me he had seen everything. I looked up and another dark form had taken the place of the first. What should

I do? How many more of them were out there? I reached over and pushed Tex's weapon down signaling him not to shoot. We sat there listening to the rain and watching as sixteen figures crossed in front of us.

I was worried about the men who were all strung out behind me. Had I let the enemy go to save my own ass? Now I might get someone else killed. I couldn't move back to warn them--if I did, I was likely to get shot by one of my own men. I just hoped some idiot didn't make any noise.

Minutes dragged into hours as we waited for daylight. The damn rain kept pouring down. I felt something crawling down my cheek. Was it a damn leach? I hated to take my hand out from under my poncho, but I had to feel. Relieved, I realized there was nothing there but water. My head kept dropping as I tried to sleep but would jump awake as soon as I would doze off. Tex was breathing hard again--that damn guy could sleep through a firefight.

Tex was a man's soldier, a soldier with the raw nerve of being raised on the street. No one pushed Tex. He was his own man, and he knew his job and did it well. He was the kind of person you wanted beside you in a fight. You knew he would always have your back and be with you till the end.

Gradually, morning began to creep in around us as a heavy fog covered the whole jungle. With the light came the chirping of the frogs or some damn insect.

I crawled back until I could find the lieutenant. He had watched the VC go past, telling me that one of the other men was almost stepped on as they moved past. We gathered up our troops and followed their trail until we came to the edge of the rice paddies. There under a large tree the dumb bastards were cooking breakfast right at the edge of the brush. Pulling back, we worked our way around until we had them with the open space to their backs.

Hell, it was like a damn turkey shoot. We mowed them down before they could pick up a weapon. Slowly walking into their camp, we shot anything that moved or made a sound. There were only fourteen bodies; I was sure I had counted sixteen last night. We put two men out on guard as we searched the bodies and waited for the chopper to pick us up.

I stood there looking at some of them. They didn't look like they were even fifteen years old. But even a small child with an AK-47 can kill you. I hadn't been in Nam two months yet and already I had been in two firefights. How long would my luck last?

I heard a slap and the guy next to me went down with blood splattering all over my face and neck. Everyone hit the ground and dug for cover as the cracking sound from an AK-47 rang through the morning fog.

I searched the rice paddies trying to find out where the fire was coming from and not get my damn head shot off. Tex came running past me firing the 16 from his waist. Two other men joined him in the rush and the fight was over. We had found the other two VC, but it had cost us another man.

Chapter Two

The ambush we had set up was over quicker than it started. We had killed sixteen of the enemy and lost only one of our own. I guess that is a pretty good score if you want to keep track of such things. I still feel the senselessness of this war--we are killing and getting killed for people who have never known anything but being ruled by someone stronger. These people wouldn't know what to do if they were free to make their own decisions. This whole form of government they live under is so far removed from democracy that most of them would starve or be killed by the stronger party if they were suddenly given the freedom to make their own rules and decisions.

My thought is we can never force our way of life on another country. If you want freedom, you have to want it, fight for it, and even die for it if necessary. Most of these people just want to be left alone to farm and raise enough food to feed their families. They aren't willing to die for someone else's freedom, nor can they see or even reason why anyone would die to set free someone they don't know.

Unless you have been born or lived in a free country, it is hard to understand the personal restraints that come with being free.

I slowly walked among the bloody and bullet-riddled bodies, pausing long enough to etch each face into my mind. Some of them looked so young, but to me they all looked somewhat alike. They have the jet-black hair like the American Indian, with the Asian eyes and facile features of a race that is still pure.

I guess I am getting hardened to all this. It doesn't seem to bother me like the first time I was involved in it. I shot deer back home in Missouri and helped my father butcher hogs, so death isn't anything new to me. But these were humans, men fighting for a cause they believed in or, maybe like me, fighting because their leaders ordered them to.

I am sure if they had caught us out in the open like that the situation would have been reversed. We called for a pick-up and, as the Hueys came in, we set out a smoke and made clear a landing area. I hated carrying the dead men and loading them into the chopper. It seemed like I always had to take one last look into their glazed-over eyes as I lay them down. We got back to the base and thank God didn't have to help unload the dead.

I walked over to the dugout where my bunk was and lay down. I lay there thinking of how easy it was to kill another person. I felt dirty and sick at the same time. Pulling off all my clothes, I grabbed a towel and my shaving kit and walked across the compound bare-ass naked to the showers. The hot water felt good running down over my tired body. As I relaxed I began to cry, why I have no idea. I guess it was nerves. I stood there and cried for several minutes.

Going back to my quarters I could feel myself shaking and knew it wasn't from the cold. I put on a pair of shorts and a t-shirt, then lay back on my bunk. Every time I shut my eyes the faces of those dead soldiers were staring at me. The blank emptiness of their eyes and the soiled smell of their bodies still lingered in my senses.

I soon gave up on sleeping. Getting up, I dressed into clean ODs and walked over to the mess tent. I didn't have much of an appetite but did want something cold to drink. I bummed a coke from one of the cooks and asked if he had some rum for it. Giving me a dumb look, he said if he had any he would drink it himself. Noticing Tex and a couple of the other black guys at a back table, I walked over and sat down, asking if this poor white trash could join them. A solder we called Slick looked up at me and said, "We don't want to put up with no honkey-ass sergeant tonight unless he got some damn good weed to share with the poor folks." Telling him I was tapped out, I stood up to leave, but he grabbed me by the shoulder and said, "Sit your white ass back down. We done got used to the smell of you by now."

Tex spoke up and said, "Men it is time we put in for a little R and R. I need some of that Saigon pussy and a week of good hard drinking." The five of us walked over to headquarters and requested seven days of rest and relaxation. Coronel Hawkins told us we could have four days starting tomorrow. And if we screwed up in Saigon we would be humping the brush for the next six months, that he was damn tired of getting men out of the brig and that hell-hole they call a jail.

We sat and talked most of the night. Come morning we were at the pad before they ever got the supply chopper preflighted. We offered to help the crewman, but he refused us saying he wanted to get killed naturally, not in a damn crash caused by a bunch of dumb-ass ground ponders. We got aboard and soon were on our way. It took almost two hours to get to Saigon. We made arrangement for our return flight and headed for the first tavern we could find.

All of the bars seemed alike. There was the high piercing music from some stringed instrument with a tenor sound, plus the lonely haunting sound from a flute. The B-girls were all dressed in the short satin skirts that clung to their slender bodies, each with a slit up one side that showed the cheek of their ass whenever they moved. Their almond-shaped black eyes added to their strange but somewhat beautiful appearance. Hell, after three months in the bush the damn water buffalo were starting to entice me.

Tex said "I'll see you later" as he grabbed a couple of beers and disappeared immediately with some girl dressed in a short blue satin skirt that showed her ass. I bet she would have to push it to make fourteen. I had a couple beers and a stick with some kind of meat on it. I just hoped it wasn't dog; somehow eating Lassie just didn't appeal to my appetite. A couple of the B-girls came over and sipped that damn tea we buy for them that is supposed to be a drink. I guess it fools some GIs, but not me. I've tasted it.

We stayed there and had several more beers while playing grab-ass with the girls and waiting for Tex to come back. Knowing him, he may be gone with that little girl all week. I was getting a buzz and that damn goat or whatever I was eating didn't taste that good. Walking over to the bar I got some weed and papers from the barkeep. Sitting back down, the three of us all rolled a joint, sucked it in and let the smoke drift around while our minds went numb to everything except for that haunting sound of the flute and the twanging music of the stringed instrument some old man was playing over in the corner.

All of this young stuff started to look good to me. I reached over and pulled some little thing down on my lap. I kissed her neck and squeezed things I probably shouldn't have as she didn't have much to squeeze. All of these girls have a peculiar smell to them; it must be from the rice diet. It is similar to the smell you get from going into a Chinese restaurant back home. They try and mask it with cheap perfume, but it doesn't help much.

These people are basically a clean race and take pride in their appearance. It is a struggle for most of them to make a living, and with the war going on they have been burned out of their farms or are so scared of the Viet Cong that they feel safe only in the cities.

The effect of the weed was now hitting me along with the dozen or so beers. I wanted to lie down someplace as that damn dog on a stick wanted to leave my stomach by the same path it got there.

I asked the little girl how much to go to her room. "Five dollar," she said. I gave her a ten and we walked around behind the bar and up a couple flights of stairs. The dog made it only up the first flight. I hung over the rail and puked all over everything and everyone below me.

After I got my asshole shoved back down out of my throat, I felt pretty good. I don't remember much about the sex; I guess we had it. The next thing I knew the little gal was shaking me and saying, "Wake up, Joe." At first I couldn't figure out where the hell I was. The room was spiraling around and my stomach felt like that dog had pups in it. Sitting up on the side of the bed, I reached over and pulled the little half-dressed girl over to me. I kissed her stomach and she pushed me away saying, "No more, Joe, you got no more money."

I came to enough to realize she had probably cleaned me out. I looked down to see if I still had my socks on, which I did. We always carried most of our money in our socks. I reached down and felt for the bills I had stuffed alongside my ankle. They were still there. I grabbed her, threw her down on the bed and gave her a rough going over, then got dressed and headed back down to the bar with her shouting cuss words at me as I went out the door.

Mutt, the other black guy, and Slick were still there. I am sure these two had real names but I had never heard them. They were both out of it. Having gotten hold of some hard drugs they were stoned out of existence. Tex finally showed up and we walked across the street to the Saigon Hotel and rented a couple of rooms. We had to make two trips dragging Slick and Mutt up to a bed. We went down to the lobby and then to a little eating place for breakfast, leaving our two stoned friends to sleep it off.

It was now the middle of the morning and Saigon had come to life with bicycles, cars and motorcycles going in every direction. There was so many I couldn't see how they kept from killing each other. But they all seemed to move about in a fast, orderly fashion with only the constant honking of horns and a lot of hollering at each other. We spent the next three hours just walking around the city, getting checked by every MP we came across. I guess it was their job to make sure GIs stayed out of trouble and didn't overstay their passes.

By the time we got back to the room, Slick was sitting with his head in a puke bucket and Mutt was lying in the middle of the bathroom floor naked. When we put him in the tub and turned on the cold water, he came out of it pretty fast. I learned some new words and some things about black people I hadn't known. They don't cuss like white folks. Hell, they can lay out a line of swear words like you never heard. And they like to mention your mommy in most of them.

Tex asked them what they had gotten a hold of. Slick said they had some poppy juice, which was damn good shit. "Yeah," I said, "as fucked up as you two are it must have been rat poison." I guess one of the bar girls had introduced them to black tar heroin; Slick still had a ball of it rolled up in aluminum foil. "Man," he said, "it will make you feel so damn good that sex doesn't even compare to the feeling you get from this shit. Get a little of this in your blood and you couldn't give a shit if this whole damn world blows up into one big ball of fire. Man, you don't feel nothing. All of your pain and memories are gone away; it is just you and the music of life. Only thing is it sure leaves you with one bitch of a hangover. My head is throbbing like a sick robin's ass."

Slick called down to the lobby and had a large pitcher of cold beer sent up. After a couple of glasses of suds, we all slept.

The sounds of nightlife finally brought us awake. We showered, changed into clean uniforms and hit the street. The guys were hungry so we hunted up a place to eat. I had some more dogs on a stick--I could get to like that stuff. I wondered if lab and collie taste anything like poodle.

These people eat rice with everything, sort of like we do potatoes. Most of it is a long-grain brown rice. I am still not sure about the meat. Hell, it could be rat at far as I know. Little fat pigs are everywhere so I think most of their meat is pork or some water buffalo that drowned in a rice field.

We walked around after dinner to let the meal settle before doing some serious drinking. Everyone agreed to go back to the hotel bar so we wouldn't have any hassle getting back to our rooms. Things were pretty quiet in the bar, but it was early yet. There was some good-looking singer that had on a long red silk dress filled out in all the right places, her long black shiny hair added to the color scheme. She was trying to do a Patsy Cline song but couldn't get all the words right. After a couple of beers we just looked at her body as she twisted around. To hell with the music--she could ride me anytime.

Slick talked us into going back up to the room so he could fix us a shot of poppy juice. I had heard all about heroin and wasn't really sold on the idea. That damn stuff will mess you up for life. He cooked up a spoonful and sucked it into a syringe, giving Mutt the first shot. Tex tried the next one and I shot myself with a little of what he left. I didn't feel much after that.

We went back to the bar and danced with some of the B-girls. The three guys all went off with women, leaving me sitting there alone enjoying the music. Anyway, I think that was what I was doing. I couldn't keep my eyes off the singer and one of her band members didn't like me talking to her as she sang.

When they took a break, I walked over to her and asked if I could buy her a drink. She smiled and said; "Okay, Joe." She spoke pretty good English, and I found out later she was born in San Francisco and that her father worked for the government. We were getting pretty chummy when her damn boyfriend came over, grabbed her by the arm and pulled her up from the chair, saying something to me in Vietnamese. Normally I would have knocked his damn ears off, but the heroin and beer was working good. I was in such a pleasant mood that nothing could anger me; I just laughed at him and threw her a kiss as they walked away.

The music started playing and I just sat back and listened to it echo through my stoned-out mind. At times it sounded like I was in a tunnel or far away from it. Tex finally came back grinning from ear to ear and still had the same little girl hanging onto him. They tried to dance, but he was so stoned all he could do was hang onto her and try to keep from falling.

We never saw the other two that night, so I have no idea where they ended up. I hoped it wasn't in some dark alley with their throats cut. This was a bad place at night. The VC came to town for fun and games, killing Americans wherever they can. More than one man died in the dark alleys and back rooms of this place where they had been lured by some half-naked little bar girl that in all actuality was a Viet Cong soldier.

The MPs were thick and tried to keep an eye on everyone, but they knew better than to go into some of the back-alley places. Drugs of all kinds were as plentiful as candy is at a local market. They tried to keep all the heavily intoxicated men picked up and stopped most of the loners who were wandering around looking for trouble. That's why I liked to drink in a hotel bar where I didn't have to go out on the street with a snoot full. I always chose a table away from any door or window as they will ride by on a motorcycle and throw a satchel charge into a bar.

If you wanted anything the barkeeper could get it for you. Prostitutes kept a steady parade of their wares coming and going all night. And as the night wore on, the price comes down as quickly as their panties. A lot of the men got more than they paid for and suffered the effects the rest of their lives. The thought of this kept me pretty leery of most of them.

Tex had disappeared again and I was worn out, so I finished my beer and staggered up to my room. I never heard anyone come in, but when I woke up everyone was sprawled out on a bed snoring. I got up, took a quick shower and walked down to the now empty bar and had a cup of the worst coffee I ever tried to drink. I ordered a shot of booze and poured it into the cup. Now it tasted like rotten coffee with rotten booze. I sat there and sipped that half-cold junk for over an hour thinking about what I was doing over here. I had nothing against these people except the ones who were trying to kill me.

I had learned a lot about being a soldier and surviving while I was in the ROTC program at South West Missouri State. I might even have made a good officer; I knew people and could recognize a man's good and bad points quickly. I knew how to get along with people and could discipline a person and still leave them with their self-respect and feeling good about themselves. This is something many of these damn college boys never learn. They have been yelled at and scolded by their fathers until that was the only way they knew how to treat someone.

We had one more night on the town before we were to fly back to the "palace," as we called it. I hated the thought of going back into the bush with all the damn rain and leeches. I was never too fond of getting my ass wet unless it was in a nice hot shower. I still had nine more months to serve over here. I just pray I can stay alive and keep all my arms and legs. I have thought about shooting myself in the foot but know I can't get away with it.

I don't figure I am any better than anyone else so I will do my time like I believe everyone should. Most of these men over here are guys who are too dumb or else couldn't afford to go to college. It is definitely a poor man's war.

Chapter Three

The last night in Saigon was one I can't remember much about. We were all stoned on poppy juice before we hit the bar. I was determined to lay that little singer tonight or get my ass kicked by her boyfriend. We had packed our bags so that we would be ready to go in the morning. All we had to do was survive the night and be at the airport by ten.

Tex took off with the same little girl as soon as she showed up. Slick and Mutt went across the street to some other joint. Me, I just ordered a cold beer and got as close to the stage as I could. When the singer showed up and reached over and gave me a kiss, I knew then that this night was going to get exciting. I had taken only a light hit on the heroin (that shit will kill you) because I wanted to remember what I was doing. The little girl in the red dress was really in tune tonight--her songs rang out loud and clear.

I must have gone through ten beers before she took a break and came by my table. I reached over and pulled her down on my lap. She laughed and gave me a big kiss. The next thing I know I am on the floor with some bastard kicking me. I blocked the next kick with my shoulder and came up with a bamboo chair that I drove down over the little slant-eyed bastard's head. They never called me "Mean Mike Malloy" in college for nothing. I grabbed him by the shirt and head-butted him in the nose. He spurted blood as red as any American. Before I could hit him again, two of the biggest damn MPs I have ever seen had me in a head and body lock and were dragging me toward the door. I still had a lot of fight in me so I kneed one in the groin, spun loose and caught the other big bastard with an overhead right that shook me clear to my shoulders. He just shook his head and kept coming. I caught him with my best left hook and half turned him around. By then the other one was up and coming at me with a nightstick. He landed a good swing against the side of my head and I knew then that my fun and idea of romance for the evening was over.

I tried to talk my way out of it, but they said I should have thought about this before I started fighting. One of them laughed and said: "We love fighting you tough boys," and tossed my big badass into the back of a paddy wagon where I was greeted by Slick and a half dozen other drunken soldiers.

At the brig I explained to the sergeant that we had a flight out at ten in the morning. He lay his hand on my shoulder and said, "Be a good boy and sleep it off and I will see that you are there on time."

The damn brig sergeant's word was about as good as confederate money. Hell, it was almost noon when I woke up and everyone else in the place was still asleep. Even the guards were sacked out. I started hollering, which brought a string of cuss words from everyone around. I screamed at the sergeant that I was supposed to be on a plane at ten. He just laughed and said, "Soldier boy, you shouldn't have gotten your ass thrown in here if you needed to be someplace else."

About four o'clock the MPs came and took me and Slick to get our gear from the hotel and then to the airport. We sat on our asses all night waiting for a ride back to Ben Wa.

Coronel Hawkins wasn't a damn bit impressed by my story as to why I was a day and a half AWOL. The veins stood out on his red scrubby neck as he screamed and said, "Malloy, I told you what I would do to your sorry ass if you got in trouble. You will never get another R&R day while I'm in command here. If you ever get another piece of ass it will be from humping some damn water buffalo. Now get the hell out of my sight and get your ass ready to hit the bush. And I don't mean the one between some gal's legs. I promised you what would happen if you got arrested." He ranted on about how this made the whole outfit look, as if I really gave a shit. Hell, I just wished he would shut up.

Slick stood there weaving back and forth. I thought once he was going to fall across the old man's desk and land in his lap. He was feeling the pain of the poppy juice and needed a fix in the worst way.

After the Coronel got through with his fit, he said to get our gear and get ready to hit the brush, and he didn't want to see our sorry asses for a month. I sure didn't need this shit; I needed about twenty hours of sleep and a shot of booze, which I was about as likely to get as I was that little singer in Saigon who caused all my pain and misery.

The damn rain kept on falling and I knew it was going to be another lovely wet-ass experience out in that leech-infested jungle with some Vietnamese asshole trying to shoot my frigging head off.

Slick and I walked back to the hooch where we slept and packed our gear. He took some tar heroin out of his pocket and cooked up a syringe full. He injected most of it and gave the rest to me. It gave me enough of a buzz that I could care less about where we were heading. We got aboard the chopper with ten other men, Tex and Mutt included.

We had some new Lieutenant who was just out of the academy. I knew from the start this was going to be a disaster for someone.

Slick was asleep before the chopper ever left the ground. Tex took one look at him and grabbed me by the sleeve. Shaking me, he said, "What in the hell are you two on?"

I just looked at him and grinned. Pushing me back, he muttered, "Shit, this is just what we need, two stoned motherfuckers in a firefight. You stupid bastards will get your asses shot off before you ever get out of the Huey. I should have both of you thrown in the damn stockade. You better snap shit when we land or the Lieutenant will really have your ass. Lucky for you he decided to fly up front. Damn it, Malloy, sometimes you just try to fuck up."

I don't know how long we were in the air, but when we landed it was in some rice paddy surrounded by thatch huts. We were relieving another squad that was glad to be headed for warm food and hot showers.

Slick and I slept while the new Lieutenant wasted an hour talking with the squad leader and went over maps of the area. I wish I had paid attention. Hell, I knew we were lost before we ever left the landing zone. The rain had washed out the fog to where visibility was probably more than a mile. I could see some jungle-covered hills in the distance and knew immediately that was where we were headed. For some damn reason the army never likes to walk or fight on flat ground. It's always in some wet-ass rice paddy with no cover or else in the damn jungle with the fucking brush so thick you can't see the end of your dick.

The new Lieutenant was like a scared rabbit. He clung as close to Tex as I did, knowing that he was probably the only one who had any idea where we were or where we were heading. Slick was dragging along behind us and I knew I should go help him; if we got hit he would get his ass shot off for sure. We had a bunch of new guys with us and they were all pissing their pants with every step they took, each one trying to hide behind the guy in front of him. I kept trying to get them to spread out or at least back off from each other; this was a disaster just waiting to happen.

Tex looked back at me and just shook his head. Now I got worried-- when something bothered Tex it had to be bad and Tex was as nervous as I had ever seen him. His black eyes darted from one side of the trail to the other with each cautious step he took. I worked my arms free from the cover of the poncho and checked the load in my weapon. I had four grenades and six clips, not much killing power for a long fight.

We had just gotten inside the tree line when they opened up on us. The new Lieutenant never knew what hit him. He was blown backwards bouncing off one of the new guys as they both went down. Tex was down on one knee firing the M-60 and trying to get out of his poncho at the same time. I came up beside him letting loose a long burst on full auto, not knowing where or at what I was shooting.

The fight was over as quickly as it had started. We had four men down. The Lieutenant was dead, two of the new men were hit and Slick was all shot to hell. He must have stayed standing until he couldn't catch anymore. I cursed myself for not watching him; I knew he wasn't in any shape to be with us. The medic was working on him with all the skills he had. The new guys just stood there wide-eyed and staring like they didn't think any of this shit was for real. I screamed and told them to take a good look. "This is what happens when you come out here all fucked up and don't pay attention. You little fuckers better quit playing with your dicks and learn that this place will get you killed."

I called in our position and asked for a medivac. Tex took two men and scouted the area. We never saw anyone; they hit us quickly and disappeared. We dragged the dead and wounded about fifty yards to a small clearing and set out a smoke. Everyone spread out and took cover while we waited for the chopper.

The rescue unit came in low over the trees accompanied by two Cobra gunships. They searched the area flying back and forth over us while we loaded the dead and wounded. I took one last look at the Lieutenant and thought what a waste. He had spent four years in the academy and wasn't in this country long enough to get his uniform dirty. I reached over and squeezed Slick's arm and told him to hang in there.

Then they were gone, just a black dot moving out over the trees. The two gunships made one low pass over us, the door gunners giving us thumbs up, and they, too, were over the ridge and out of sight. The popping sound of their rotors was just an echo in our ears as we stood there, eight scared men, wet, cold and hungry.

I looked at Tex and said, "I guess you're it. Which way do we go?" He pointed to my sleeve and said, "White boy, you got one rocker on your sleeve that ain't on mine. You are the boss man now." I just gave a quick smile and turned toward the other men.

We stood there with the rain dripping off our ponchos looking at each other. It was then I realized I knew only two of the eight men with me. I never listened for names so I asked the new kid where he was from. "Georgia," he said. From that minute on he became Georgia Boy, whether he liked it or not.

The rescue unit had left us a couple cases of field rations and four cans of ammo. I told Mutt and Red, another new kid, to grab the ammo can and for the rest to stuff as many field ration packets into their packs as they could carry.

Tex asked where we were headed. There was a small hill about twenty clicks from us with an old abandoned thatch hut at the base of the hill. I told him, "It's time we found a dry spot. With only eight men we can't do much and I'm not going to look for trouble or call for reinforcement until I have to."

We found the old hut before dark. It hadn't been burned and most of the roof was still intact. The damn rain was pouring down in sheets and it looked like it would all night. We scraped together all the old thatch bedding that was dry and made a nest against the back wall. I kept one man on guard while the rest of us sacked out. It was dark when the guard kicked my boot and said, "Sarge, can one of the other men relieve me? I can't stay awake much longer." He helped me rig a trip wire about fifty yards from the hut and we stacked some bamboo poles in a pile so they would fall and wake us if the wire was hit.

I didn't figure anyone would be out moving in a rain like this, but to be safe I made an exit door in the back of the hut and checked out a place to run in case we were found.

Tex came over and sat beside me as everyone sacked out for the night. He sat there in silence for a long time. Speaking in that slow Texas draw, he said, "Malloy, this is my third trip over here. I have never been scared until today. I had a premonition that the new Lieutenant wouldn't make it through the first fight. It was like I was seeing into the future. I want out of this mess; I want to go home to sunny days, good smelling girls, horses and laughter. I've got two Bronze Stars, two Purple Hearts and more damn campaign ribbons than I can pin on my shirt. I ain't no damn hero. I came back because I'm good at what I do and I think I have kept a lot of boys alive with my experience. At night I wake up sweating and shaking. I dream about being home, walking across paved streets with people hollering and waving to me from fancy cars and trucks. Then it is like someone pulls a black curtain in front of me. I can hear people crying and calling out my name. Malloy, I believe my ticket has been punched! I'll never get out of this damn jungle alive." He sat back as a tear ran down his cheek. Seeing him cry scared the hell out of me.

Listening to him made my hair stand up and a lump came into my throat so big I couldn't speak. When I tried all that came out was a little moan. I reached out and touched his leg. He placed his large hand on mine and gave it a squeeze, then moved back over against the wall. It was so dark all I could see was his large form lying there.

I was really shaken; you just didn't expect something like that from a man of Tex's caliber. I lay back listening to the rain run off the thatch roof, shut my eyes and tried to sleep. Each time I would doze off I would wake up with a start. Everyone around me seemed to be sleeping soundly. My mind turned to home, back to the little town in Missouri where I grew up. I played football and basketball in high school. Being small during my senior year I was intimidated by the older kids, but I hid it by being stubborn and aggressive. I never really had many girlfriends in school--not having a car made it hard to date anyone and most activities around town were either church or school events. But there was one girl named Sarah who was still on my mind.

It was light when I woke up; everyone else was still asleep. Slowly I stretched out my tired muscles and got to my feet. The damn rain was still pouring down as I slipped on my poncho and crept slowly from the hut. I made a round circle into the bush and up a little trail that led to a toilet fashioned under a crude thatch roof that had been hung in a small tree. I moved on up the trail several hundred feet and hid in a clump of bamboo. I sat there listening to the rain falling around me thinking, here I am not even twenty-one, yet half a world away from where I would love to be. I thought about my Mom and Dad, wondering what they were doing. I know Mom is worrying if I am safe and why I don't write. The people back home have no idea what it's like over here--most of my friends are married and working or else going to school, enjoying life, not caring that men are dying. Dying for what? I really don't have a clue as to why we're here except that some damn politician sent us.

Catching a movement on the trail, I leaned back farther into the clump of leaves, watching the spot for several minutes. I caught the shape of someone coming slowly up the hill. I could tell it was Tex by his size and movement. As he came by, I said, "Bang. Your black ass is shot full of holes." He laughed and said, "Hell, Malloy, I could see your lily-white ass shining clear back to the hut. The only way you could hide out here is if this damn place was covered with snow, and that ain't likely."

He said, "I heard you get up and figured I better come out and check on you before you got your ass lost out here in these woods. The reason I made any noise at all was in case you were out here choking your chicken. I didn't want to embarrass you, but I doubt if you could even find that little white thing unless you got a big fat leech latched onto it. How do you white boys aim those little peckers when you only have enough to hold in one hand or with two fingers like in your case. Those little girls in Saigon done told me all about you short-peckered white boys. They say they can never tell if you do anything with them or not."

He grinned, showing a mouth full of perfectly aligned white teeth. I explained to him that it was all in how you use what you are given. It's not how you cut the cake but the way you lick the frosting. Laughing, he said, "Man, if you was hung like one of us black men you would faint from lack of blood going to your brain every time you got a hard-on."

We both smiled and changed the subject. "What are we going to do?" he asked. I said, "I believe we will sit tight and rest our worn-out asses for a few days until the grub runs out or some stupid gook tries to chase us off. I'll call the old man on the radio and give him our location just in case we get our tit in a wringer. I will make up some story about checking out some suspicious activity over the hill so he won't send us someplace else. We should put out a guard farther up the trail, especially during the daylight hours. Go back and send Georgia Boy and one of the new men up to help me. I'll scout up the hill a little farther. And tell the trigger-happy bastards not to shoot my balls off when they come up."

At the top of the hill I found an old landing zone. The hilltop had been blown clear and most of the brush around three sides had been clipped clean. Logs and trenches were placed around the sides. It looked like this hill had been defended before. Finding a dry bunker, I crawled inside and removed my poncho. Digging through my wet maps I found our position. This was hill 739.

Hearing noise I crawled out of the bunker, scaring the hell out of Georgia Boy and a new kid he called Snake. I looked at the new man and could see where his name comes from--he was tall and skinny as a snake and had the facial features of a pit viper. We walked around the area and found an old machine-gun bunker that was dry and overlooked the back side of the hill. I left the men there, telling them I would send a relief in four hours and if they see anything moving for one of them to come for us. If it looked like things were going to heat up for both of them, to get their asses out of there.

Going back to the hut, I called the old man on the talker, telling him our location and asked for a flyover as we had seen some movement in the valley. This was all a lie but, hell, the damn colonel didn't know it. I also asked for a water drop and four more men to replace those we lost. I needed a man with a grenade launcher in the worst way. He told me to sit tight, that help was on the way. I had barely gotten off the radio when two A-1 sky raiders screamed in from the south, banking hard over us as they swept across the valley, then rolled over and came back along the side of the hill laying a wall of napalm about a half mile long.

This scared the shit out of me as I figured they had hit Georgia Boy and Snake. My worries didn't last long for the two of them came streaking down the trail like a damn tiger was on their ass. My guts churned with the fear that the planes had seen something we didn't. I told Tex to take three men and scout the left side. I would take the others and go back to the top. We left everything but our water and ammo and shagged ass out of there, going back up the trail in record time. Once on top I set the men up, telling them not to shoot Tex and the others as they come around below us.

The damn rain didn't seem to let up at all, the mud was getting stirred up and sticking to our boots. Most of the trenches had a half foot of water in them but it was better to slosh along than to expose your ass to the enemy.

It seemed like it took forever for Tex and the others to come around the hill. I glassed the burned-over area where the napalm had been dumped and couldn't see anything. Tex came up over the back of the hill and reported everything was clear. "Hell," he said, "I think those damn flyboys were just having some fun and putting on a show for us. I looked at Tex and smiled, saying,

"It's about time we had some damn fun, maybe get some more R and R and even a medal for everyone."

"Malloy, just what in the hell are you planning?" he asked.

"Just watch and see. We're about to win one hell of a firefight and get the hell off this hill and maybe earn another trip to Saigon. Have everyone load and lock and, on my signal, each throw a grenade and empty a clip."

"Don't do it, Malloy. You will get all of our asses thrown in the damn brig for the rest of this war."

I called the command center and as soon as they answered I dropped the mike and started screaming and firing my weapon. Everyone cut loose and the damn noise was deafening. I kept yelling into the phone, not making sense to what I was saying. I was General George Patton directing fire from every direction. The old man was on the phone screaming in my ear. "Malloy, what in the hell is going on up there?" I lay the radio down, grabbing it long enough to call for ammo, then shooting a new burst before letting go of the transmitter button.

Everything got quiet as we listened to the old man scream into the radio. "Do you need reinforcement up there?" I shut off the mike and asked the men if we needed reinforcement. Tex said, "Like hell, no. All eight of us just kicked the shit out of the whole North Vietnamese Army." We laughed and then I screamed, "Hold on" and shot another half clip with the transmitter wide open.

I gave the old man the numbers and had artillery blow the shit out of the hill across from us. Those damn cannon jockeys were pretty good--they missed us by two hundred yards and blew that hillside to shreds. I had the men keep firing a few rounds as I talked to the Colonel.

"We got hit hard by a patrol but have fought through it without any casualties," I reported. "We're low on men, ammo and beer," I added.

"Can do on two of those," the old man said.

About that time two Cobra gunships came roaring over us with guns blazing. "Be careful they don't hit us," I warned the men. We watched as they sprayed fire into every nook and cranny on that hillside. Coming low over us we gave them a thumbs-up. Returning the gesture, they circled behind the hill and disappeared. Then it was the Navy's turn as two jets about took our heads off when they came screaming in over us. Rolling and climbing into a tight turn they went up the canyon between the hills and we heard a couple of rockets blow something up. They wiggled a wing as they flew back over and were gone.

I sat the men down and told them if one damn word of this gets out we will all be doing time in Leavenworth, Kansas, or some place worse. Hell, it was fun and relieved a lot of stress, which probably cost the taxpayers only a few hundred thousand. We can just call it a training mission.

It wasn't long before a dozen helicopters came into the landing zone. Men were unloading faster than I could count. More Cobra gunships kept circling and firing. Hell, it looked like the old man had sent out a whole damn regiment. More jets were screaming in low overhead and blowing hell out of the backside of the hill. The new Lieutenant wanted to be briefed on the situation, so as we walked over toward the hut, I told him we had been hit by a force of twenty-five to thirty men. And the firefight didn't last long as we held the high ground.

We didn't search for enemy casualties and didn't have time to observe much as the rain kept visibility to only a few hundred yards. It was then I noticed it had quit raining. I thought, this is just great. I now had half the base out into the field and not a one of them is going to get his ass wet after we just spent a week getting ours soaked. The Lieutenant told me and the men to grab our gear and get aboard the chopper as the old man wanted us back in for a debriefing.

I looked at Tex and said, "We better give the boys a good story to tell." "Hell," he laughed. "Let them make up their own. We might all get the

Silver Star for this."

I shook my head and told him I didn't want it pinned to my ass. "It is like the army to take a little fun and blow it up into a full-scale battle. After the old man gets done telling headquarters about his part in this, he will probably get a promotion. After all, he was on the phone directing the firefight. We couldn't have survived it without him, so we all want to thank him for his moral support and expert guidance in a time of real pandemonium. Just having him on the phone was like he was standing shoulder to shoulder with me guiding each shot. I could have panicked without him and gotten someone hurt."

Slapping me on the back, Tex said, "Malloy, if everyone in this world was as full of shit as you are, it would be a smelly place."

Chapter Four

On the flight back I told the men to tell the old man whatever they wanted, just as long as it wasn't the truth. I knew in my mind I would never get away with this, but maybe they would give me a section eight (which is a nut case) and ship me home. I could always claim battle fatigue.

The old man met us on the chopper pad and saluted us as we crawled from the Huey. He told Tex and me to grab a hot shower and be in his office in fifteen minutes. Tex looked at me as we walked toward the hooch. He said, "I don't like the feel of this shit, Malloy."

"Don't worry, I gave the orders for the whole thing," I replied.

The shower felt good, but the walk to the old man's office was full of apprehension; we could hear the big guns still firing and the sky was full of gunships heading out.

Colonel Hawkins met us at the door, slapped me and Tex on the back and told us to take a chair. He gave each of us a cigar, lit up, then sat back and let the blue smoke rise as he looked at me and said, "Malloy, when you got here I took one look at you and decided you were the biggest fuck-off I had ever seen in this man's army. But let me tell you, what you and your men did today was one of the bravest things I have ever been involved in. For eight lightly armed men to engage a force that size takes balls as big as coconuts. You saved this base from getting overrun and probably all of us from getting killed."

I looked at Tex, who had turned a sick gray color. I didn't know if it was from the cigar or the Colonel's speech.

"You men, through your bravery and bulldog determination to stay and fight, stopped the enemy, giving us time to head off one of the largest attacks ever aimed at this area.

"There are more than four hundred North Vietnamese Army regulars pinned down across from hill 739. And Malloy, if it hadn't been for you and your men searching them out and engaging in battle, we would have been overrun tonight. That was the fiercest firefight I ever listened to. Man, you should have stayed in officer's school. I am putting all eight of you men in for a promotion and a Bronze Star, and recommending you and Johnson for a Silver Star."

My stomach churned, and I don't think it was from the cigar.

However, my Missouri blood clicked in about that time. I looked at Tex sitting there with his big mouth open looking like he was going to puke. I said, "Colonel, you don't know how encouraging it was to hear your voice on the radio. I was scared shitless and your suggestions and guidance helped calm me down and kept us fighting. I could never have directed those men and kept them from panic if it hadn't been for you reassuring me that help was on the way."

Tex picked that time to get choked on his cigar and made a run for the door gagging and puking. Colonel Hawkins sat straight up in his chair, looked in the direction that Tex had run, reached over and knocked the ashes from his cigar saying, "I don't believe that boy appreciates a good smoke." I laughed and said, "We don't often get a good cigar out here in the brush, sir."

He told me to write out my battle report and, if I cared to, I could mention the help that he gave us. I assured him it would all be written out just like it happened. Standing up, I saluted and asked if he wanted to talk to the other men. He assured me that he didn't find that necessary, but for me to give all of them his appreciation of a job well done. He saluted me and said, "Malloy, keep up the good work. You will go far in this man's army."

Tex was still bent over the trash can coughing when I came out. He stood up, looked at me with tears in his eyes and burst out laughing. "Malloy," he said, "you should become a damn politician. Anyone who can spread bullshit under pressure like you just did is wasting his time killing dinks."

The thunderous explosions from the big guns could still be heard and the red glow of napalm from hill 739 lit the sky. The damn rain had started again as we walked back to the hooch. Tex said, "Man, you are one lucky mother that the dinks showed up when they did or else your white ass would still be in there explaining your so-called training mission."

As we came into the dugout everyone gathered around, wanting to know what went on with the Colonel. Tex sat down on his cot and said,

"You men ain't about to believe this shit. There was a whole damn dink army on the other side of that hill. Our reinforcements now have them pinned down and, thanks to us, they are flat-kicking some gook ass. The old man is putting each of us in for another stripe and a Bronze Star. Hell, if Malloy here don't get us all killed or court-marshaled, we will leave here with more medals than we can pin on our chest."

The Colonel sent his orderly over with our two-beer ration and word for us to take things easy for a couple of days and rest up. I told the men to be careful about what they wrote home; that the mail sometimes gets read around here and I wanted to remain a hero in the old man's eyes, not some dumb-ass private in the brig.

We finished our beers and headed for the mess tent. The place was almost empty. I guess everyone was out fighting the big battle. They had gotten in a shipment of fresh milk and I drank it until I was almost sick. The steak and potatoes we had were excellent. I thought this would be a good place except for the rain and the fact someone was always trying to shoot your ass off.

After dinner we went back to the hooch and sacked out. I lay there thinking about what had gone on. Someone told me one time in Sunday school that the lord worked in mysterious ways. And I guess in our situation he really did.

Then I remembered the report that the old man wanted. I dressed and walked over to headquarters and into the orderly room. I found some paper and wrote out a report about the mission. I gave all the men credit for their bravery and their actions under fire, smearing it on some about how Tex kept going from man to man directing the attack. I really laid it on for Colonel Hawkins, explaining about his superb guidance over the radio, how he kept encouraging us, talking us through the battle, telling us to hold on and keep fighting, that help was on the way. And how quickly he got the A1s there with the napalm, and the accuracy of the artillery fire he had guided, how each round landed precisely where I had called it. I was going to add about what a pleasure it was to serve under a man like him, but Tex came in about that time so I handed him the report. He read it over, coughed and snickered a little then asked, "Are you really turning this in?"

I yanked it out of his hands, signed it, walked over and placed it in the Colonel's basket, telling Tex that he just wasn't officer material, that you have to learn to think like a leader and let everyone around you know that you are the man. "That's why you're still a dumb-ass sergeant."

He laughed and said, "Malloy, if I hang around you much longer I will be lucky to get out of this army as a private."

We walked back over to the mess tent and had a cup of coffee with a couple of fresh hot rolls that had just come out of the oven. Sometimes it pays to be in the right place at the right time. We sat and talked about everything in general. I asked Tex when his tour was up. He smiled and said, "I believe it is this month. And Malloy, you ain't going to see my black ass around here no more. I am heading back to Austin and them sweet-smelling Texas women. Three tours in this godforsaken place are enough." He laughed and said. "Wish I could take you with me, old buddy. Them Texas folks would like you, even if you are white and as full of shit as a young robin."

It was dark now as we walked back to the hooch, the big guns had quit firing and all was quiet over toward hill 739. I lay down on my bunk with my clothes still on and was asleep before I ever knew it. Awakening sometime during the night, I got undressed and crawled under my blanket, listening to the rain beat on the plastic roof. Morning was a long time coming as I slept hard, waking up ever so often then drifting back into a deep restful sleep.

Tex kicked my cot sometime around nine and asked if I was going to sleep all day. Rolling over onto my stomach, I stuffed my blanket under my head and said, "By god, if I can, I am."

Tex said, "You're taking an awful chance lying there like that, with your lily-white ass sticking up in the air. One of these boys is liable to drill you before you know what got you." He laughed and said, "Let's go get some chow. This nigger is hungry."

I sat up and looked for my socks. Everything was scattered out of my reach so I had to stand up and search for things. Getting dressed I headed for the latrine and washed my face. My beard hadn't gotten too bad so I let it go. Tex was still bitching and telling me to hurry up. I told him someday he was going to make someone a good wife. He grinned and shoved me out the door.

The damn rain was still falling--a steady downpour that made a muddy mess out of the whole base. Drainage ditches had been dug but they never seemed to catch it all, and those that did ran over because some dumb-ass private had dug them in the wrong place.

Breakfast was good. We had ham, eggs and hotcakes with lots of fresh cold milk. I ate slowly and enjoyed every bite, finishing up with a halfway decent cup of coffee. The cooks had a poker game going in the back corner and asked us if we wanted to contribute. We still had a few dollars so thought that would be a good way to kill some time. They played mostly five- and seven-card stud with a few hands of draw poker thrown in to keep it interesting. I held my own most of the morning while Tex lost his ass and all of his fixtures. I kept loaning him money until his luck changed.

And once it did, that boy knew how to play poker. If he didn't have a good hand he bluffed his way through. By noon the cook boys had all gone bust and I had my money back. Tex laughed really loud and said, "I was just letting you men build your confidence. This here money is going to be spent on some little Texas gal in just a couple of weeks. For boys, my black ass is leaving Nam forever."

We hung around the base for the next three days drinking our two- beers-a-day allowance, trading and buying more from the guys who didn't drink. The battle for hill 739 was winding down and some of the minor wounded were returning to the base.

I started to thinking and that ain't good for me. I got scared when I thought of what could have happened to the eight of us up there on that hill. It's a wonder we all weren't overrun and killed without anyone knowing what hit us. Now I'm not a real religious man, but it had to be the intervention of the good lord that made me pull my stupid stunt the exact time I did. Any sooner would have alerted the enemy, and any later they would have mowed us down.

We were scheduled to go back out on patrol the next day. Tex was really getting jittery as his time was short and this would most likely be his last trip out. The old man had given us two new men so now we had a grenade launcher and an extra grunt. We were being sent up to some valley near Da Nang Air Base to try and ease the problem of rockets being fired at low-flying aircraft as they approached over some of the taller hills.

Tex and I were up early going over maps and charts in the mess hall while we sipped our after-breakfast coffee. We were to be dropped off about forty miles from Da Nang and were to make a four-day patrol over the hills and across the valley to the air base, then catch a hop back to Ben Wa. Colonel Hawkins told us he hated to send us on this patrol but didn't have anyone else.

We were ready to take off when a Marine lieutenant came running across the helicopter pad with a full pack and all his battle gear. Seems like he had only gotten here the day before and already wanted to go on a patrol. He introduced himself as Lt. Wolf and assured me he was along for the ride only to get some experience in the field.

Tex and I looked at each other and told him to get aboard. The flight to our drop zone took nearly two hours. Why in hell they didn't send a patrol out of Da Nang beats the shit out of me, but I learned early to never question anything the army does. The landing zone was on the wrong side of a big river and I talked the pilot into setting us down in a clearing near a rice paddy on the right bank. He laughed at me and said, "Can't you boys swim?" I smiled and said, "We're Army, not Navy."

We unloaded and strung out about twenty yards apart, making our way along the dikes until we came near the jungle. Once inside the brush we closed up a little closer so we could keep everyone in sight. The rain had turned into a light fog that hung like a grey curtain just above the ground, making it hard to see very far and was spooky as hell.

The first hills were about eight miles ahead of us on the chart, but in this damn fog we could be climbing them for all we could tell. The French had logged this region and left mile-long strips of timber, then logged clean the next mile. I hated coming into the clearings and moving across them. We kept the men stretched out as far as we dared and not have someone get lost. I would rather have the rain; at least I could see what I was walking into.

We stopped for the night on the downhill side of a heavily forested slope that allowed a little shelter under some of the trees. We dug in a defensive position beside a large log and set sentries out about fifty yards on each side.

I told the Lieutenant that the academy must really have messed with his brain for him to want to come along on this patrol. He laughed and said, "They're going to have me lead one of these patrols one day and I want to have some idea what I'm getting into."

He seemed to have his head on straight and was eager to learn. Tex and I briefed him on what to expect. He was an

Indian from somewhere in Oregon and a damn good egg, even insisting on pulling guard duty. You don't find many like that in this outfit. He had the sharpest eye for detail that I have ever seen. I wouldn't mind serving under someone like him.

Morning brought more of the fog; we sat tight for several hours hoping it would lift. We were too bunched up but it had to be that way or lose someone.

Coming to the river I could now see why they put the landing zone where they did. I cussed Tex and told him he got us on the wrong bank. He said, "Malloy, you always did read a damn map upside down. It's a wonder you can find your way to the shit house."

The water was muddy and deep. We had no choice but to put our packs on top of our heads, hold our weapons high and wade across. We were almost in the middle of the river when they hit us. I heard the crack of an AK-47 fire but couldn't locate it. The Marine lieutenant raced to the bank throwing down his pack. He ran into the brush as the rest of us followed. He had been grazed by the round but didn't seem to pay any attention. He opened fire and threw a grenade into the wash ahead of him. Following the grenade blast, he jumped into the ditch and opened fire. Tex and I followed, only we weren't needed. Four men lay dead. Lt. Wolf was pointing toward the trees; he had seen a couple more run in that direction. We got everyone gathered up and dug in while Doc fixed up the Lieutenant's arm. I joked with the Lieutenant about his wound and getting a Purple Heart. I told him I would write it up so that he could get a medal if the Marine Corps. would believe some army sergeant. He laughed and said, "Don't tell them I was so scared I pissed my pants or I will never live it down. Glad I was in the river--that way no one noticed."

We waited for over an hour and nothing happened. It must have been a small patrol and thought they would get some of us while we were in the water. Only one of them must have gotten trigger-happy--they could have wasted most of us. I wanted to get out of here before they came back, so we traveled at an angle away from where we were.

At the next clearing we had to cross, I had the men stay back as far as they could and still see the man in front of them. This took a lot longer but would keep a lot of them alive if we got hit again. By evening we had covered over fifteen miles and the fog had blown away. We were now facing a strong wind coming in off the gulf. We dug in on a hilltop and spent the night as the wind blew constantly, making it impossible to hear anything or see any movement.

It's suicide to travel when the wind is blowing in this jungle. You need every one of your senses to survive. The constant movement of the leaves and the noise keeps your nerves on edge. So we sat tight until the weather calmed. By afternoon it was just a light breeze as we hotfooted it across another clearing about two miles wide. There were a series of rice paddies along the outer edge near the bush. We were really strung out now, walking single file along the dike with Red on point followed by Georgia Boy and the Lieutenant.

An old man was working in the water planting rice; he bowed and waved as we went by.

The silence was interrupted by a loud explosion; the ground shook as Red screamed and his body was thrown skyward. Georgia Boy and the Lieutenant were blown back toward me. At first I thought it was a mortar round. I lay there thinking the next one should go off pretty quick. I could see the Lieutenant trying to get up; it was then I realized it had been a damn mine.

Chapter Five

I called for the medic who was on the other side of the dike. By the time I got to Red, the Lieutenant had a tourniquet on his severed limb. I turned to help Georgia Boy who had a nasty-looking head wound left by a piece of shrapnel that had hit him squarely in the forehead along his scalp. It wasn't deep but was bleeding profusely. Grabbing a pressure bandage, I wrapped his head tightly as his whole face turned a blackish blue. He kept trying to get up until Doc shot some morphine into him.

Lieutenant Wolf had a bad gouge to his upper thigh, but he kept helping everyone until the medic made him lie down. We got some sulfur powder on his wounds and got him bandaged. I called a medic flight in from Da Nang as we took care of the wounded as best we could. The rest of the squad was now light-footing it across the dikes to the tree line in case we got hit. The rescue chopper was there in minutes, accompanied by two Cobra gunships that flew the area all the time we were loading the wounded. The Lieutenant refused to go with the medics saying he was okay. Doc and the rest of us tried to get him aboard but he wanted to finish the mission.

We moved to the cover of the forest and set up a defensive position, just watching and waiting. I figured the sound of the explosion would bring the Viet Cong on the run. I kept looking at the old man in the rice field as we waited. He would stand up and look in our direction, then turn and look back across the dikes. As I watched him it seemed to me like he was looking for someone to come from the rice fields.

I told Johnson that we needed to talk to that old bastard, that I believed he knew the mine was there and let us walk into it. I said, "Just watch that old gook. He keeps watching us then looking back over the dike."

Tex said, "Hell, he's just an old man that's scared to death, just leave him alone. There are more mines on that side or someone is hiding over there."

I stood up and grabbed my weapon, leaving everyone behind. I waded out toward the old man. At first he started to run but knew he couldn't get away. Tex followed me saying, "Malloy, this is stupid. That old fart doesn't know anything."

I grabbed the old man by the shirt and pointed to where the mine had been, asking, "How many?" The old man just shook his head and waived his hands muttering something I didn't understand. Tex said to leave him alone; he doesn't know anything. I pulled my forty-five from the holster and shoved it into the old man's face, again asking, "How many?"

He tried to pull loose from me just as I caught movement coming over the dike. I whirled to look and felt the forty-five jump as the old man's body jerked in my grasp. As I turned back I could see the water behind his head turn a bight red, at the same time hearing Tex shout, "Malloy, you crazy bastard, you killed him! What in the hell are you doing?"

At the same time I could hear the screams from an old Vietnamese woman as she came running and splashing toward me. It was all like a horrible dream. I looked at the bloody face of the old man half submerged in the dirty water with one eye bulging out and his mouth hanging open.

The woman was screaming and crying as she beat on my arm and chest with blows that I scarcely felt. Tex yanked the forty-five from my hand saying, "You've gone fucking crazy. That man wasn't hurting anyone."

I stood there stunned, looking into the black teary eyes of the old woman, with her wrinkled skin and flat nose features of the tribal people. A look of hate and sorrow was written on her face. Standing there too numb to move, I had just killed her husband and probably her last means of support in this war-torn land. We had come here to stop this from happening to these people, now I was guilty of what I had come here to prevent.

I watched as she clung to the bloody, limp body of the old man while tears ran down her dark face and cascaded over each wrinkle, mixing with the blood and water of the rice paddy.

I could hear Tex talking to me and felt him pulling on my arm. I looked up and saw the anger and frustration on his face. "Come on," he said. "We've helped these people enough for today."

My mind and body were drained as he led me back across the rice field to the waiting trees. The men were all watching as I walked over and sat down. Putting my head in my hands, I sat and cried, begging God to forgive me. I screamed at this dirty fucking war and everyone around me. I wanted to run, to run back out there, to explain that I didn't kill the old man on purpose, that it had been an accident. I could hear the Lieutenant asking Tex what happened.

"You don't want to know, sir," he said. "Just let it be. It's just another casualty of this damn war."

He got everyone up and moving, walking off into the jungle leaving that old woman alone out there with the only person she had who cared for her lying dead. And I had just killed him.

It had been an accident; I had no intentions of harming that old man. The sudden movement of the old woman coming over the dike caused me to jump and pull the trigger. Hell, I can't even remember cocking the hammer on that damn gun.

I took point. If anyone else was going to get maimed or killed it was going to be me. I was sick of this damn war, sick of killing and sick of living. I walked on without looking; each step was as if I was in someone else's body. In my mind all I could see was that old man's face looking so helpless at me.

Without caring I moved across clearings without checking what was on the other side. I drove the men hard all day; we must have covered ten miles or more. Tex kept trying to get me to slow down and use more caution. "Hell, man," he said, "this ain't going to make anything easier. You're only going to get yourself killed and some good men with you."

I had no feelings. All I wanted was to get as far away from that place as possible. Every time I shut my eyes I could see the old man lying there in my grasp with one eye protruding from his face and the bloody water all around us. I can still hear the screams of the old woman in my mind. Tex and the others looked at me like I was crazy, and maybe I was. I tried to talk to Lt. Wolf, but he said, "Let it go, it's just another part of war."

I wish it was that easy. It's one thing to fight back in battle and kill someone who is trying to kill you, but to take a gun and shoot someone who isn't hurting anyone is another matter.

We made it to the Da Nang Air Base the next afternoon. Lt. Wolf checked in at the infirmary while the rest of us got a hot meal and showered. I made arrangements for a flight back to Ben Wa.

Tex wasn't talking to me much. I asked him to write a report on our patrol. He asked me what he should put in it. I told him to write the damn thing the way it happened, especially about Lt. Wolf and how he chose to stay with the unit even after he had been wounded twice, and the men he killed at the river.

Tex looked at me and said, "What about that old man?"

I told him to write it as he saw it, that I didn't give a damn what they did to me. It had been an accident. I didn't pull the damn trigger, it just went off. He looked at me as if I was a total stranger. It was then I noticed how old and haggard he looked--this damn war had taken a lot of years from him.

I forced a phony grin and walked over to the non-commissioned officers' bar, drew my two-beer ration and found a table in the back. I sat there not hearing or noticing anything as I sipped on the cold beer and tried to get things right in my mind. I wondered if the old man I killed had any sons. I can recall how happy my father was when I would hit a long ball or make a touchdown; he liked to brag to his friends about my athletic ability.

It had been several weeks since I had heard from my folks; mail had a way of getting lost out here, sometimes it took weeks to find you. I thought about Sarah, the girl I used to go with in high school. We were in love, but once I got with the college crowd we drifted apart. Mom was very upset with me; she loved Sarah and always hoped I would marry her.

I lost all track of time as the night wore on. A janitor told me they were closing and asked me to leave. I walked back to where I had left my gear. It was then I realized I didn't have a place to sleep. I wasn't about to go to headquarters this time of night and ask for a bunk.

Grabbing my gear, I walked over by one of the buildings and sat down, leaning up against it in the dark. Every time I shut my eyes, all I could see was that poor old peasant farmer staring up at me with one bulging eye, asking me, "Why, Joe, why?" I wanted to cry, but no tears came, just an uncontrollable shaking. I felt cold and damp even though the rain had quit hours before. I prayed to God to forgive me and to look after that old woman.

How long I had been sitting there in the dark I have no idea. I became aware of someone lifting up on my arm and saying, "Come on, Malloy, everything's okay." Even in the dark I could tell it was Tex; he had been looking for me all night. Picking up my gear he took me over to the infirmary, telling the Doc that I was in bad shape and needed a place to lie down and something to help me rest.

Whatever they gave me really worked--it was almost noon before I awoke. I started to get up and realized my clothes were gone. I was lying there naked between clean white sheets. Sitting up I could see rows of beds with men in them. I started to panic--was I in the damn psycho ward? Where in the hell was I?

I started yelling and a nurse came in and told me to quiet down. I asked where my clothes were and she told me I didn't need them as I wasn't going any place. I said, "Lady, if I don't go piss it's going to get awfully wet in here." She pointed to a table and said, "There is a gown or there is a urinal by your bed. Take your pick."

After she left an orderly came in; giving me a slip of paper. He said, "Here's a message for you."

It was a note from Tex, saying he hoped I had a good sleep and that he would see me back in Ben Wa; that is, if they let me loose in time. And for me not to worry about the report because he would write it like I had taught him, and "P.S. If you ever get to Austin, look me up. My ass is headed home. I'm done with this fucked-up war."

I told the orderly that I needed to get going, that I felt fine. He said, "You should feel good, you been asleep for three days. Man, you were one beat individual. Your blood pressure almost blew the cup apart. You're going to be with us for a spell, so lay back and enjoy the comforts of Da Nang Army Hospital." He would see if he could stir up something for me to eat.

All I wanted was to piss and get the hell out of this place. Hell, I was okay. My nerves may be a little frayed but a good shot of booze and some little Saigon sugar would take care of that. I put on that damn backless gown and, with my bare ass hanging out, I headed for the john.

After I did my thing, I washed up and looked in the mirror. The reflection looking back at me wasn't anyone I recognized. Had I aged that much in the short time I had been here? My face was thin and wrinkled and my hair was much lighter than it had ever been. I stood there looking at myself for a long time.

What was this war doing to me? I had noticed that look in Tex's eyes and now I could see the same in mine. It was a cold, hollowed-out dark look that people get when they have lost all hope. I first saw this look in pictures of people in the concentration camps from World War II. It was the same look on the face of the old Vietnamese woman when I killed her husband.

My stomach started churning and I became sick. I stayed there in the can trying to heave. An orderly came in and led me back to my bed.

I lay there staring at the ceiling, then the tears came. I cried and cried with body-shaking sobs. I couldn't quit, my whole body shook uncontrollably. Soon a nurse came in and gave me a shot; I was still crying when sleep overcame me.

It was dark when I awoke. Everything was quiet except for the large fan over my bed. It made a slight squeak with each turn of the blade. I lay there watching and waiting for the next squeak; it turned so slowly I don't see how it could do any good.

My mind was numb--a deep, dull depression had come over me and I never felt so heartsick in my life. I just wanted to scream, to get up and run from this place, to find some dark corner where I could be alone and shut off the whole damn world. I thought about death, how restful it would be. Maybe I had done that old gook a service by killing him; he no longer had to spend all day working in that damn leech-infested rice paddy. I shut my eyes and his face kept appearing in my mind, along with that of my father. I tried in vain to remember what my mother looked like; I could no longer form a picture of her.

All I could see were dead bodies; all I could hear were men screaming. Am I going out of my mind? Has this damn war driven me completely insane? Is that why I am in here?

I knew then I had to get out of this place and get back with my men. If I didn't leave now, they would never let me go.

Chapter Six

I knew if I didn't get released before I had another breakdown, I'd be shipped to the loony ward and kept there for God only knows how long. I searched the closets along the hallway in the ward, finding only cleaning stuff and a few old torn-down beds. I asked the orderly what they did with my gear and clothes. He said everything was kept in an orderly room locker in the basement. I convinced him I needed to get some papers out of my pack so I could write my reports.

He took me down and told the sergeant who was running the place that I needed to get some things out of my pack. We had to look up my name and find what locker it was in. Giving me a key, he said to go to number 17. Everything was there, even my forty-five along with the M-16. They had even washed my clothes and hung them on hangers. Now all I needed was to figure out a way to get dressed and get out of here.

I took my pack with me and locked the lock, giving the key back to the sergeant. He walked over and looked at the lock, then went across the hall to a little office. Going through my pack I made it look like I was studying a map. Taking out some paper I wrote a letter to my folks. I sat there trying to figure out a plan to get out of this place. I knew I could catch a hop back to Ben Wa most anytime, and they weren't about to ship me back here once I was with my unit.

There was a glass of water on the table with a soda straw in it. I picked up the straw and cut several short pieces from it. Going back down to the basement I asked the sergeant for the key to number 17. He took the key off a hook and tossed it to me. The lock was just a standard master lock. I unlocked it, opened the locker and tossed my bag in checking to make sure everything was there.

Hooking the lock back in the door I took a short piece of the straw and shoved it over the curved part of the lock, pushing the other end into the hole. It looked like it was locked; now all I had to do was get past the orderly somehow and get out of this damn place.

I waited until dark. Grabbing a towel I walked down the hall; it looked like I was headed for the showers. Slipping down the stairs to the basement, I found the men's room and went in just in case someone had seen me. No one was at the office of the orderly room so I tried the door to the lockers and it was open. I was afraid to turn on a light and it was darker than a black cat's ass in there. I felt for the locker doors and ran my hand along each lock until I found the one with the straw over it.

Getting dressed in the dark was a real bitch. I couldn't find any underwear so I just put my pants and shirt on without any. I forgot about socks and pulled my boots on, lacing them as quickly as I could. I buckled on the ammo belt with the forty-five, grabbed the 16 along with my pack and headed for the door. In my haste, I ran into a damn stool with my shinbone that hurt so bad it almost made me piss my pants and made more noise than a damn bull in a china shop.

I think I felt every inch of that wall before I found the door. Easing it open I could see someone sitting in the office talking on a phone. I must have waited ten minutes before the dumb bastard ever turned his back. Slipping from the room I walked across the basement to an outside door and was free. I felt like some inmate who had just broken out of prison. I walked around the building trying to figure out where to go. Seeing a plane coming in I decided that was where the airfield was. I walked over to a light post and dug through my pack among the maps and charts. I still had the orders from Colonel Hawkins for the patrol. If the damn gate guards didn't check the dates too closely, I had it made.

Getting through the gates wasn't any problem; now if I could just get a hop back to Ben Wa without causing too much suspicion I'll be home free. The hospital won't miss me until after eight and they will look around for me for a couple of hours before they declare me missing. By then, with a little luck I will be on my way.

I knew where the flight operations office was located so I walked on over and asked about a flight to Ben Wa, explaining that I had been delayed due to a staff infection and had to get back to my unit. The officer in charge checked my papers, telling me to grab a cup of coffee and he would see what he could do.

As soon as it got light I was in a Huey headed for Ben Wa. I leaned back and listened to the whapping sounds of the rotors and went to sleep. It seemed like I had just shut my eyes when we were setting down. Thanking the aircrew for the lift I grabbed my gear and headed for the Colonel's office. He was in a staff meeting so his orderly offered me a cup of coffee and told me I could wait, but it might be a couple of hours. Seemed like one of his men had run away from a base hospital in Da Nang and they are looking everywhere for him. He said, "The guy's a real nut case, if you know what I mean."

Smiling at him I said, "Maybe I can help. You see, I'm that 'real nut case' they're looking for. And to make it worse I have an M-16 and a forty- five with lots of ammo and I am just itching to shoot the bloody hell out of something or someone."

I never knew a private could move his ass that fast; his feet didn't touch the damn floor as he flew out of his chair and through the door to the staff meeting.

Colonel Hawkins came out chomping on a cigar with the scared private and three other officers peeking over his shoulder. Reaching out his hand, he said, "Malloy, where in the hell have you been? Come on in here, we were just discussing what a damn fine soldier you have turned into. But I must admit that right now you look like death warmed over."

It was then I realized that my shirt was buttoned crooked, I had no t- shirt on under it and the top button was undone. I tried to straighten things up but the Colonel said, "Hell, boy, it isn't your uniform I am talking about. It's the look in your eyes. Man, you look like you haven't sacked out in a month. A shot of good booze and a piece of Saigon pussy would kill you deader than hell right now. You better get some rest."

The Colonel dismissed the others in the room and told me to sit down. Reaching into a drawer he came out with a bottle. Grabbing a couple of coffee cups, he poured each of us generous shot of whisky.

Taking a long drag on a cigar and a sip from the cup, he leaned back in his chair and asked, "Now what's this shit about you escaping from some hospital in Da Nang?"

I took a long swig from the cup, cleared my throat and told him that they were about to send me to the loony bin and I wasn't that far gone yet, so I just took an early release."

Getting up, he walked around and lay his hand on my shoulder and said, "Malloy, you scared the living shit out of my orderly. He come running in here pissing his pants saying that damn crazy man we were looking for was outside the door and he had weapons. What in the hell did you say to him?"

I finished drinking the whisky and told him about our conversation. He laughed and said, "You know they want you back up there for observation. They think you're suffering from severe battle fatigue. I explained to them how you're the best damn sergeant I've got and, Malloy, after the report Sergeant Johnson turned in about you single-handedly killing the gook that was planting mines along the dikes hits the front office, you will most likely get the Silver Star. Hell, man, you're gathering more metal than Audie Murphy. You better watch out or those Hollywood types will be making a movie about you."

"He's dead you know. Yeah, I heard he got it in some plane crash back in Virginia."

"What?"

The Colonel looked at me and said, "I didn't mean him. I meant Sergeant Johnson. His helicopter went down on the way back to Da Nang, killed everyone aboard. Tex was a damn fine soldier. He was done with this war, on his way home he was. That's a hell of a time to get it."

A shocking jolt went through my body. I was stunned and I wanted to heave. I had never felt so much hurt or anger in my life. My whole body was shaking when I stood up to leave. The Colonel grabbed my arm and yelled for his orderly to get a medic over here, and tell them to be damn quick about it. I tried to pull away but all my energy was gone. I slumped down into the chair and slid toward the floor as darkness closed in around me.

When they loaded me on the stretcher it was like I was drugged or paralyzed. My mind wouldn't work and I couldn't get up. I tried to tell them I was okay, but couldn't form the words.

The base infirmary wasn't much more than a big tent; most wounded men were airlifted to Da Nang or some larger base. The only thing they could find wrong with me was low blood sugar and exhaustion. They let me lie around there for three days then turned me loose back to my unit.

Things weren't the same with Tex gone; I still couldn't make myself believe he had been killed. I guess it's best that way. We have a new lieutenant named Heck; the men just say, "What the heck, one name is as good as another." He is just out of the academy and they expect us to keep him alive and obey his orders. I hate these new officers. They can't make a quick decision and when they do it's usually the wrong one.

We are due to go back on recon the next week. I am sure looking forward to this. With Tex gone I will have to pull the whole load as they haven't promoted a new sergeant yet. Red and Georgia Boy were both sent home. Too bad because either one of them would have made a damn good leader.

When I got back to the hooch I had a couple of letters from Mom. She said everything was going good at home. Sarah wrote a footnote on the bottom of one letter asking me to write to her.

My mind still wasn't working right; I turned to ask Tex something and he wasn't there. For a moment I just sat and stared at the empty place where he bunked.

Stretching out on my back I tried to sleep, but weird dreams keep coming to me. Tex and I were in Saigon and the Viet Cong were chasing us down this alley. My legs wouldn't work right. He was hollering at me to run, but I could hardly move. One of the VC fired at me and as the flash of the gun went off I awoke screaming. I sat up covered with sweat and everyone around was staring at me.

Word soon spread through the compound that I had been in the loony bin at Da Nang and escaped. Everyone in the outfit seemed to steer clear of me. I've become a loner, seldom ever talking to anyone. I eat alone and drink alone. It's amazing how quickly one can get labeled in life, even Lieutenant Heck talked at me, not to me. It was like he was afraid I would start screaming and climb the walls.

After the aggravation of the whole deal wore off, I tried to have a little humor with it. I would tell stories about huge snowball mice that ran the hills in Missouri. They were hell to see when the snow was on the ground, and that was about the only times they came out of their caves. I told how they ate only snow and it kept them near frozen. Once full of snow, they could hibernate until the next winter. That was why it was always so cold and damp in the dark caves of Missouri.

Most of the men would listen to my stories then walk off shaking their heads. Maybe I am nuts; hell, who cares.

My promotion to Staff Sergeant came through along with four medals; one was the Bronze Star with an oak leaf cluster. Colonel Hawkins made a big show out of pinning the medals on me and handing me my new stripe. I thought I could hear Tex Johnson snickering in the crowd. The Colonel slapped me on the back and said, "Don't be adding a Purple Heart to that chest full of medals now, Malloy. We need you around here."

After the ceremonies were over I went back to the hooch, cleaned my weapons and wrote a note to Sarah. I tried to remember all the things we did together--it seemed like it had been such a long time ago. I really loved her once, and I still have a soft warm feeling for her. Maybe we will get together again, if I survive. It's hard to write a decent letter from here.

The daily routine is always the same, unless we are getting out butts shot off. This place is hours and hours of boredom with brief minutes of pure terror. And I don't think the loved ones want to hear about all of that. I try to describe the beauty of this country, and it really does have some beautiful scenery if you could look at it without searching for a rifle barrel poking out of the brush.

We are to go back on recon so everyone is busy cleaning weapons, getting ammo and enough field rations for five days. The rain has stopped but now the heat is building up. The only good thing about this is that the damn leeches go to the water and don't bother you unless you have to cross a stream.

Come morning we loaded into two Hueys and flew about forty minutes north of the base, landing in a swampy rice paddy. They can never set us down on dry ground; we always end up walking all day with wet feet. No wonder half the squad has jungle rot.

I took point as we had never been in this part of the country before. Lt. Heck followed me with the rest of the squad strung out about forty yards behind in two lines. We stopped as quickly as we got to the tree line and everyone put on dry socks, like this was really going to help. I told everyone to use powder on their feet; most of the old guys were smart enough to carry it.

Moving along a gully that ran between two hills, we came to a large clearing where we stopped to set up a perimeter. The Lieutenant wanted to study the maps and get an idea where we were headed.

I had the men dig in just in case we were being watched. It was decided that we would bivouac here for the night. We posted guards out about fifty yards on all four corners and settled in. I looked the clearing over several times trying to memorize every tree and bush in it. It gets dark here as soon as the sun fades out of sight. The moon hadn't come up yet when I looked through the night scope and noticed something under one of the trees. From the green outline the heat image looked like someone sitting down aiming a rifle at me. I had the Lieutenant take a look along with a couple of the other men. Setting up a stargazer scope, one that gives more detail, I realized that I was watching a damn big tiger.

I asked the Lieutenant to look and by then it was gone. I sent men out to warn the outpost guards to be on the lookout. It wasn't long before everyone was back in camp sitting pretty close to each other. Seems like no one wanted to be tiger bait tonight. All of the post watches said we could shoot them if we wanted to, but by God they weren't standing out there in the dark alone with a damn tiger prowling about. We all got a chuckle out of this, but I noticed that it got really quiet as everyone strained to hear movement.

We knew the tigers were eating on dead bodies; we had seen the results several times. I don't think anyone slept well that night and come morning we found tracks pretty close to us. I didn't relish the thought of being chewed on by a big cat, so I made sure my weapon was ready and close at hand. We spent a lonely five days out in the brush without seeing anymore tigers or anything else. Making our way back out to the rice fields, we called for pickup and waited most of the day for the choppers to get there.

Seems like the big brass got word of an attack pending at Da Nang and our whole unit was being shipped there. We were only at Ben Wa long enough to shower and catch a hot meal. I had mixed emotions about going back there, wondering if they would put me in the loony bin. I decided if they did, it beat sleeping with the mosquitoes and leeches, plus the food was hot.

Chapter Seven

The trip to Da Nang was like all of the army moves--no one knew where to put us or why we were sent there. The base had been receiving mortar attacks every night. They would shoot a few rounds, move and fire a few more. We had patrols out but no contact with the enemy was ever made, so it must be coming from a small unit.

I knew that as soon as we got settled we would be sent on patrol. I didn't really care; at least out there you didn't have to shave, shower and do the whole army bit. I have given up on going home alive. When I go I want to take as many of the little slant-eyed bastards with me as I can, especially now that Tex is gone. I never asked to come here and I sure as hell ain't a hero. It still bothers me that I shot that old papa-san. I'm having trouble sleeping and the bad dreams just won't stop. I'm afraid to ask for sleeping pills because I know they would keep me.

I have turned into a walking zombie, barely talking to the men in my unit unless I have to. I don't have a close friend here and don't want one. I don't even want to know the men's names so I just call them some name until it fits. You don't want to get close to someone who is most likely will get killed any day. The loss of Tex Johnson is enough to last me two wars.

After chow I sacked out on my cot and read a letter from Sarah that had just been delivered. I lay there holding it on my chest thinking of the stupid things we used to do in school. It seems like I think of her more and more as the days go by.

I must have fallen asleep or else I was just in deep thought. An explosion half blew me off my cot, only to be followed by more and more explosions. We were under attack! From who and where I had no idea. Hell, I wasn't even familiar with this damn base.

Everything was as dark as it could get except for the blinding explosion of the mortar rounds. We had no base defense position assigned to us. I gathered my squad, knowing we couldn't fight from where we were. Remembering a drainage ditch that ran behind the hooch and down toward the fence, I led my men out of our quarters and into the fight. We set up a light machine gun and two M-60s, plus two grenade launchers. We had a lot of fire power.

I had everyone hold their fire and dig in as best they could. We sure didn't want to fire on our own men. Lt. Heck hadn't found us and probably wouldn't until morning. All hell was coming down on and around us; most of the choppers on the line were burning along with several big planes. The flight terminal was on fire as were most of the wooden buildings. It seemed like the whole damn North Vietnamese Army was attacking us. I left the Corporal in charge and told him to hold fire unless he knew damn sure what he was shooting at.

Slipping over the back side of the trench, I made my way toward a machine gun that was firing without hesitation. This was a bad move on my part as they were receiving as much fire as they were giving. Twice I felt something tug at the back of my flak jacket as round after round spit dirt in my face. Sliding into the trench with the gunners, I asked where their commander was. One of the marines had been hit but was still feeding the gun. He asked me if I could run some ammo for them as they were on their last can. This sure as hell wasn't what I had in mind when I came over here. Getting directions to the ammo dump, I slid over the backside of their bunker and crawled out of the line of fire.

Finding the ammo dump and a bunch of scared marines, I sent two of them back to the bunker with all the ammo they could pack. Grabbing two cans of ammo, I made my way back to where my men were. They were heavy in the firefight, shooting everything we had toward the surrounding fence line. The Corporal told me that twice they had shot men off the fence trying to come into the base. I picked two men as ammo runners and told them to keep it coming until they were told to quit and to grab anything that we could use.

I had noticed the machine-gun bunker behind us had quit firing. Taking a private called Snow with me, we worked our way back over and found both marines wounded and in bad shape. By now flares were being fired every few minutes and we could see enemy soldiers working their way through the fence. Reloading, we shot a full belt without stopping and then realized we were about out of ammo. One of the wounded marines fed the gun for Snow as I made a run for more.

I could hear the bang-bang sound of forty-fives being fired along with the clashing of bayonets and the screaming of scared men. I knew then that a lot of hand-to-hand combat was taking place as we were being overrun. The smoke and smell of explosives was so thick that it was hard to breath, the ammo dump was on fire at one end and everyone was trying to move as much ammo as they could. I grabbed two cans and made a run back to the bunker. I could see Snow and the marine standing up firing their weapons from the hip. Sliding into the pit I grabbed my 16 and ran a full clip through it as fast as I could fire. Reloading, I could see several bodies lying along the fence with others trying to get through the wire. We reloaded the machine gun and set up a steady fire until nothing was moving.

Snow and I put pressure bandages on the two marines and called for medics, who I knew were too busy to get to us. Snow had a couple minor wounds from grenade fragments to one hand and arm, but he was still in the fight. One of the marines needed more help than I could give him. Picking him up in a fireman's carry I climbed over the sandbags and headed for the first-aid station. Feeling a jarring pain in my shoulder I almost dropped the marine as I stumbled into a couple of medics. Leaving him there I made a dash toward my men.

The fires were lighting things up now and, along with the flares, men could see and were starting to get organized. We were still getting hit by a few mortar rounds, only now we were pouring out ten times more than what was coming in. There was sporadic fire coming from along the outside perimeter as men fired at anything they thought was moving.

With daylight came the rain, which helped with some of the fires but turned the trenches into mud holes half full of water. The base was a total mess, wounded men were lying everywhere; half the base had been blown to shit. The hospital that I had been so afraid of was half-wrecked with broken windows and smoke coming from parts of it. My back was hurting me from carrying the wounded marine and I was having difficulty breathing.

Getting back to my squad, I was happy to learn that we hadn't had any casualties. Snow had been sent back over to us as the marines replaced those wounded. We got busy filling sandbags and digging a drain for the trench. It looks like we will be here for awhile.

The damn cloud cover is so low that nothing can fly in to help us, and most of the Cobra gunships got hit with the first wave. It was like they knew where everything was, and I believe they did. A lot of civilians work on the base. The little bastards will smile at you and be friendly during the day, only to come back at night and cut your throat.

My back is really hurting me now and to make matters worse, I have started coughing and spitting up blood. I must have bruised a lung climbing over the sandbags. Lt. Heck finally found us--he had been helping fight some of the fires. He took one look at me and asked, "Malloy, are you hit? Your back is covered with blood and you look white as a ghost." I told him the blood came from a wounded marine I carried over to an aid station. About that time I went into a coughing fit and started spitting up blood again.

The Lieutenant made me sit down and take off my flak jacket. Turns out I had a wound that went in under my right arm and out my back. The fragment was still in the fiber of my flak jacket. I hadn't felt a thing, but now the pain is almost more than I can take. Clayton, our medic, put a bandage on me and had a couple of the men help me to the aid station. They gave me a shot of morphine and told me I could wait. I lay there in the rain covered with a piece of clear plastic. After the morphine kicked in I could have cared less; the rain beating on the plastic sounded like a drummer playing. Hell, this stuff is almost as good as that damn poppy juice we tried back in Saigon, only I hear it is twice as addictive.

I feel good enough to go back to my men, but think I will just lie here and listen to the rain. Everything is so quiet and peaceful as I drift off into a deep sleep.

My wound wasn't life threatening. They put a couple dozen stitches in a large cut and put my right arm in a sling. The doctors were so busy I never got to thank the one who took care of me--the tent I was in was full and getting fuller.

I asked to rejoin my men and was told to go ahead, but once things settled down or if I started coughing up blood again to get back over here. I must have been nuts to leave a dry warm tent and go lie in a trench half-full of mud. Some of the men had rigged corrugated metal over the top and covered it with sandbags. At least the rain didn't hit us but ran through under our feet. We gathered some old wood pallets and broke them to fit the bottom of the trench. Now all we needed was some beer and a television and we would have all the comforts of home.

The morphine had worn off and my shoulder was hurting. I should have asked for some pain medicine. Calling our medic over I asked if he had any more morphine. He laughed at me and said, "Hell, Malloy, I can't give you that stuff." Shaking out a bottle of pills, he handed me a couple and said these will have to do. They were little more than aspirin, but did help the ache some.

Just before dark we got hit again, only this time it was artillery rounds and some pretty heavy stuff. I can't see how they got anything in close enough to reach us. Small arms fire and mortars kept coming all night long. They were continually testing the outer perimeter and trying to come over the fence. A lot of air force boys got to find out what hand-to-hand fighting was all about.

We got a mortar round almost inside the trench. I took a piece of shrapnel to my leg as did two other men. Our flak jackets took the worst of it, but the explosion made our heads hurt for hours. My wound was nasty looking but didn't do much real damage--it was a deep gouge with a lot of bleeding. The medic put a tight bandage compression on it and sent me back to the first-aid tent.

This time I chose to stay in a dry place for awhile. I had been wounded twice in two days so figured I deserved a rest if I could get one. Only thing is I felt a lot safer in the trench than I did in that damn first-aid tent in the middle of the compound. The sides were covered with sandbags stacked up about seven feet high, but the roof was just heavy canvas. I lay there and tried to sleep but nearly jumped off the cot with each explosion. Finally I asked to be released and made my way back to the cold, wet trench. At least I had something over my head and we stacked sandbags on each end to keep another mortar from getting in on us.

Most of the men thought I was nuts to come back until I explained how unsafe I felt over there.

With morning came a change in the weather. The clouds rose some and the rain slackened allowing for the Cobra gunships to come in and fly the area. We sat in the trenches and watched the show as they fired rockets and machine-gunned the whole area.

The mortar rounds ceased coming and we were allowed to take a quick shower with what hot water we could find. We also got our first hot meal in three days. My back wound was really causing me a lot of pain and had some infection in it. I went back over to the hospital and checked in. The doctor took one look at my wounds and, after checking my records, told me I was going to be on the next flight of wounded going to Japan.

He wouldn't allow me to go back to my unit for my gear, saying that it would be shipped to a military warehouse in San Francisco. Smiling at me, he said, "Mr. Malloy! You're done with this war; you'll soon be going home. You have been twice wounded and suffered severe battle fatigue. I believe you have done enough for your country. I hope your wounds heal fast and you become successful in whatever you do."

I lay back on the bed while a flood of emotions ran over me--I wanted to laugh and I wanted to cry. I had been in this country seven months and a few days, most of it just walking or sitting around in pure boredom, with a few hours of pure hell thrown in just to liven things up. I had seen a lot of men killed and wounded on both sides, and I still can't figure out why in hell we are here.

I really thought we were doing good until I killed that old man. That one accident seemed to undo everything I had done that was good. Every time I shut my eyes I see that old woman's face with all the hurt, hate and anger she has in her wrinkled stare. I can still hear her scream and still feel the old man's body go limp in my grasp. I know I should talk to one of the doctors about this, but they would just lock me in the loony bin. Maybe that is where I belong, but I'm sure as hell not going to help them put me there. One thing I know is I am no coward; I have been so damn scared I pissed my pants, but I stood and fought with everything I had. This damn war has changed me, and I don't know if I can handle civilization again. I do have questions about my own sanity. Only time will tell.

Chapter Eight

The flight to Japan was quiet; we were accompanied by some of the friendliest and best-looking nurses I'd seen. I was wishing they hadn't given me a sleeping pill so I could have gotten to know them better. I guess you just call that the luck of the Irish. At least I am still in one piece and have my arms and legs. Some of the men on the flight were really crippled and in bad shape.

My wounds are really bothering me. I guess it's because I have more time to think about it. I still don't remember getting hit the first time; it must have been while I was carrying the marine because I remember a burning sensation in my shoulder as I sat him down at the aid station.

The military hospital in Japan is a big place. It is good to sleep between clean sheets and have hot meals. I feel guilty for not finishing my full year out. It seems like I left all those other men back there to do what I was supposed to. I never knew many of their names, but I can shut my eyes and picture each one of them. The new men have a scared, worried look about them, while the old guys have a cold, haggard look on their faces.

Each one of them has a goal of getting out of there alive and in one piece. Twenty-year-old men look thirty and seventeen-year-olds look like scared schoolboys. But each of them can put his fear behind him and fight when the time comes. They laugh and joke in a carefree manner, trying to hide what is really on their minds.

Tex was halfway through his third tour when I met him. I was looking out for Number One and picked the most experienced guy I could find to learn from. It was a good move as he taught me how to survive. I loved him like a brother; it was like I had always known him and we shared things with one another that we would never talk about with anyone else. I felt a need to go visit his family and I planned to when I get back to the states.

Tex wasn't bitter about life like some men are. He took things as they came and dealt with them in his own way. I am sure he would have been a very successful man no matter where he went in life. I will always remember Tex and thank the good lord for letting me know him.

I hate lying around in this place; you have too much time to think. All of the wounded men here keep my mind on what I have just been through. I must be screaming in my sleep again because they want to do a sleep study on me. I don't like the idea but have no choice if I ever expect to go home. They have put me on some kind of drug that is supposed to relax and calm me. Hell, all I need is a good-looking nurse and a bottle of bourbon.

Just let me go on a three-day drunk, then see how good I sleep. Even with the drugs they are giving me I still have dreams of being captured or else being chased all over hell. Sometimes I am on the street back home and other times I am still in Nam. It is always the face of the old Vietnamese woman screaming at me. Sometimes she has a knife or a gun and I always wake up before she reaches me.

I see the twisted and mangled bodies of dead soldiers, but the faces are always so blurred I can't tell who they are. In my last dream, Georgia Boy and I were being chased by Tex and that old woman. Each of them was carrying a machete and kept swinging it at us. We tried to run but our legs would hardly move; when I awoke I was sitting up in bed covered with sweat. Two nurses were trying to hold onto me, but I kept pulling away until I got out of bed. I still couldn't figure out where I was or what was going on. The lights were on in the ward and everyone was awake and looking at me. A doctor came in and gave me a shot, telling me that it would help me rest.

Now I believe I am going insane. I want to get away from this place to go back to the jungle; I can hide out there. I need to be alone and have time to figure this out. The walls are closing in on me, making me feel trapped. I am being cared for by people I have never seen before--are they the enemy? Have I been captured? Or am I really in a hospital in Japan? I need to find out what's going on.

I can't get dressed and leave as all I have are these army pajamas and a pair of paper slippers. I start thinking of how I can steal some doctor's clothes; they have to have a dressing area around here someplace.

It is the middle of the day when I awake. Whatever they gave me really makes me feel tired and slow. Some nurse comes in and asks if I am ready to eat. I tell her yes, but I haven't got any appetite. Maybe the sight of food will make me hungry.

Looking around I realize they have moved me to a room by myself. I don't like this at all. Maybe I have something that will contaminate everyone. The nurse wasn't wearing a mask so it must not be too bad. I guess it is because I woke everyone up last night. Before I could figure things out a Japanese orderly came in with a tray of food, set it on a little table and swung it over toward me. He said something that I couldn't understand as he left the room.

I had one egg, two sausage links, a piece of toast, half a banana and a little bowl of dry cereal with a pint of milk. I sure as hell wasn't going to get fat. I wondered who got the other half of my banana. I picked at the food until it was all gone, then I realized I had been hungry.

Another nurse came in with a cup of pills and told me to take them. I argued with her that I didn't need any more damn pills, that I wasn't sick and had just had a good night's sleep. She insisted I take them so I put all of them in my mouth and pretended to swallow them with a drink of water. After she left I spit them out into the milk carton and bent the top over flat.

I don't know what they were, but part of them had dissolved in my mouth leaving me with the worst taste ever. I had to get up and brush my teeth and mouth to get rid of it. She came back in later with some damn machine and started sticking little round patches all over my head and chest.

I asked what was going on and she said they were going to do a brain- wave study on me while I slept. I told her I had just woken up and didn't feel sleepy; she smiled and said you will pretty quickly. It was then I realized the pills I was supposed to take were to relax me and put me to sleep. I bet that milk carton is the most relaxed one in the trash. Hell, you can probably hear it snoring if you walk by the dumpster.

They must have had fifty wires connected to me, so I just lay back and shut my eyes. I could feel my pulse beat through the ones hooked to my temples. I fell asleep and the next thing I knew I was in a deep ravine covered with vines and brush. I couldn't find my way out; I was tangled in the vines and they stung my face as I pulled on them. Then the old Vietnamese woman appeared. She just sat crouched on a hillside and watched me as the vines pulled me deeper and deeper into the darkness. She had hold of my wrist and was pulling me into the mouth of a dark cave. I was kicking and screaming as I fell into space.

The next thing I remember is standing beside my bed with all those damn wires dangling from me and that fancy machine was turned over. Some nurse and an orderly had hold of my arms. They were talking to me, trying to get me back in bed. My heart was beating faster than I can ever remember. My leg wound had been torn open and blood was running down onto my paper slippers. How I got them on I don't know.

I lay back on the bed while the nurse unhooked all the wires from me, leaving all those damn patches stuck to me. I curled up in the fetal position and lay there shaking. God, I am so afraid of what is happening to me. Now I'm afraid to shut my eyes; I might not come out of the next dream. I don't want to be locked up with a bunch of crazy people who just crawl around on the floor and talk to themselves. I need to get back to my unit, back to the leeches and the rain, back into the dark jungle where I can lose myself and all of my tormenters.

I am a soldier, a sergeant in the United States Army. I am a fighting man who leads other men into battle. What am I doing here curled up in bed crying like a child? I must be doped by these people; only drugs could make my mind do these things. I have got to escape and get back to my men.

Getting up, I walked out to the nurse's station and asked if I could take the patches off. The nurse tells me they want to run another study on me as soon as I get tired. Trying to look normal, I walked around the halls telling her I need some exercise; when no one is looking I peek into every room I can find. Most of the closed doors are to linen closets or are full of cleaning gear.

Going back to the nurse's station, I ask to go down to the cafeteria and have something to drink. She tells me it is in the basement and how to find it. My plan is working now. Once in the basement I watch as the doctor's drive in. I pick up my coffee and follow them as they go to a locker room where they change into their scrubs. I pretend to be looking for a Dr. Heck, which was the first name that came to my mind. None of them knew him but said there were new doctors coming and going all the time.

Thanking them, I walked back over to the cafeteria, sat down and worked on my escape plan. A lot of the doctors wore civilian clothes; I need to steal a uniform so I can move about more freely. Now I know I can get out of this place and I am sure Colonel Hawkins will cover for me once I return to my unit. I went back to my room and read from some paper I picked up in the hallway. I have got to be normal for awhile or they will put me under guard.

Once again I fake taking the pills, and when it gets later they come in and hook me up again. I tell myself to sleep light, not to let any of the dreams seem real. My plan is to realize I am dreaming and to wake up when they start. I am having a hard time getting to sleep with all those damn wires. I can't turn over; I just have to roll from side to side.

Soon I am asleep and the dreams start. I'm in a cage. It's like they have put me in a cell. I tell myself to wake up, that this is only a dream, but the old woman is standing laughing at me. Pulling on the bars I scream and shake the bars. They feel loose so I pull on them harder. The door opens but I am tied with wires to the wall. I can't break free.

The entire time that old woman is taunting and laughing at me, pointing her skinny finger in my face as she laughs through rotten teeth. I feel her grab me and I fight with all my strength. I can hear another voice calling my name and people shaking me. Someone is holding me down. I open my eyes and look into the face of several nurses. They all have a scared look on their face. One of them runs her hand through my hair, pushing it back as she tells me to relax, that I have just had another bad dream. They unhook the wires and take the patches off me. One of the doctors comes in and sits down next to my bed. He starts asking me what my dreams are about and when they started. He wants to know if I have the same dream or if each one is different.

My session with the doctor lasts several hours. Finally I tell him about the old man I killed and the old woman who comes in every dream. He explains that this is a normal reaction to something that traumatic and that the pills should help me relax and sleep better. He said he would increase the dosage. Now I got worried to the point I told him I hadn't been taking them.

He stood up and smiled, saying, "I can't help you if you won't cooperate."

I promised him I would take them for awhile. He shook my hand and said he would see me tomorrow. I bet he really thinks I'm nuts.

After the evening meal the nurse brought me the pills. This time I swallowed them and opened my mouth like a little kid so that she could see that they were all gone. She smiled and patted me on the chest, and said; "Good boy." I was tired and after the lights were out I relaxed. I was afraid to go to sleep but couldn't stay awake.

The next thing I know some nurse is shaking me and asking if I was going to sleep all day. It was after nine and I had slept all night without having a dream. Maybe those damn pills do work.

I asked to go down to the cafeteria for breakfast. She told me to hurry or else I would be eating lunch. Once in the basement I checked out the doctor's dressing room but didn't go in. I want to stay around awhile and see if they can help me. I feel good for the first time since I have been here.

Chapter Nine

The medication seemed to help with the bad dreams, but it left me feeling doped and listless. I felt like I wasn't in control of myself; anytime I would sit down for awhile I would fall asleep. I tried to write to Sarah and my folks but I could never seem to put anything down that would make any sense. I'm still not sure where I am--I believe it is Hitachi, Japan.

I have been here more than three months. The dreams still come once in awhile but I can handle them now. I have been able to tell myself I am dreaming and wake up. My promotion finally came through, along with a notice that I was to receive two Bronze Stars, and a Silver Star that I got for killing the old man, thanks to Tex Johnson's report. I also was given three Purple Hearts even though I had been wounded only twice. I guess they gave me one for going nuts. I should make a stink about all of it, but what the hell--if the army's happy so am I. All I want is to get away from this place.

One day they talk about sending me back to my unit and the next they are going to send me back to the states. I just want out of here; there isn't anything else they can do for me. They have done more studies on me than any ten men. I have had a couple of bad nights but they went unnoticed so I didn't say anything. I've decided these dreams don't do any more than scare hell out of me and anyone else who may be around.

One morning the doctor came in and asked me how I would like to go home. My heart jumped with excitement at the thought of seeing my family and Sarah again. That afternoon I had a long talk with the psychologist. I asked him about my condition and if I was safe to go home. I told him I was still having the dreams but that they weren't as violent as before and I thought I could handle it.

He wanted to know if there was a veteran's hospital close to where I lived. I told him that there was one in Springfield, Missouri, that is only a few miles from my folk's home. Standing up, he lay a hand on my shoulder and said, "I think you are okay for daytime, but I want you to spend your nights in a medical facility. You don't seem to be violent when you have one of these dreams, but you sure could traumatize anyone who didn't understand. You scared hell out of some of our nurses and most of the men who were in the ward with you. That's why we moved you down here to a private room.

"We still don't completely understand all of what the human brain goes through when something this traumatic happens to it. Everyone seems to react differently to these situations. You are a young man and given time your brain will heal itself. That's not to say you won't have flashbacks from time to time but they, too, will eventually cease. The thing we need to do is to get you interested in other matters so that you completely quit thinking about what happened.

"Part of the healing process is to get you back around friends and family and doing a job or something where your mind is busy with other thoughts. Sitting around here you have too much time to reflect on what happened. And no matter how many times you run it through your thoughts, you can't change it.

"Malloy, what happened to you was so against everything you have always been taught and believed, it is impossible for your mind to accept it. This was just an unfortunate accident. What you have got to learn to do is accept it as something you had no control over. It's just an incident that you can't change. It is okay to blame yourself and feel remorse.

"But remember, you didn't volunteer to go to Vietnam or even out on patrol that particular day. You were involved in a war, where people other than soldiers get killed.

No one plans to kill them, they just happen to be in the wrong place at the wrong time. "If you believe in God, turn to prayer each time you think of what happened. Go back to school and learn to study, get an education and learn new things that will keep your mind busy. Spend time with someone, write about your childhood, do anything that will get your thoughts off Vietnam. Go for long walks, get plenty of exercise, and make your body so tired that all it wants to do is rest; you won't have time for bad dreams.

"We can keep giving you medication that will have to be increased to stronger and stronger doses the longer you are on it. I don't want to see you dependent on some drug in order to function normally. All drugs have side effects, especially ones that alter the process of thinking. Over time they will actually damage thought procedure and can lead to severe mental illness.

"I'm not telling you this to scare you, but to explain what can happen if you just give up. Your illness is common among combat veterans; we have seen it and successfully treated it since World War I. So Mike, let's get you out of here and back on the road to recovery. I will put in the orders to transfer you to the veteran's hospital in Springfield. Missouri. They will take good care of you. I expect a complete recovery in your case, so take care of yourself, soldier."

He shook my hand and walked from my room. I don't know if I really understood what he just told me but I think he believes I'm nuts. Hell, I could have told him that. They don't call me "Mad Mike Malloy" for nothing.

Days dragged by as I lay around the hospital. The dreams continued but I handled them as best I could. Days finally turned to weeks and I still hadn't gotten transferred. I asked to see the doctor again; he was surprised to see that I was still there. I wanted to be sent back to my unit but he told me I wasn't fit for combat anymore and I was going home. I told him I heard that several months ago, but I was still here.

After he left an orderly came in and had me fill out a bunch of papers and sign another bunch that I didn't even take time to read. Two days later I was on a military transport headed for San Francisco. They had given me a new uniform that didn't fit very well but it was better than a hospital gown. There were about a hundred people on the plane, most of them military personnel who were going home.

I leaned my seat back and tried to sleep. My folks don't know that I am headed home so I won't have to deal with seeing them until I am ready.

I'll have to fly commercial airlines to Kansas City, then on to Springfield. I hope I don't have a long layover because I need to stay awake. I don't trust myself; it would scare hell out of everyone if I had a bad dream on one of those flights.

The flight over the ocean was rough and the plane bounced around a lot. It would keep me awake just enough that I knew where I was. I started dreaming again but this time it was about Sarah. We were together in my folk's truck going down a long hill. We were going too fast and the brakes wouldn't work. I was pushing on the brakes as hard as I could but we just kept picking up speed. I could feel Sarah holding on tight to me and telling me we were going to be okay. It was then I realized I was dreaming again and opened my eyes to the prettiest nurse I have ever seen talking to me and running her hand through my hair, telling me that everything was okay. I was scared and embarrassed at the same time. She asked if I wanted anything, and I sure did, but I didn't think it was proper to ask. I just shook my head. It's funny--that is the first time I have even thought about sex in a long time. They say a man thinks about sex every thirty seconds. Well, let me tell you that in combat you think about everything else, like not getting hit and staying alive. Then anger takes over and you want to fight to kill and destroy. The adrenalin rush is something else.

Each man handles it differently. Most men are totally consumed by fear but their training and the need for self-preservation take over. I have seen quiet men go into a killing rage and stay that way for hours. After a firefight they would be screaming and talking as loudly as they could. It would take hours for the adrenalin to leave their bodies, usually leaving them sick to their stomachs.

I noticed that these men were never the same again. Some would become quieter and withdraw into themselves, while others became bullies and wanted to fight everyone. I know I have changed; my thinking is a lot different from when I first came to Nam. I didn't care about much, just having a good time and getting stoned. Now I realize how fragile life is, how quickly it can be snuffed out. Those who haven't been physically wounded have mental wounds that will take a long time to heal.

I sat there covered with sweat thinking about all of this. I needed to rest in the worst way, but was afraid to go back to sleep. I looked around the plane at all the young faces; most of them have a hallowed look of fear and a darkness around their eyes that makes them look old. It's like they are afraid of going home. I have seen this look on old men who went through the Great Depression, men who worked hard all their life just to live. Most of these young men aren't old enough to buy a beer, but they have lived through a hell where they witnessed death and destruction on a daily basis.

We have been told about the war protesters that will be waiting for us. I wonder how some of these men will handle them. I just hope they stay away from me.

We landed in Hawaii and were given a couple hours to look around. Most of the men just stayed at the base terminal. I walked around looking things over for about an hour. Hawaii sure wasn't what I had it pictured to be. I guess I was expecting girls in hula skirts and sunny beaches; maybe I never got to the right place. I might as well have been in Long Beach, California. It was just as crowded and busy as any town on the mainland.

I ate and made my way back to the terminal in time to get back on the plane. It was dark when we arrived at San Francisco. I think they had it planned that way so that the war protesters would be gone.

A bus met us and took us to a military receiving facility. We were taken to a large building and given a place to sleep. I was exhausted and went to sleep immediately; I didn't have any dreams and slept until the lights came on. We were told to get dressed and where the chow hall was. They told us to be back here at nine and they would start processing us. I wasn't sure what that meant but I was hoping that I was getting released.

I was a little late getting back but no one seemed to notice. They finally called my name and I went into this office where several men sat at desks shuffling papers. They asked me a lot of questions and finally told me I was being given a medical discharge. I was given orders to report to the veteran's hospital in Springfield. I was allowed to draw three hundred dollars from my pay. They told all of us to go to the base store and buy civilian clothes as it would help with the war protesters if we weren't in uniform. I thought what the hell, here I almost got my ass shot off for this country and they can't keep some pantywaist little bastard from harassing me.

Chapter Ten

After staying four more days at the medical facility in San Francisco, I was finally booked on a flight to Springfield via Kansas City. Checking out with what few possessions I had, I headed to the airport in a cab.

Wearing my civilian clothes like they told us, I tried to stay away from the damn war protesters, but they were all over the place. At first no one paid any attention me until I got to the ticket counter. Then someone noticed my haircut and came toward me. A long-haired sleazy-looking bastard walked up to me and asked if I was one of those damn baby-killers.

I didn't like his looks or his smell, and he spit when he talked. Telling him to get out of my face, I shoved him back and tried to walk away. A stringy-haired girl with buck teeth started screaming at me and the whole damn bunch joined in yelling and cussing. I turned around and slapped that bitch, then hit her boyfriend with my best shot. He hit the floor screaming and holding his mouth. I could see two policemen coming so I lit into the whole damn bunch, going through those hippie bastards like a pit bulldog in a hen house.

Two sailors jumped in to help me and we were really giving it to them when the riot squad arrived. I couldn't believe it when they handcuffed us and let that bunch of creeps go. We were taken down to the police station and thrown in a cell with about ten other men. I thanked the two sailors for their help. They said they had been harassed by that bunch ever since they got to the airport and the police wouldn't do anything to help them. Everyone was glad I smacked a couple of the mouthy bastards.

After about four hours I was taken to a desk and a report was filed on me. I had to be fingerprinted and have a mug shot taken. I guess I was now a real bad-ass criminal. A military lawyer from the provost office showed up and talked to the three of us. The two sailors told him they were just trying to keep me from getting hurt, so they were released and told to stay out of trouble. The officer found out that I was headed to a medical facility for mental evaluation and convinced the police to release me, especially since none of the protesters had filed a complaint.

The officer drove me back to the airport and talked to the security people. They let me stay in a small room until time came for me to board the plane. The protesters were still screaming and pointing fingers at me while I stood in line to board. This was hard to take; I had just spent eight months getting my ass shot at while these milk-suckers smoked dope and protested the war.

The flight to Kansas City took about four hours; I was afraid to sleep so I just sat there and thought about what I had just been through. It sure as hell wasn't the welcome home I had expected, even though we had been told what might happen. That was the first time I ever slapped a woman; it sure shut her up until I lay her boyfriend on his ass. Then I think she tried to hit me, but I can't remember--I was just throwing punches at everyone I could reach. I wish the cops hadn't arrived so quickly, especially after the two sailors jumped in. We were really kicking some hippie ass. Those dope- smoking bastards were as weak as a bunch of little kids. I bet it was the first time anyone had ever smacked some of them. I know it sure did feel good to release some of my frustrations on those long-haired assholes.

After we landed I sat there and let everyone get off the plane. One of the stewardesses smiled and asked me where I was going. I said, "Home. I have been in Vietnam for the past ten months. She just smiled again and said, "It must be hell over there," as she turned and walked back into the cabin. I was worried about protesters here, but it was now three in the morning and I guess they do sleep sometimes. I had a long walk over to the American Eagle terminal where my flight to Springfield was departing.

I found the terminal and checked in. There was a two-hour wait until my flight left, so I went into the bar and had a beer. I really needed something to eat but didn't see anything open. The beer wasn't bad so I had another while I sat and watched the war news on television. Just seeing the country again brought back a sick feeling in my stomach and I started thinking of the old man I killed. Knowing this wasn't good for me I gulped the beer and walked back over to the waiting area, sitting so that I could watch the planes come and go.

I must have fallen asleep for I was again back in the jungle with VC all around me. I was crawling through the underbrush when I crawled up on a dead body. It was the old man I killed, covered with blood and the one eye bulging out staring at me. I must have screamed or hollered for I was standing up when I awoke. There were only three other people in the room and they were on their feet and walking away looking back at me with a scared look on their faces.

Looking into a mirror I saw that I'm really a mess. My face looks like an old man and I am white as a ghost. I have lost about twenty-five pounds and these clothes don't fit me well. I hate looking at myself.

I sat back down and covered my face with my hands. I could never go home like this and take a chance of scaring Mom. What if I was with Sarah and I had a bad dream? It would traumatize her to the point that she would never want to be around me again.

I never felt so scared and alone in my life; at this moment I wish I had gotten killed over there. I feel so helpless and confused. I want to run back into the jungle and hide from everyone and everything. I know now that I have to go directly to the veteran's hospital when I get to Springfield. I'm glad I never told anyone that I am coming home. At least this way I can try and work things out. I am having more and more thoughts of committing suicide. This would be the easy way out, but Mom and the rest of the family could never handle it. God, how did my mind ever get so screwed up?

I finally get on the flight to Springfield. It is one of those little prop jets, but the ride is good, and we flew low to get around all the thunderstorms. The closer I get to Springfield the more I wish I was back in Nam; at least out there I knew what I was doing. I sure wasn't the soldier that Tex Johnson was, but he did train me well. I knew how to stay alive and keep most of my men out of trouble.

I haven't given much thought to what I will do in civilian life. I think I will go back to college if the army will pay for it. First I have got to get released from the damn nut ward. Why didn't I listen to Johnson when he told me to leave the old man alone? I'm bone tired but afraid to lean my seat back and rest. If I started yelling in this little plane it would scare all these old farts half to death. We will be in Springfield in about thirty minutes so I can stay awake that long.

I watch the dark clouds and the lightning flash as we fly around the storm. Everything below looks so neat with all the fields fenced off and the limestone rock formations along the roads. I wish that there would be someone to meet me. Mom would throw a fit if she knew I was coming home and didn't tell her. I wonder how many other men are coming home to an empty airport with no one to greet them. At least I can walk off the damn plane, a lot of those boys can't. I will probably call my older sister Vera in a day or two and let her know where I am. She can keep a secret pretty good. Vera is a nurse at one of the

Springfield hospitals so maybe she will know what I am going through.

The seatbelt light just came on so now I am really getting nervous-- what if I run into someone who knows me? The landing jolts me back to reality with the squealing of the tires and the shaking of the plane as they reverse the engines to slow down. It seems like I have been away for a lifetime, but it has been less than a year.

It is just a little past seven a.m. and the airport is filling up. I wait for my one piece of luggage, which seems to take forever to come around on the conveyor belt. Picking up my bag I head for the front door, then start thinking about where in the hell I am going. I get into a cab and tell the driver to take me over to a restaurant near the college because it is the only place I can think of. On the way I tell the cabbie to drive around a little bit as I have been away and want to look things over. Sitting back I look at the city, all of the old places are the same, and they all bring back memories. Finally the cab driver asks if I still want to go to the restaurant.

I tell him to drop me off at a good motel, one that isn't too expensive. He tells me about a Motel Six on the off-ramp of Interstate 44 that is close by, so I have him take me there. It has a vacancy sign in front. I pay the driver and walk into the lobby. A middle-aged lady asks if she can help me. I ask for a room on the top floor as I don't like the noise of people moving around above me.

The room is small but clean. I throw my bag on the floor and drop onto the bed. Lying there I stare at the ceiling wondering what to do next. I need a shower but decide to take a nap first. Getting up I lock the door and turn on the television.

Finding a news channel, I lie back on the bed and take in what is happening in the world. There is a lot of news about college kids protesting the war, so I change the channel. I have learned to hate those long-haired maggot-infested little bastards. I just wish some of them had to go through what I have in the last ten months.

There is some old Gary Cooper western movie on so I watch it until I fall asleep. It is dark out when I wake up. I can remember having a lot of silly dreams, but none of them made enough sense that I can remember them. I am starving but decide to take a shower and change clothes before I go eat. I don't like the clothes I have and the first thing tomorrow I am going to buy some new threads.

Standing in the shower I let the hot water cascade off my scarred body. I run my hands over the old wounds and look at them as best I can. My back is still sore, and the damn handcuffs the cops put on me tore something in my shoulder. When I was hit, the projectile went through my shoulder blade and did considerable nerve and muscle damage. The scars are still a bright pink color and there is some tenderness in the tissue. I look at myself as I shave. There are lines in my face and my eyes look so dark and shallow, like I have been starved for a long time. My body is thin now; I have lost a lot of the heavy muscle I used to carry.

No one would recognize me as thin as I am. Well I am going to do something about that. I splash on some aftershave and get dressed. I am ready for a good steak and all of the trimmings. Going back down to the lobby I ask the lady if there is a good steak house close by. She tells me about a good restaurant two blocks down the street that isn't really a steak house, but that they do cook up a good rib eye with all the trimmings. Thanking her I walk out into the night air. It seems cold to me, then I realize it is October--what day I don't know. I think it is the fifth, but could be later. Walking down the street I feel strange but happy. I sure wish Tex was here with me, but I guess he is as long as I keep his memory alive. One day I am going to go to Texas and find his folks. That would be the least I could do for him.

Finding the restaurant I go in and am greeted by the prettiest little blue-eyed girl I have seen in years. She gives me a big smile and asks if I am alone. I say, "Yeah, but you can join me if you wish." She smiled again and said, "Sorry, but I have to work." She walked in front of me, leading me to a table as I watched every move of her slender body. Pointing to a chair she handed me a menu and said, "Someone will be right here to take your order." Turning she asked if I would like anything to drink. I hadn't taken any medication so decided I would have a beer.

After ordering a medium-well rib-eye steak with mashed potatoes and gravy, I sat back and enjoyed the beer as I looked at all the other people around me, searching for a familiar face, yet hoping I wouldn't see one. The meal was delicious and the second beer hit the spot. Now I wish I had a smoke, but I have given them up somewhere along the way. You learn quickly not to smoke while out in the field; tobacco smoke can get you killed.

Sitting there I realize how tired I really am, so I leave the little gal a tip, walk up front and pay my bill, then head for my room. The night air is cold but feels good as I watch the traffic move slowly along the street, thinking how long it has been since I have driven a car. I guess I still know how. Coming to the motel I go up to my room, undress and lie on the bed. I have got to go to the VA hospital tomorrow. I don't have enough money left to spend another night here. I was supposed to report today, but what the hell. I can't see where they can do a lot to me, and I need some time alone.

Sleep comes quickly. Sometime during the night I wake up enough to crawl under the covers. Then I go into a deep sleep and the dreams come again. I am back in the jungle with Tex sitting under a large tree with the rain beating down. The leeches are crawling all over me and I can feel the raindrops soaking my skin. Suddenly the old woman is standing before us dressed in the olive-drab uniform of a North Vietnamese soldier. She just stands there in the darkness looking at us.

I reach out for Tex and he isn't there. Looking up, the old woman is gone. I tell myself to wake up, that this is only a dream. When I open my eyes I am covered with sweat. I had forgotten to turn the heat down before I went to sleep and the room is smothering. Getting up I threw open the door and look out, the night is cold and quiet. I stand there in the doorway with only my boxer shorts on, taking a deep breath and listening to the night sounds. I can hear a siren off in the distance and think it might be exciting to become a cop.

I walk over and turn the heat off, leaving the door open until the room cools down. Going back to bed I lay there and think of Sarah. That little girl at the restaurant stirred feelings in me I haven't had since Saigon. I lay there thinking about the women in my life until I fall asleep. I rest well until morning with no more dreams.

My arm and shoulder are really sore. I get up to shower, then head down to the restaurant for breakfast. The place is packed and I have to wait for a table. I study the people around me while I wait, wondering what each of them does and what they are thinking.

Everyone seems to be busy as they eat fast and hurry out. I finally get a table and order biscuits and gravy--something I haven't had in a long time. After breakfast I walk back to the room, get my bag and walk down to the lobby. After paying my bill I ask the lady to call me a cab.

Chapter Eleven

I hated going back to the damn hospital. I knew I would be filling out papers and answering questions for the next two hours. It was just a short cab ride and I had the driver drop me off at the admittance office. After paying for the cab I took a long look around before going in and giving them my records. I had to sit out front for over an hour before some orderly took me into an office and had me fill out all of their stupid forms.

I was assigned to a room and given a pair of blue pajamas and some damn paper slippers. I hate those things. Wonder who gets the million- dollar contract for selling them to the army. At least I was in a room by myself and I was allowed to go to the lounge where they had a television and lots of stuff to read. I wasn't scheduled to see a doctor until the next day so I went back to my room and read until I fell asleep. It was evening before I awoke; I couldn't believe I had slept that long without dreaming.

My stomach was growling and I was hungry, so I walked out to the desk and asked to go to the cafeteria, explaining my plight to the nurse. She looked at her records, which showed that I wasn't scheduled for a meal in my room, gave me a meal ticket and told me where the cafeteria was.

The place was almost empty except for a couple of haggard-looking individuals over in the corner drinking coffee. They looked worse than I did. The meal was good and I had a glass of cold milk with some cake for dessert. Now I was stuffed.

I ventured out back of the hospital where there was a small park by a little lake. It was a peaceful place and I sat and watched the ducks splash around in the water. Some man in pajamas and a woman were standing with a little boy who was fishing. I watched him untangle his line several times and remembered how Dad used to get mad at me for tangling up mine.

It came to me that I should call my folks. I didn't have to tell them where I was. Since it had been several weeks since I wrote, Mom might be calling the army asking about me. My parents have no idea I was wounded and I don't want anyone telling them; it would just add to their worries.

Going back up to the nurse's station, I asked about making a call. I was told that as long as it was local I could call from my room. I tried to remember their phone number. Why is it you can always remember everyone's number but your own?

Pulling up a chair, I sat and held the phone for awhile, trying to think of what I am going to tell them. With shaking hands I dialed their number. Mom answered on the second ring. All I could say was, "Hi, Mom." She burst out crying and asked how I am. I tell her I am okay and on my way back to the states. She hollered for Dad and told him it is Mike. Dad grabbed the phone and started asking questions faster than I could answer. He wanted to know if I had been in any battles and how the country is over there. I just tell him I have only been in a couple scrapes and that the country is either jungle or rice fields.

Mom told me I need to call Sarah as soon as I can. She gave me her number. Of course, I have to find something to write on, so I lay the phone down and go back to the nurse's station for a pen and paper. After getting Sarah's number we talked about everything from crops to neighbors. I told them I will call back in a couple of days as soon as I get located. Mom told me she will keep praying for me, that she has said a prayer every day that I have been gone. Dad told me to take care of myself and to hurry home, that he has a lot of work for me to do.

After I hung up I sat there and thought how lucky I am to have a great family. My folks have always supported me and followed me in all my school activities. I decided to call Sarah while I was in the mood. Her phone rings and some girl answers. I ask if this is Sarah and she tells me Sarah is in the shower. I just say, "This is Mike. Tell her I will call back," but the girl had already yelled, "It's Mike!" Sarah was on the phone in a split second, telling me how she was standing there naked and dripping water all over the place. I told her I could hang up while she dries off and gets dressed. She said, "Don't you dare hang up this phone, Mike Malloy. I have been waiting for months to talk to you. Why haven't you written to me? I waited every day for a letter from you and very few ever came."

"Well, Sarah, it's hard to come up with things to write about when every day is the same; anyway, I figured you had found some cute college guy by now."

Sarah said, "All these guys are a bunch of jerks. All they think women are good for is sex."

I couldn't come up with a witty answer so I just sat in total silence. She says "Not you, too." All I can say is, "Well, if I remember right, it is fun."

"Where are you?" she asked. I wanted to tell her that I am only a few blocks away but I am afraid to, so I just say I am on my way back to the states. She told me that when I get home we are going to have to have a long talk about the letters I wrote and the ones I didn't write. Now I am trying to remember what I might have said. So to get out of it, I started telling her how I thought of her every minute I was awake, and even had a couple of good dreams about her.

She said, "Yeah, I just bet you did," then she laughed. It was good to hear her laughter again; I had forgotten how much fun she was.

We talked for over an hour, I never did ask her if she put on any clothes. She probably dripped dry standing there in the nude talking to me. I tried to form a picture of that in my mind but never succeeded. After I said goodbye and hung up, I wanted to go find her, to hold and kiss her. She really stirred me up, especially the thought of her being nude. Maybe I ain't dead yet.

I go to sleep thinking of her. Again I make it through the night without any dreams. Maybe that doctor in Japan knew what he was talking about when he said I needed to get other things on my mind.

After taking a hot shower, I put on clean pajamas and walked out to the nurse's station. She told me I could get what I wanted to eat in the cafeteria and to just give them my room number. And that I had a doctor's appointment at ten, so be in my room at least ten minutes before.

My appetite has returned so I ate a big breakfast, following it up with a good hot cup of coffee. Afterwards I went for a walk out by the lake keeping a close watch on the time so I won't be late for the meeting with the doctor.

The session with the shrink went okay. He asked me a lot of questions and checked my records to see what kind of pills I was on. I told him I hadn't been taking anything for a few days because I wanted to wean myself off of them. He wanted to know all about my dreams and if they were always the same. I told him I hadn't had a dream the last two nights

and I wasn't on the medication either. He told me he would write a lighter prescription for me, that he wanted me to take them for awhile longer.

I talked to him about my arm and shoulder hurting, and he scheduled me with another doctor for the next day. He informed me I was due to get my separation papers soon, but I could still stay on at the hospital until I felt secure enough to leave. I was to draw my same pay for ninety days, then have a reevaluation. This really got me to thinking about what I wanted to do. I wasn't fit enough for the army, but was I fit enough to work someplace?

I walked down to the personnel office and asked about getting paid. I had almost three thousand dollars on the books with my combat pay figured in and what I would get for being released. If I enrolled back in college, I would get two hundred and fifty dollars more a month. I had them draw me a check for the whole amount. The next day I walked over to the bank a couple blocks away and opened a checking account. This was a first for me. I held out five hundred dollars since they wouldn't have any checks for me for a couple of weeks.

Walking uptown I bought everything from shoes and socks to underwear, a couple pairs of pants and three shirts. Going back to the hospital I checked in and did the therapy secession with my shrink. I have only had short dreams lately and they weren't bad, so maybe the medication or else new surroundings are helping.

My duffle bag arrived one day with all my uniforms and other clothing. I never thought I would ever see them again. I guess the army does work miracles at times.

I got called into the personnel office and was informed that I was going to be given a medical discharge, but that it would be subject to review every year until I was found fit for civilian life, whatever that meant. I would get a pension of five hundred and eighty dollars a month, plus another two hundred and fifty if I went back to school.

Going back to my room I lay on the bed and thought about all I had been through. I kept thinking about Tex--what would he think of me? Would he think I was a nut like everyone else? Hell, I even believe it myself after one of those damn nightmares.

I drifted off into a sound sleep. Soon I was standing on the edge of a deep gorge with a spiraling river at the bottom that was so small I could hardly see it. I could hear the wind whistling as it pulled me toward the center. Then I was falling, reaching out, searching and grabbing frantically for anything that would stop me. I could hear the old Vietnamese woman shrieking and laughing as she watched me fall farther and farther into the darkness of the gorge.

I could hear myself screaming and felt people grabbing my arms as I fought to catch hold of something. Feeling a hard slap to my face, I opened my eyes. Several nurses and orderlies were holding me, telling me to relax, that I was all right, that I had only had a bad dream. I pulled away from them as embarrassment set in. Getting up, I walked over to the window and turned my back to everyone. I stood there as tears ran down my face and watched as darkness fell on the hospital grounds. Everyone just left me alone to think things out.

I was still standing there looking out into the darkness when a young nurse came in and asked, "Mr. Malloy, are you okay?"

"I don't know," I answered without turning around.

She asked if she could get me anything. I turned and said, "A new mind would help. I think I have about worn this one out."

Walking over she took hold of my hand and asked if I wanted to talk about it. Just the touch of her soft hand made me want to cry. Fighting back tears, I said, "I sure as hell need to talk to someone." She suggested that we go to the cafeteria for a cold drink.

Getting a coke, we walked over and sat at a table in the corner. She smiled and asked me if I had it rough in Nam. I said, "I guess I didn't have it any rougher than anyone else." I told her about Tex and the things we did, about him getting killed on his way home. Finally I told her about accidentally killing the old Vietnamese man and how the old woman beat on my arms and chest as I held on to his body. How I can't forget the look on the old man's bloody face or the red-stained water that pooled up all around us.

I added that I hadn't gone home to see my folks or my girlfriend who lived only a few blocks away. They didn't even know where I was.

She told me her name was Kay and that she was in her last year of pre- med training to become a physiologist. We talked about her training and all the schooling she had been through. Unofficially, she recommended that I put on my uniform with all my ribbons and go see my folks. Also that it might help to see Sarah, that getting other things on my mind would help me stop having the bad dreams.

I squeezed her hand, looked into her blue eyes and told her she could help me forget a lot of things. She squeezed my hand back and smiled saying, "Sorry, Mike, but were not allowed to date patients, plus I have too much of a workload to get involved with anyone right now."

She walked back to the elevator with me and asked if she could visit me again. I told her I would look forward to it. Giving me a light kiss on the cheek, she turned and walked off down the hall. I watched her disappeared around the corner, thinking what a great person she was, when the opening of the elevator doors drew me back to reality.

On the way up to my room I decided to call my folks and Sarah to let them know where I was. Returning to my room I dug out my uniform and tried it on. Everything still fit me pretty good even if I had lost some weight.

Taking my uniform to the laundry, I asked to get it cleaned and pressed. I went to sleep that night planning the visit with my family and Sarah. I slept well with no dreams.

Morning came early and I was excited and hungry on the way down to the cafeteria. I ate a good breakfast. Sitting and sipping my coffee, I remembered I had another session with the doctor at ten. Feeling better than I had for days, I hurried back up to my room. I had a note to contact the personnel office.

Having an hour to kill I walked over to the administration building and into the personnel office. They checked my records and told me that there would be a Colonel from Fort Leonard Wood coming down the next day to present medals to all the veterans, and for me to be ready for inspection and medal presentation at one p.m.

I called Mom and told her I was now at the VA hospital in Springfield. She scolded me and asked why I didn't tell them I was coming in so that

they could meet me at the airport. I made some excuse about war protesters and told her we weren't allowed to tell where we were going. I asked if she and Dad could come to the hospital at one the next day for the medal presentation ceremony. She wanted to come over right now, but I told her I had a lot to do to get ready for tomorrow and I still had a couple of doctors to see. She had a million questions about why I was in the hospital and how I was. Making excuses, I told her it was all routine army stuff I had to go through before getting discharged.

By the time I got her off the phone, the shrink I had to see was in my room waiting for me. He wanted to know all about the dream I'd just had and about what happened to me in Nam. Damn I hated answering all those questions, but guess they are necessary. I told him about the incident with the old Vietnamese man and all about losing Tex. These were the two things that seemed to bother me the most.

He wanted me to go over every patrol with him. I didn't want to put myself through all of the killing and all the wounded men I had seen, but he thought it would be helpful if I could face everything.

Chapter Twelve

The session with my shrink lasted several hours. I was exhausted afterwards, both mentally and physically. I took him through each patrol and firefight I had been in, telling him the truth about our little skirmish that we faked on the hill that turned out to be the real thing. He just smiled and said, "I guess I missed a lot not being over there. I can see where one could come home with some problems."

He reassured me that my dreams would stop after I got interested in doing more things. After he left I lay there thinking about everything I had told him. I'd forgotten to tell him about the tiger; I guess that wouldn't have any effect on me.

The next thing I know I'm back in Nam and that damn tiger is coming toward me carrying the old woman in his mouth. She is screaming at me but I can't make out what she is saying. I just stand there frozen in place watching as the giant cat comes closer and closer. The cat turns into Tex. He is carrying someone over his shoulder as he walks past me and goes on into the jungle. I awake as he disappears among the trees. I listened to my heart beat thinking about why I had this peculiar dream. I believe it is because I fell asleep thinking about the tiger situation. I wish I could have seen who Tex was carrying--maybe it was me!

Remembering the medal ceremony tomorrow, I got up and checked all my clothing, making sure I have everything ready. I noticed that it was after two, no wonder I'm hungry. Going down to the cafeteria I picked up a tray and looked around hoping that Kay was there. I enjoyed talking with her and I wanted to tell her about my last dream.

The place is practically empty, just a couple people sitting and drinking coffee. I would like to have someone to talk with while I eat but don't see anyone who looks like they would be interested. Sitting down, I nibble at my lunch and think about what few friends I have, if any. I had friends while I was in school but have no idea where any of them are. My relationship with Tex was the closest I had ever gotten to anyone.

I could feel the depression coming over me, so I tried to think about Sarah and how good it will be to see her tomorrow. I hope she won't be disappointed in me. I know I have changed; the carefree person I used to be got lost somewhere in Vietnam. Someplace over there in a jungle or rice patty, all of the softness and caring I had disappeared. I became aware how fragile and precious each moment in life is, realizing that it can all be gone in one short step.

I can still remember the faces of the men I saw get killed, but I can't put many names with them. I guess war has always been like this-- sometimes it all seems so useless. Then I remember the refugees and how they struggled to survive, all because someone stronger was trying to force another way of life on them. Then it all seems worthwhile. I would go back if asked, for the strong have to help the weak or we will all become enslaved under a stronger force. My mind wanders as I pick at my food; my appetite is gone so I guess I wasn't as hungry as I thought.

I put my tray away and walk out back to the little park. Chairs are being set up and everything is getting prepared for the big ceremony tomorrow. I have had enough of this place for the day. Going back to my room and trying on my dress uniform with all the ribbons and medals that I will wear for the ceremony tomorrow, I decide that while I am dressed I might as well go for a walk. I stroll around the block to College Street and head down it. I guess I am hoping to see Sarah. I should have called her, but she is probably in a class at this time of day.

Going toward the little coffee shop where the kids all hang out, I can see a lot of long-haired hippie types coming and going. Some of them stop and stare at me. I start to realize that I am in the wrong clothes to be in this part of town. As I turn to head back I hear someone one holler, "Mike!" Turning around I see Sarah running toward me with her long hair blowing in the wind. She keeps hollering "Mike! Mike!" and then she is in my arms almost knocking me over. I stand and hold her tightly, remembering how good it always felt to hug her.

She looks up through teary eyes and with wet, trembling lips she kisses me. We stand there on the sidewalk and embrace each other for what seems like an eternity. Stepping back she holds my head with both hands and said, "Let me look at you, Mike. You look terrific!"

"Sure I do! I look like I have been dragged through hell frontward and backwards."

She laughs and said, "I haven't checked out the back yet, but up front you look real good."

I tell her that she hasn't changed much, that she was always the prettiest girl in high school and college has improved on that.

Taking me by the hand she leads me toward the coffee shop, telling me she has some friends she wants me to meet.

The place was pretty crowded and it seemed like everyone in it stopped what they were doing and looked at me. I sensed trouble and tried to tell Sarah that we should leave, only by now she was introducing me to some of her friends.

She seemed to know everyone there. I smiled and tried to be polite, but I could feel the tension in the air. Some guy got up and walked past me muttering something about a damn baby killer.

Two long-haired freaks walked past, one of them bumped me intentionally and said, "You better watch yourself, soldier boy." I let it go and sat down.

Sarah ordered us a cold drink as one girl asked me about the military. I told her I had gotten drafted while I was in college and was sent to Vietnam. She wanted to know if I had killed anyone over there.

This started to anger me and when she asked how many civilians I had killed, I about lost it. I told her that everyone shooting at us wasn't wearing a uniform, so I wasn't sure if they were civilians or not. She had a silly smirk on her face that I wanted to slap clear across the room. I told her you are just as dead no matter who pulls the trigger on you.

Then she smiled and asked, "How many little kids did you shoot?"

I leaned forward and whispered, "Lady, if you want to know so damn much about it, why in hell don't you enlist and go serve a tour over there?"

I looked at Sarah and she was sitting there wide-eyed like she couldn't believe what she was hearing. I grabbed my hat and stood up to leave when some jerk behind me said, "It's about time the damn baby-killer left."

I hit him while he was still sitting down. The chair he was in flew, overtaking him and the table with it. Glass went flying and I could hear it breaking as I headed out the door.

Sarah grabbed me by the arm and tried to apologize for her friends. I told her it was okay, that I should never have come down here in uniform knowing how people felt about the war.

I could hear sirens and knew the cops were on their way. Trying to hurry, we hadn't gone three blocks when a police car pulled up and an officer told me to come over and put my hands on the car. Sarah was crying as I walked over and asked what the trouble was. The officer pushed me and said, "I told you to put your hands on the car."

Grabbing my arm, he tried to force it down behind my back. I tried to tell him that I had been wounded through the shoulder and my arm wouldn't bend back that far. Putting a handcuff on my other wrist, he yanked it back and tried to force my bad arm around to close it. I screamed in pain and again told him my arm wouldn't go back that far. Giving it a hard twist he pushed it back and fastened the cuff as my shoulder felt like it was separating from my body. He said, "Soldier boy, it'll go back if I have to tear it off and put it there."

I was in so much pain by now I couldn't talk. Grabbing me by the shoulder he opened the back door of the patrol car and shoved me in. I am begging him to take the cuffs off me, at the same time thinking, "Is this what I fought for in Vietnam?" Hearing a voice, I looked up as another officer leaned over and opened the door, asking some bloody-nosed, long- haired hippie if I was the guy who struck him.

Sarah was crying and begging the officer to let me go. They just shut the door and left me there in agony. The pain in my shoulder was almost more than I could bear. I keep asking the officer to uncuff me. He just smiled and said, "Soldier boy, if you can't take the pain, don't play the game."

I asked to be taken to the VA hospital, but he tells me the only place I am going is to jail. I again ask him to take me to a medical facility, telling him he has torn the wound in my shoulder loose. Looking back at me he said; "I don't see any blood so you'll be all right, boy."

They finally took the cuffs off me at the jail and I couldn't move my arm for the pain. As they go to fingerprint me, they tell me to put my right hand on the ink pad. I try and use my left. The booking officer grabs my right arm and yanks it up, asking if I am so stupid I don't know my left from my right. I grimace in pain as I tell him I have been wounded in that shoulder and the other officer re-injured it putting handcuffs on me.

He apologizes and asks me to remove my shirt so he can look at it. Slowly I unbutton my shirt with my left hand and slip my bad arm out of it. Raising my t-shirt the officer looks at my scarred shoulder blade. "Damn," he exclaims, "that had to hurt." I explain to him how I was carrying a wounded marine at the time and didn't realize I had been hit until later.

Calling the officer in that arrested me he has him look at my shoulder. They decide to file a report and take me back to the VA hospital. The officer apologizes for hurting me, saying he hears all kinds of excuses as to why people can't have cuffs put on them. I said; "Maybe you should listen to some of them." He apologized again and said, "I suspect I will after the sergeant reads the report on this and gets through chewing my butt."

On the ride back to the hospital I start worrying about Sarah and what she must think of me. I doubt if she will show up at the ceremony today.

The officer drops me off and apologizes again. I walk down to the emergency room and ask to be seen. After filling out a dozen forms with my left hand I get to see a doctor. He wasn't very thrilled with the way the police treated me, or with me for hitting someone. Some of the scar tissue in my shoulder had been torn and my arm would be in a sling for several weeks. He gave me some pain medication and sent me back to my room.

I thought how great it's going to be meeting my folks with my arm tied up. Mom will know I have been wounded and worry herself sick about it. Taking a look at my uniform I see it is a real mess. With one arm I clean it the best I can and hit the sack.

My body aches all over. Why did I even go down to the college? Especially in uniform! I should have known I was asking for trouble with all the stupid protesters running around.

Sleep came quickly but didn't last long enough. It was morning before I knew it. At least I didn't have any dreams. Maybe I should do this more often. I moved my arm and pain shot through my whole body, much worse than the original wound ever hurt.

I manage to get my robe on and the arm back in the sling. Making my way back down to the cafeteria, I got in line and slid my tray along, taking more than I would probably eat. Carrying my tray in my left hand, I balanced it with my right as I headed for a table in the corner.

Kay hollers at me as I pass by a row of tables. I ask her to join me. Excusing herself from the people she had been talking with, she joins me, asking about the sling on my arm. She wanted to know if I'd had surgery. I explained that I ran into a mean cop. Smiling, she asked what really happened. I told her the whole woeful story, even about being with Sarah and how I doubted that she would be at the medal presentation today.

Kay said, "I bet she will be here, and if she isn't, I'll sneak down for your part." I told her I had never been to one of these big ceremonies, that the other medals I received were pinned on me by my commanding officer at morning formation. Standing up, she reached over and patted my hand and told me she had to get to work, and for me to get my speech ready. Smiling at me, she walked away, leaving me there thinking, do I have to make a speech?

Chapter Thirteen

Once back in my room I checked over my uniform and got everything ready for the presentation ceremony. Looking at my uniform I remembered the young lieutenant who got killed, how neat and perfect his uniform fit. All the creases and folds were in the proper places and it was tailored to fit. It was a shame; he hadn't been in the field a week before he got wasted on his first patrol.

God, I don't need to start thinking about this shit again. I have enough problems without trying to add more to them.

I still have a couple of hours to kill. Stretching out on my bed I lay back and look at the white square tiles on the ceiling. I would love to sleep, a long restful sleep. Hell, I don't care if I ever wake up. Moving my right arm I try and make it work without it hurting. That damn cop really did a number on me, but I guess I can't blame him for doing his job. He probably meets assholes of all types out there every day. I don't want to put my arm in a sling, but I know if I don't I'll have to salute and that won't work, so I'll just put the sling back on and let Mom worry.

I lay there over an hour as time clicked by. Finally I got up and headed for the shower. The hot water felt good on my sore arm as I stood and let it beat against the tender skin on the scar tissue, remembering the young marine I was carrying. I wonder if he made it. I guess I was lucky, maybe the round passed through him before it hit me. It did enough damage, and I guess I should be thankful I am still alive.

Stepping from the shower I dry off and get dressed. I still have over an hour until the ceremony is to begin. One of the nurses came in and helped me into my jacket, straightened up my sling and smoothed down my collar. She patted me on the arm and said, "You're one good-looking soldier, Mike. How many pretty girls are waiting for you down there?"

I managed a smile and said, "Just one, I hope, plus my Mom and Dad." She patted my arm and told me she would be watching.

Walking down to the ground floor I look out toward the little park. There were a lot of people already seated. I can see my folks and Sarah, along with my sister Vera and her husband James. Walking back to the front of the building, I go out and down the sidewalk that runs past the park, cutting across behind all the chairs I walk up behind Mom and ask, "Do you live around here, lady?"

She came out of her chair like a bee had stung her. Grabbing me around the shoulders, hollering "Mike, Mike," she about ripped my sling off. I grimaced with pain as she squeezed me, but held my composure. Dad and Sarah were up hugging me and asking questions faster than I could answer. Mom kept asking why I had my arm in a sling. I guess Sarah hadn't told them about my little wrestling match with the local law. I said, "I had a minor wound, just enough to give me a Purple Heart and maybe make me a US Senator someday."

Dad took a look at my ribbons and said, "I see you have had more than one minor wound." Then he noticed the Silver Star. Reaching out, he touched it and said, "I am afraid to even ask about that one."

"It's a long story," I said. "Some day when you have a lot of time, I'll tell you about it."

I hugged my sister and shook hands with James. Mom wanted to know why I didn't let them know I was coming in or why I hadn't been home. I said, "I was worn out and looked pretty haggard when I got here. And I wanted to wait until I could look my best for you and Sarah."

We sat and talked until time for the ceremony. I had to move up and sit with the other military people. Looking around me I could see young men in wheelchairs and on crutches, some missing arms and legs. I really felt stupid worrying about a damn sling on my arm.

After a long dry speech, the Colonel finally got to handing out the medals. When they called my name, he read a long report of my exploits and recommendations by Colonel Hawkins. I was awarded another Purple Heart, a fourth Bronze Star, and several commendation medals along with a couple of medals given by the Republic of Vietnam. I felt very humble, especially when I thought about Slick, who had gotten shot all to hell, and about Red whose leg was blown off, and Lt. Wolf, who was wounded twice and stayed on patrol with us, and Tex Johnson, the best soldier I ever knew. These are the men who should be standing here being honored, not me. I really don't feel like I earned most of these medals. Hell, I'm no hero. I'm just some unlucky bastard who got his ass put in a bad situation and made the best of it.

Asking if I had anything I wanted to say, the Colonel brought me out of my trance. I started to decline when I heard the war protesters out on the street yelling and clapping their hands. I know they have a right to protest, but I would love to throw a grenade in the middle of them and watch as they haul ass. I stood there holding back tears and anger as I told everyone what an honor I thought it was to serve my country--and to serve with all the brave men I had gotten to know. That a lot of good men had died and gotten injured in this war, but at least they were fighting for something they believed in. Not like that bunch of sickos out there on the street. Everyone stood and applauded as I sat down.

After the ceremony Mom must have made me pose for a hundred pictures--standing with Dad, then Sarah, then with my sister. She must have burned up a dozen rolls of film.

A banquet meal had been prepared for everyone in the cafeteria. The food and drinks were good and relaxing. We sat and talked about each other, the crops, and everything in general. A tour of the hospital was offered so I went along with them. I had seen enough of this damn place to last me a lifetime. When we got to my floor I excused myself from the crowd, telling my folks I wanted to go change and would meet them in the cafeteria in a few minutes.

Getting to my room I shut the door behind me as I stood there shaking and sweating so badly I could hardly stand. Sitting down on my bed, I wanted to cry but no tears came. Standing up and going over to the mirror, I took a long look at myself. Who was this figure looking back at me? It sure as hell wasn't the happy-go-lucky kid who was in college a year back. My eyes looked sunken and dark. I was a lot thinner and the look in my eyes was that of a lost animal. Had Mom and the other folks noticed this? Depression was starting to sink in as I turned around and slid my arm out of the sling and took off my coat. I thought about Tex and all the others--what would they think of me? I had survived that damn war for some reason. Surely God must have a plan for me. I took a couple of pills to relax and changed into civilian clothes. Stuffing a change of underwear and some more clothes into a small travel bag, I washed my face in the sink, ran my hand through my short hair, and made my way back to the crowd.

Sis and her husband gave me a big hug as they said goodbye, telling me they would see me Sunday. Dad was anxious to get going, asking me if I wanted to drive. I said, "I don't believe you will want to ride with me until I've had time to scatter some of the gravel on the back roads." Sarah and I got into the back; she leaned over and hugged and kissed me, which took me by surprise. I looked into her blue eyes and realized what a beautiful woman she had become. The small gangly girl I loved in high school is now a full-fledged woman.

Sitting there holding her and looking at my folks, I can't believe how everything and everyone has changed. Dad looks so old and frail; I used to think he was the strongest man in the world. Mom's hair has turned gray and she wears it differently. I started to wonder--are they the ones who have changed? Or is it me?

Sarah kept talking to me and Mom was still asking questions. As I sat and watched the familiar landscape go passing by, Sarah squeezed my arm and said, "Mike, are you ignoring us?" This brought me back to reality. I said, "No, not really. It's just that in the army you digest things longer. What were you saying anyway?"

Everyone laughed. It felt good to be with friends and family again.

As Dad pulled into the yard, my old dog Sparky came out to meet us. I got out of the car and called him. He wagged his tail, came over and sniffed my hand, and then walked over to Sarah.

Mom said, "I don't believe he remembers you."

"Oh, he remembers me all right; he is just showing his displeasure at me being gone."

Dad laughed and said, "After you see all the work I have lined up for you to do, you'll see all the displeasure I have at you being gone, too!"

Taking Sarah by the hand we walked out through the back lawn and past the barn. Once we couldn't be seen, I took her in my arms and held her tight. She lifted her head and kissed me long and hard, saying, "Mike, I have really missed you. Even before you went to Nam I wanted to be with you. What happened to us after you went away to college?"

I just stood and held her tight as thoughts raced through my mind. Finally I said, "I guess it was all the excitement of being in college, away from my folks and feeling freedom for the first time." I kissed her and said, "I always thought of you and wanted to be with you, but college takes up so much of your time you just don't ever seem to get done what you really want to do."

She put both arms around my neck as she kissed me again, saying, "We better get back to your folks or they are going to come looking for us."

The house was pretty much like I remembered. My room was the same, all my clothes still hung neatly in the closet. For the first time since I came back I really wanted to be here. It's amazing the things we take for granted--I guess in my mind all of this would always be here. I picked up a baseball trophy that I had won in Little League. I had been so proud of that trophy that I had sat and held it for hours. Mom finally made me put it away. All of that seemed like such a long time ago.

Dad called to me--he wanted to show me their new television. He had a control so that he could change channels without getting up out of his chair. I laughed and said, "I wondered who would change channels for you after I left." He said that was when he missed me most, when the television needed changing and the chores needed doing.

I sat there in the living room looking at all the little knickknacks and pictures Mom had placed around the room. Some of the stuff I didn't remember.

Dad asked me what my plans were now that I was back. I told him I still had some time left to serve, and didn't know if I would be sent someplace else after my wound healed.

"What happened?" he asked.

I said, "I got hit with a stray round during a minor skirmish. I was carrying a wounded marine back to an aide station. I didn't even know I was hit until I got back to my men a few minute later. The round went in under my arm, missing my flak jacket, and came out through my shoulder blade. It felt like a bad muscle pull."

"What about the others?" Dad asked.

I told him I got hit in the leg by some shrapnel from a mortar round. I started to get nervous as I knew the next question that was coming. I just sat there and waited. "And the third one?" he asked

I didn't want to lie to him. "It was just something minor," I said. "Nothing that even required a bandage."

He laughed and said, "I guess they give them out pretty freely."

I just looked at him and smiled, saying, "If you bleed for the cause they will hang something on your chest."

I tried to change the subject several times, but he kept asking questions about the war. Finally I told him that it was just a hot, miserable, boring place where good men got blown to hell. Getting up I walked into the bathroom, sat down on the stool and shook uncontrollably. I must have been in there awhile because Mom knocked on the door and asked if I was okay.

I answered, "Yeah; I just felt sort of sick for a moment. All this good food I have been eating lately doesn't always agree with me."

I would have loved to lie down but didn't dare take a chance on falling asleep. Washing my face in the sink I went back to the living room. Dad was almost asleep so I walked out on the porch and called the dog. He came up and licked my hand, then stepped back and looked at me as if he was asking, "Where in the hell have you been?" Gently I reached out and stroked his head and said, "Old fellow, you don't even want to know."

Chapter Fourteen

I turned as Sarah came out. She walked over and stood beside me running her hand down the back of my neck. Leaning over, she kissed me on top of the head. I reached out and got her around the waist, pulling her to me and burying my face against her breasts, smelling the scent of her perfume and feeling the softness of her body. I thought how easy it would be to really fall in love.

She spoke, asking me what I was doing out here. I looked up at her and smiled, saying, "I'm just trying to renew a friendship with an old friend."

She sat down on my knee. I told her I wished I had two good arms so I could really hug her. Standing up, she pulled me to my feet and threw both arms around me, saying. "I have two good arms so I will hug you for both of us." We were standing there kissing when Mom came out the door. Mom was somewhat embarrassed as she excused herself and went back inside.

I laughed at Sarah and told her she had embarrassed Mom. Smiling at me, she gave me a little peck on the lips and said, "I don't think so. We women understand these things."

Taking her hand I sat down on the steps and looked out across the fields and meadows, thinking how different they looked from the rice patties and jungles of Vietnam. My thoughts turned to war. I wondered if we will ever have to fight on this soil, going from fence row to fence row, while our homes and barns burn. Will American children ever have to be refugees of war, scrambling ahead of the battle trying to stay alive, carrying what few possession they have?

Sarah reached over and placed her hand under my chin turning my head toward her. "Where are you, Mike," she asked. "You haven't heard a word I said to you."

I stood up and embraced her. Wrapping my arm around her I whispered into her ear that I was sorry. "I was a long way from here," I told her. "I was back in the jungles of Vietnam. I can't seem to get that place out of my mind. Let's take a walk and I will tell you about it."

Taking her hand we walked around the house and out through the field that led to the pond, neither of us saying a word, just wrapped in our own thoughts.

We sat down on the pond bank and I told her the whole horrible story. All about the men who died and the ones I killed. I explained to her that was why I didn't tell anyone I was coming home. I told her about the terrible dreams I have of the old man and old woman in the rice patty, how I wake up screaming and fighting to get away from my own mind.

Sarah was sitting there with a lost look on her face as tears ran down her cheeks. She reached out and squeezed my hand and kept saying, "It's okay now, Mike, you're home, everything is all right."

I tried to explain to her how I was afraid to spend the night in my folk's house. She encouraged me to tell them everything I had told her, saying, "Mike, they will understand."

"How can they understand," I said, "when I don't?"

I reached over and drew her close to me. Holding her tight, I said, "Sarah, I am so scared, sometimes I think I am going crazy." I told her about Tex and how he knew he was going to die in that god-awful place. I never believed him the day he told me he thought his ticket had been punched. He tried to get out and almost made it.

Sarah was shaking all over as we sat there holding each other. Neither of us spoke for a long time. Our silence was interrupted by Mom's voice calling us to come eat. Holding Sarah at arm's length I looked into her blue eyes and asked her if she was sure she wanted to get mixed up with me after what I had just told her. She stood there dabbing at her eyes with a Kleenex the way women do. Looking up, she kissed me lightly and said, "Mike we will work it out together."

Mom had prepared my favorite meal of sausage patties, mashed potatoes and gravy, and hot biscuits. We ate pretty much in silence. Dad spoke up telling me about the improvements he wanted to do on the place. Mom started talking with Sarah about the neighbor girl and the big wedding she had. She said, "Half the county was there. It must have cost her folks a fortune."

I looked at Sarah and winked, saying "Mom's trying to talk us into eloping; it's much cheaper that way."

Mom blushed and said, "Mike Malloy, you just mind your manners. I never meant any such a thing."

Dad scooted his chair back, saying he was going to watch the news, leaving the three of us sitting there. Even though I was about to bust I ate another piece of sausage with gravy poured over it. I then excused myself while Mom and Sarah were chatting and walked into talk with Dad. He was already asleep in his chair with his head down on his chest. I stood and looked at him for a moment, thinking how much life had aged him.

Quietly I walked out to the front porch and sat down. Sparky must have heard me--he came up and lay his head on my knee wanting it scratched.

Rubbing his ears, I said, "Sparky old boy, if I could I would change places with you, even if you do only live a fraction of a human's life."

I watched a robin and a mockingbird fight over the cherry tree. Next thing I know I am back in the jungle as darkness creeps in around me. I can hear the chatter of people talking and the patter of rain on the leaves. I try to crowd back deeper into the trees. I can't find my weapon. All I have is a stick, a long curly stick with a handle on it. Someone is coming toward me. I reach out and swing the stick striking them. I can hear their cry of pain. The force of the blow woke me up.

Sarah shouted, "Mike, wake up." She was sitting there holding her arm.

"Did I hit you?" I asked.

She had a strange expression on her face as she said, "Yes. Yes, you did, and it hurt. You were making all sorts of strange sounds and I tried to wake you up.

"I'm sorry," I told her, "but don't ever touch me if I am sleeping. I have been through hell and I'm not sure I am back yet. I'm awfully jumpy when I first wake up. Are you okay?" I asked.

She smiled and said, "I think I can live through it."

Mom was standing there holding the hose as water ran everywhere. She laughed and said, "I'm sure glad I didn't squirt you with the hose, we probably wouldn't have a porch left!"

My arm had come out of the sling and it was hurting. I decided to see if I could go without the sling for awhile. Standing up I took Sarah in both arms and hugged her even though I did have to grit my teeth.

Walking out into the yard, I told Mom that she had some really pretty flowers. She laughed and said, "If I could keep the bugs and deer out of them, it would help."

We walked around the house looking at every flower and bush. Deep in my mind I was thinking that back in Nam, there would be a rifle barrel sticking out of half of them.

It was getting late when I asked Dad if he would drive me back to the hospital. A look of disappointment came over his face as he said, "We thought you were home for a few days."

I said, "All my medication and stuff is still at the hospital. And I have to see a couple of doctors tomorrow."

Mom was very disappointed with me, but I knew I had to get away. There was no way I would trust myself to spend a night here. I had just struck Sarah, what if Mom came in while I was sleeping and I hurt her? I could never live with it.

Dad gave the car keys to Sarah and asked if she would drive me back, telling her he would pick up the car at her place the next day. Giving me a hurt, puzzled look that went clear through me, he turned and went back into the living room. Mom had a sad look on her face as she wiped her hands on her apron. She said, "You're not leaving here without having dessert. I spent all morning peeling apples and you're going to eat a piece of apple pie before you go."

I laughed and said, "Okay, Mom, if you're going to twist my arm."

I was still stuffed from dinner, but the pie went down just fine. I drank part of a glass of milk to help send it on its way. We sat there and talked for over an hour. Dad never did come in and join us. I guess my refusing to spend the night really upset him. I walked in and tried to explain to him why I couldn't, but he looked at me with old tired eyes and said, "Son, you don't have to explain anything to me. If you don't want to stay, you don't want to stay. I'm sure you have your reasons."

I reached out and lay my hand on his shoulder. "Dad," I said, "When I sleep I have these horrible dreams. I wake up screaming and running into things. I am still killing people in my sleep. It's not like I don't want to stay the night, I am afraid to. It would scare Mom to death and probably shock you a little. That's why I am in the hospital."

Placing his hand on mine he looked up with tears in his eyes, and said. "Son, you will always have a home here as long as I'm alive, even if I have to build a special room for you to sleep in. A lot of men come out of combat suffering battle fatigue, you'll be okay." Patting my hand he said, "Now get out of here and get well. Your Mom and I will be up to see you in a couple of days."

When we got to the car I told Sarah I wanted to drive. Giving me the keys she slid in next to me. As I backed out of the driveway I thought how good it felt being behind the wheel again. I hadn't lost any of my skills as I wound down the gravel road to the interstate. Once we were back in Springfield I headed down Walnut Street toward the college. There was a little coffee shop and bar on the corner. I pulled in and asked Sarah if she wanted a cold drink. She hugged me and said, "No, but a cup of coffee would be good."

I noticed the place was full of college kids as we came in and took a table near the door. A young girl came over and I ordered a Bud Light and a cup of coffee for Sarah. I wasn't supposed to drink with the medication I was taking, but surely one beer wouldn't hurt anything.

The place was dimly lit and the music was a little loud. If it hadn't been for all the loud talking and the cigarette smoke, it would have been a nice place to sit and relax. But it was hard to talk over the roar of the crowd so we sat and watched everyone as we sipped our drinks.

Two long-haired drunks came in. One took a look at me and said, "What's with you, skinhead? You just get drafted?"

I tried to ignore him but he turned to his buddy and said, "Bill, I bet we got a real war hero here."

The whole place got quiet except for the jukebox blaring out some screaming rock-and-roll song. A knot started to form in my stomach as fear crept into my mind. I knew a fight was coming and I had no way to avoid it.

I looked around the room for some way out. This wasn't going to be like a fight in the jungle where you were jumped and fought with everything you had learned from months of training.

I thought about running out the door but my pride wouldn't let me. I lay the car keys on the table in front of Sarah. As I picked up my beer and took another drink, the sour mash taste of hops almost choked me as it met with the bile that was building in my throat. I hated the sickly feeling I was getting in my stomach as fear built up inside me. I tried to look away but the big-mouth bastard wasn't having any of it.

He reached over and lay his hand on my shoulder, saying, "Come on, soldier boy, tell us all a big hero war story."

Gripping the bottle by the long neck, I laid it across his face with a backhand blow, breaking the bottle as its contents flew all over. Coming to my feet I stuck the broken jagged bottle into his face, grabbed his shirt and pulled him in close to me, telling him, "If you want to see blood and war, asshole, let's use your blood for show-and-tell." A small trickle of blood was running down the side of his nose as his buddy and everyone else cleared back to give us room.

Some three-hundred-pound bouncer came from behind the bar wielding a small wooden bat. I pushed big-mouth back toward him and said, "You come at me with that club, fat boy, and I will cut forty pounds of lard off your ass before you can swing it." This gave him something to think about--he stopped and stood there glaring at me as he fumbled in his feeble mind for some heroic words that would give him courage enough to finish his charge. All the time Sarah was saying, "Mike, don't do it! Let's just get out of here."

The big-mouthed drunk had sobered up considerably and I noticed the young waitress was on the phone. I didn't need another round with the local police so I backed out the door pulling Sarah behind of me. There were fifty pairs of eyes following my every move; none of them had balls enough to do anything.

I took the keys from Sarah and unlocked the car just as two police cruisers came sliding into the parking lot. Giving Sarah a kiss on the cheek I said I've got to run, pointing toward the door as the cops got out of their vehicle. I hauled ass as fast as I could toward the back of the building. Looking back, I could see Sarah pulling out onto the street and hoped she would go on home before the cops could talk to her.

Coming to a long chainlike fence, I climbed over and found myself in a golf course. I walked around a water hazard to a small building that had a long bench in front of it. Sitting down I tried to recall what had just happened. My hands were still shaking and my heart was beating a hole in my chest. The little bit of beer I drank mixed with the drugs was making me lightheaded. I can still see the flashing lights of the police cars in front of the coffee shop.

I kept hoping that Sarah wasn't driving around looking for me. If she was, the cops will stop her for sure. Nobody in that place knew me, and I don't think any of them knew Sarah, so I should be home free. From where I sat I can see if they come into the golf course. If they do, I will slip off into the cattails that are around the pond.

I saw Sarah drive by several times but I didn't want to move. The cops have no idea where I went and I'm not about to go stumbling about in the dark and run into them. Feeling sick, I lie down on the bench and soon fall asleep. I can hear the rain hitting the bushes all around me. In my sleepy haze I crowd closer to the building. The rain was coming down in wind-blown sheets. I can hear the clicking of a tank wheel as it rumbles closer. Tex is screaming for me to run, but my legs seem paralyzed. I can hardly move—it's like everything is in slow motion. I am on my feet, but in the dark I can't figure out where to run. As I stumble along a blast of rain water hits me, then it's gone. I can hear the hissing of a tank engine and the clicking of the tracks. Another blast of rain soaks me as I try to work my way through the darkness.

Chapter Fifteen

Wiping my hand across my face I can feel the water drip off my hair. It is difficult to focus. The booze and drugs have left me in a daze. Another blast from the sprinkler brings me back to reality. It is light out now and I stand like an idiot as a lawn sprinkler hits me each time it rotates. I turned back toward the bushes and ran into yet another blast of water, standing there until I can figure out where to go.

I walked toward the clubhouse in the corner of the golf course and tried to look like I belong there. Seeing a gate I exited into the street. My clothes were soaked and water was dripping off my hair. The beer I drank along with the pills still made my mind work slowly. I needed to find a place to dry off and think about what I was going to do.

Fear grips me as a car pulled alongside. I wanted to run and I'm afraid to look; I sure don't need another run-in with the police. I just walked on without looking.

Sarah's voice broke through my curtain of fear and brought me to a stop as I heard her say, "Mike Malloy, where in the hell have you been? I have been driving around all night looking for you."

She grabbed hold of my arm, asking how I got so wet. Leading me over to the car, she opened the door and reached in. She pulled out a small towel and started rubbing my head saying, "Mike, you're soaked."

Giving me a little shove, she said, "Get in the damn car."

As I sat down, shut the door and asked where we are going, she looked over at me in disgust and said, "Someplace where we can get you dried off."

When we were a couple blocks from the college, she stopped the car and told me to get out. We walked up to a big house with a porch across the front. Sarah unlocked the door and led me into a long hallway. She stopped and unlocked another door, pushed me inside and told me to get out of my wet clothes.

"Now wait a minute," I said. "I'm not in the habit of getting naked in front of every girl I see."

She walked over and started unbuttoning my shirt. "Just get your wet clothes off, Mike, you won't be the first naked man I have ever seen."

Now this got my attention, but before I could say anything she said, "Don't ask."

I just looked at her in surprise and shed everything but my socks. I was standing there wet, cold and shriveled up to the point I couldn't have found it if I had looked.

I sat down on a cold chair and pulled off my wet socks as Sarah disappeared into another room. She came back with a large blanket and started to wrap it around me. Seeing the scars on my back and shoulder, she stopped and ran her hands over them saying, "Damn, Mike, that must have hurt. You're lucky you weren't killed."

I told her about carrying the wounded marine and of not even knowing I had been hit until my lieutenant noticed all the blood on me. "After I started coughing up blood I knew that something was wrong."

Wrapping the blanket around me she pulled me close and kissed me. Just as I started to embrace her, she half turned and pushed me toward a door, saying, "The shower is in there. I'll get you a towel."

The hot water felt good as it warmed my body and stimulated my mind. My sore arm was getting better to the point I could now wash my hair with both hands. Then I thought, you dumb bastard, you used that arm to break the beer bottle and push that loud-mouth drunk around. Boy, are you lucky you didn't get your ass kicked all the way up and down Main Street.

Turning off the shower, I opened the door and there stood Sarah naked as a picked bird's ass. I stood there with my mouth open looking at her beautiful nude body, taking in every inch of her firm breasts. She smiled and pushed me back into the shower. "I need someone to wash my back."

Everything happened so fast I didn't even have time to blush. I took the soap and rubbed it over her slick, smooth skin and down over her back. With my good arm around her slender waist, I pulled her close to me. We stood there embracing as the hot water ran over our bodies. Time stood still as she pressed her wet breasts against my chest. What had been too shriveled up to find before was now making a grand appearance.

Sarah reached around me and turned off the water. Opening the door, she picked up a large towel and started drying me off. Handing me another towel, she turned as I dried her back. Draping the towel over her shoulders, I turned her around and kissed her. Picking her up, I walked to the bed and gently lay her down, looking at her naked body, taking in every curve and crevasse. Reaching up, she took my hand and pulled me to her.

I thought to myself as we embraced that if this is another dream, I hope I never wake up. I hadn't been with a woman since Saigon, so I didn't rush things. We both went to sleep lying there holding each other. I never had any dreams, just a long restful sleep that I didn't want to ever end.

Sarah woke me as she got up and went into the bathroom. I could hear the shower running as I turned over and tried to go back to sleep. I thought to myself, did this really happen? I was amazed at how quickly a couple of years of college could change a little innocent high-school girl. And what did she mean that I wasn't the first man she had ever seen naked? I wasn't about to ask--I really didn't want to know.

I could hear her messing around in the bath and decided to get up and join her. As I sat up, the bathroom door opened and there she stood wearing nothing but what God had given her. The curves of her body and the fullness of her breasts added to her beauty. I reached out my hand as she came over and stood by the bed. Pulling her close to me, I buried my face in her breasts, holding her so tightly that I was almost suffocating. Reaching down she took hold of my hair, tilted my head back and kissed me.

Pulling her down on the bed I continued to kiss her. I thought to myself, Mike, you lucky bastard, this is going to be a day you will remember for a long time. If this doesn't get your mind off those damn dreams, nothing ever will.

Halfway through our lovemaking, I thought, Oh shit! I am supposed to be meeting with a doctor about now. How could I let something like that wreck such a beautiful moment in my life?

Sarah looked at me and asked, "What's wrong?"

I said, "Oh, nothing. I just remembered I had an appointment with my shrink about two hours ago. I am over the hill."

Winking at me, she said, "Yeah, I noticed that."

I held her tightly and told her to get serious. She said, "I am. It's you who seems to be fading away to oblivion."

After grabbing a hot shower, I asked her to drive me back to the hospital. She smiled and said, "Well, I guess I can. Seems like you're finished for the day anyway."

Throwing my towel at her, I said, "Get the keys and let's go." "Okay, but you will have to buy me breakfast on the way."

As we started to leave, Dad showed up to pick up his car. He looked at us and said, "I thought you had to see a doctor about them bad dreams this morning." Smiling, he added, "Bet you didn't have any dreams last night," as he got into his car and drove away.

Sarah stood there somewhat embarrassed, not saying a word. Letting her drive, she took us out to a truck stop on the interstate called "Hoods." There must have been a hundred trucks parked around the restaurant. Sarah said, "They serve a mean breakfast here and I'm hungry. And I know you need your energy--you seemed to run out of it early."

I just picked up a menu and looked at her in disgust. I will never figure women out if I live forever.

The breakfast was great. We sat and talked for over an hour. She asked me what I thought the military would do to me for getting back late. I just looked at her and said, "After I tell the doc about this hot lady I was with, he will probably give me a medal."

Reaching over and squeezing my hand, Sarah looked into my eyes and with a smile said, "Have him give you some vitamins, too," she laughed.

She stood up saying we better get going, that "I've missed two classes already. I should make at least one today."

Pulling into the front entrance of the hospital, Sarah leaned over and gave me a quick kiss. As I opened my door, she said, "Get out of here and call me tonight. I have got to get to my next class." I stood there on the sidewalk and watched her car until it went out of sight.

Picking up my bag, I walked over and sat on a little bench out front, dreading to go back into this damn place. I didn't know what they would do to me. Hell, I was already a nut case; maybe I should just plead insanity. I finally mustered up enough nerve to go back to my room. No one seemed to notice as I walked in and took the elevator up to the "nut ward" as I had learned to call it.

Some new nurse challenged me as I walked by her station, asking if she could help me. I smiled and told her I was a patient here. Immediately she wanted my name, rate and horsepower. After shuffling through a handful of papers, she looked up at me over her glasses and said, "Mr. Malloy, you are a day late returning from your pass."

For lack of anything else to say I just leaned over toward her and said, "No shit, lady. What are they going to do, ship my sorry ass back to Nam?"

Shifting my bag to the other hand I walked down the hall to my room. I knew I shouldn't have talked to the nurse that way, but I am fed up with this whole fucking military scene. I did my bit for society and almost got my ass shot off doing it. Now I'm a damn nut case in some hospital. What I need is a good drunk, one that will last for about a week.

I went through my locker, found some clean clothes, took a shower, got dressed, and threw all of their damn pills on the bed. I walked out past Miss Snooty, telling her I would be back later.

She was still stammering for words when the elevator door shut. I smiled to myself and thought, Malloy, your ass is going to get thrown in the brig for this, but by God you're going to have a little fun before it does.

When I hit the street, I had no idea where I was going so I just walked around, ending up on old Division Street. I noticed all the drunken, homeless people sitting in doorways of empty buildings. The look in their eyes was a pleading, sad look, like life had passed them by. It reminded me of the pictures I had seen of prisoners in Germany after the war.

Some guy hit me up for a dollar. I could see the sparkle come to his eyes when I gave it to him. "Bless you, brother," he said with a breath that would have melted paint. He smelled of coal smoke and body odor. I wondered how long it had been since he had bathed. The shabby clothes he wore gave testament to the conditions under which he was living.

I noticed the old Blue Ribbon Grill had closed. With all the drunks on the street, I figured that would still be a flourishing business. I walked on until I was at the old town square. A lot of the places were closed and the storefronts boarded up. I guess the sprawl of the shopping centers was taking a toll on the downtown business.

I was blinded by the darkness as I entered a tavern. One old man and the bartender were talking. I sat down and ordered a beer. The bartender took my money and put the bottle down. Not saying a word, he laid my change beside it and walked back over to the end of the bar. The place was as quiet as a morgue and smelled of stale beer and tobacco smoke. I could hear the two men talking but couldn't make out what it was about. I sat there and nursed my beer trying to think about what I wanted to do. I felt free--a freedom I hadn't ever felt before. I know I am still in the military but to hell with them. Right now I can go and do what I want, only I don't know what I want.

I sat there and had a couple more beers until I had a buzz going. I was wishing I had brought some of my pills. That damn Valium really gives you a ride with a couple of beers. Only thing, though, is it makes you not give a damn about anything. I can see how people get killed taking that stuff.

After leaving the bar, I stopped at a Brown Derby liquor store and bought a pint of Jim Beam. I noticed that the Old Square Theater was still open and the movie Peyton Place was playing. I had always heard of that movie but had never seen it. Besides, it would be a good place to sit and finish off Mr. Beam.

I bought a ticket, went into the theater and bought a coke at the concession stand. The movie was already playing as I found my way into the dark theater. There weren't even a dozen people in the place. I took a seat in the back row where some young couple was so busy feeling each other up and kissing that they never knew I sat down. I took a big drink from the coke, poured a little of it out on the floor and filled it back up with whiskey. It took awhile for me to get settled. The Beam and coke was going down good and I was enjoying the movie. The couple next to me should have gotten a room with their movie money--they sure as hell weren't seeing the show. It got to where I didn't know which one to watch.

I took a long pull on the whiskey and coke, leaned back and relaxed. I loved the warm feeling I was getting from the booze. I was really getting a buzz on, the movie was interesting and I was getting into the plot of things.

Running out of coke, I threw the cup on the floor and took a swig out of the bottle. The last thing I remember seeing was some young chick beating a guy to death with a stick of firewood.

Chapter Sixteen

The whiskey put me in a deep, restful sleep, making me feel warm inside. I don't know how long I had been out, but things happened to me pretty fast. One minute I was with Sarah, holding her close and feeling the warmth of her body. The next minute someone was throwing me to the ground and had pinned my arms behind me with their knee on my back.

Grabbing my hair, I heard them say something. A stick pulled my head back as it is pushed against my throat. I tried to get up but my arms were locked behind me. I felt myself being dragged as bright lights burn my eyes. Blurred figures of men in uniform were standing over me. Through my drunken haze, I realized that the police had me and were pulling me to my feet. I couldn't get my hands loose; something was holding them. Struggling, I tried and get free as strong arms pushed me into the side of a building.

Sarah wasn't there to help me. Where did she go? Have these men taken her away? I asked what they did with Sarah. One of them asked who Sarah is. I tried to hang on as the world starts spinning, and I slid down the wall.

I could hear people all around me and the smell of puke and urine was so strong I fought to get a breath of fresh air. People were bumping against me; I felt someone give me a shove as I bounced off another body. I struggled to get to my feet as blurred images of people formed in my mind. Rubbing my eyes and trying to stand up, I realized I am in a crowded place with a lot of dirty, smelly people. No one seemed to be making any sense as I moved against the iron bars that surrounded me.

The smell of dirty bodies was making me sick. I tried to heave but nothing comes up. The rotten smell was starting to suffocate me. Finding a place by the bars to stand, my mind started to clear. All around me people were sitting and standing. I crowded closer against the bars and tried to clear my head. Sticking my face between the bars I struggled to get a breath of fresh air. I screamed for someone to get me out, to help me. I don't belong in this god-awful place.

I gave up and quit hollering. I stood there trying to keep from breathing the putrid smell of all the filthy bodies. After a couple of hours, a uniformed office came in and started taking down names of all of us who were standing, one at a time. Finally it was my turn. He took me in and fingerprinted me, then asked if I had ever been arrested before. I didn't want to admit it, but I told him I had been arrested for assault, that I had smacked some loud-mouth hippie bastard for calling me a baby-killer.

Sitting me down at a desk, he asked for my full name and address. I told him I was in the veteran's hospital. He wanted to see my papers, which I didn't have. I told him I got tired of that damn place, walked out and decided to get drunk. He looked at me and said, "Well, soldier, you accomplished that. You were about as drunk as I have seen anyone when they brought you in here. I didn't think you would ever stop screaming and yelling. Hell, man, you scared half the drunks in the tank into sobriety. They were giving you plenty of room. We would have isolated you but for lack of space."

He asked why I was still in the hospital, so I decided to tell him the whole story. When I was finished, he stood up, led me over to a cell, and said, "We will have to hold you here until someone from the hospital comes for you. You will have to see a judge about the drunk-and-disorderly charge."

The army wasn't in any hurry to get me. The MPs showed up just before dark and cuffed me before leading me out to a waiting car. I asked them if they thought I was some bad-ass who was liable to hurt one of them. They both were about six-feet-four and over two hundred and fifty pounds. One of them looked at me and laughed, saying, "No, Malloy, we just have to follow procedure."

Once we were back at the hospital and checked in, they took me to my room and waited while I packed up everything. Then they took me to the lockdown ward of the hospital where I was signed in. They took all my gear before leading me down the hall to a long room with about twenty beds in it. I was assigned a bunk and a locker. They gave me a pair of bright blue coveralls to wear, telling me they would bring my clothes as soon as they searched everything.

I sure as hell didn't want to be in this ward. There were bars on the windows and a guard at the door. Some of the guys in here looked like real kooks. They probably thought the same about me; none of them spoke but they all were staring. So to start things off right I sat down and let out the loudest scream and yell I could muster up, then lay back on my bunk and laughed. I wanted everyone in here, except for the doctors and nurses, to believe I am nuts. That way they will leave me alone. When I sat up everyone was busy doing something, they sure weren't looking at me anymore.

Two male orderlies came in and started giving everyone a bunch of pills. I pretended to swallow mine, but kept them in my hand. These bastards aren't about to dope me into oblivion. After they left I checked them out, but not knowing what they had given me, I flushed them down the john.

I was really getting hungry and asked some dude when we eat. He just stood there and stared at me like it was the first time he had ever heard someone speak. I looked around and checked everyone out; there were some real nut cases in here. I started to get scared. What if I never get out of this place? I remembered Sarah and thought I should call her, but there wasn't a phone in this ward. Guess they figured someone would get strangled with the cord.

Walking over to the door, I leaned over the locked gate and asked the orderly if I was allowed a phone call. He just sat there and stared at me like it really pissed him off that I even bothered to talk to him. He stood up and said, "You will get whatever your doctor orders and nothing else." Looking up at him I said, "Thanks, asshole, you should be over here with me."

I didn't like being in here. The whole place made me feel uneasy. I am afraid of some of these nut cases. Now I know I may be a little on the weird side at times, but some of these monkeys in here don't even know what a coconut is. I hope they don't give any of them sharp objects to play with--I don't want to lie down and go to sleep with some of these creeps slithering around. If I'm nuts, these guys are way ahead of me. I know I need to straighten up my act and get my ass on the other side of that gate.

They finally lined us up and we marched down to a cafeteria where we were given a tray and a spoon. We walked along and pointed at what we wanted to eat. The guys serving were having a real field day laughing at all the nuts, so I decided to have a little fun. This old guy was serving peas and when I got in front of him I just stood and stared for a long time. Then I hollered, "Daddy, Daddy, where the hell have you been? Mommy's out looking for you." The whole place erupted in laughter and the poor old fart almost had a stroke. I laughed and told him to give me a scoop of peas; he was still standing there in shock long after I left.

I guess none of these people in here ever joke with the help. Hell, they are afraid of most of us. An orderly came up and asked if I am Malloy. Before I could answer he shoved a paper in my hand and told me to report to the front desk.

Now I'm thinking, what kind of crap is going on?

Getting up I stacked my tray in the bin with the rest of the dirty dishes, gave the man my spoon and headed for the front desk. I had to let the damn dumb orderly who watches the door read my note three times before he would let me out. Walking down the hall I noticed everyone watching me. Then I think, hell, it's these damn blue coveralls. So when the next batch of nurses came by and looked at me, I leaned over and hollered, "Boo!" They scattered like a covey of quail.

I started to think that this being nuts could be a lot of fun if it wasn't for the fact that they keep you locked up.

At the front desk, the nurse handed me a bunch of papers and told me that Major Johns wanted to see me in his office. She pointed to a door across the hall that was marked "Major J. D. Johns, MD."

I thought about just opening the door and walking in, but down deep I knew better. I knocked softly and heard a voice say "Come in."

Upon entering the small office, I snapped to attention, gave a Marine salute, and stated, "Mike Malloy, Sergeant, United States Army, reporting as ordered, sir."

Pointing to a chair, the major told me to sit down and relax. He shuffled through a stack of papers, looked up and told me that I was being medically discharged from the army and would receive outpatient treatment for as long as it was needed. I sat there a moment, then asked him what all this meant. He went into details about how I would get a military pension of some kind for my injuries.

This flat scared the piss out of me as I wasn't really prepared for it. I could feel my emotions filling up inside of me, not knowing how I would survive. I could go home and stay with my folks, but I really didn't want to chance that.

"When will I be released?" I asked?

Major Johns said, "Your papers are being drawn up and will be ready by noon tomorrow."

Handing me a sheet of paper with a bunch of room numbers on them, he told me that I had to get checked out with payroll and medical offices, and to set up a date that I could report back for dental and medical check- ups. Hell, I didn't even have to go back to the nut ward except to retrieve my gear that was stored in a locker and give them back these damn blue coveralls.

The orderly took me back down to the lockup and retrieved my uniform and civilian clothes, standing by while I changed. When I handed him the coveralls, he turned and threw them into a trash bin. "Hell," I told him, "I want to keep those as a memento of all the happy time I spent here." He laughed, picked them up and tossed them to me. He said, "Throw them in your bag. I didn't see anything."

I spent the rest of the day checking out with various departments. Ms.

Snooty, the iron-jawed nurse on the ward, even gave me my old bed back.

Noticing the phone when I sat down, I picked it up and called Sarah. It rang several times before she answered. I said, "Hi, this is Mike."

There was a long pause before she said, "Mike, where in the hell have you been? I have been calling all over trying to find you. Your folks are worried sick; no one has seen or heard from you."

I couldn't think of a quick lie so I told her the truth about going over the hill, getting drunk and thrown in jail, and being put in lockdown when I got back to the hospital. All this didn't seem to faze her a bit. She said, "You could have called me or had one of the nurses do it." Now why in hell didn't I think of that? Maybe I do belong in the nut ward.

I sat there holding the phone while she ragged on me, telling me how I needed to grow up and learn to control my emotions. After a long silence I said, "I am going to be released tomorrow. Can I spend a couple days with you until I can find a place to crash?"

I could tell by her long pause that she didn't really want me there. So I said, "If it's a problem, I can find a place to rent somewhere."

She started making excuses about her roommate and that her place was awfully crowded. I told her it's okay, that I will just rent a place in town.

Chapter Seventeen

It was past two in the afternoon before I finally got all my papers releasing me from the hospital along with my separation from the U.S. Army. I was now a civilian, something I had been wanting for a long time. Only now it didn't seem like such a good idea. I had no job, no home, and no means of transportation. A deep, sick feeling hit me in the pit of my stomach. Where would I go? I sure didn't want to go back to my folks. I wasn't ready for that five a.m. alarm clock and all those damn cows to milk and clean up after. I know Dad could use the help, but I needed some time to try and find myself and shake these nightmares.

I could tell by the way Sarah talked that she didn't want me over there, so I called a cab and had the driver take me to a motel on the outskirts of town. The motel had been there ever since old Highway 66 was a main road. Now that the interstate had all the traffic, it was just a flophouse for people like me. The whole place was in bad need of a paint job--some of the siding was falling off around the edges where patrons had backed into it. The whole damn place needed to be torn down and burned to get rid of the vermin. The poor bastards who lived there either lacked enough money or enough pride to move to a better place. The walls didn't hold any insulation and were so thin that, on a still night, you could hear someone fart two rooms down. But it was cheap and clean as any worn-out motel could be.

I gave the cabbie a ten and told him to keep the change. Giving me a toothless grin, he asked if I would like him to bring me a woman later on. Smiling, I said, "Not tonight, I have other plans." As he turned to leave he said, "Bud, if you ever need a cab or anything else, just call the office and ask for Dave." Waving a nicotine-stained hand he drove off up old 66. I watched as he faded out of sight, thinking to myself, what in the hell am I doing clear out here?

It was one of those warm, sultry days where the air was so heavy a pregnant mosquito couldn't fly through it. Going into my room I turned on a small fan that was sitting on a worn-out dresser and propped the door open trying to get rid of some of the stale cigarette smoke that had embedded itself into the walls and carpet. I sorted through my bag, hung up what few pieces of clothing I had and shoved the rest into a dirty drawer.

Stretching out on the bed, I took a short nap and lay around the motel until almost dark.

I decided to call Sarah. The phone rang several times before her roommate answered, and when I told her who it was she stalled around before calling her to the phone. She answered the phone with, "Look, Mike, I don't think it will work out you moving in over here." I said, "I realize that so I have a place rented for a couple of weeks until I can find an apartment."

This changed her whole tune. Why hadn't she just come out and told me she didn't want me over there? Hell, I would have understood. I said if she wanted to come over and pick me up, I would buy her dinner. She jumped at the idea, saying, "Give me your address and I will be over in thirty minutes."

I grabbed a quick shower. The damn humidity was so bad I couldn't get dry so I got back in and turned on the cold water. I stood there and shook while my balls shriveled up smaller than a pigmy goat's nuts in a blizzard.

I was waiting at the door trying to stay cool when Sarah drove up. Walking over to her car, I opened the door and got in, leaned over and gave her a big kiss. She said, "That was worth the drive over. What's for dessert?"

"That will have to wait until after dinner," I told her. "Where to?" she asked.

I just smiled and said, "Any place that is cheap, clean and the food is good."

She drove out to the truckstop on Interstate 44, saying this is always a good place to get a quick meal. After we ordered, Sarah took hold of my hand and said, "Mike, the reason I didn't want you moving in over at my place is that I have transferred to the state university in Columbia. I will be leaving in two weeks and I didn't want you living there with my roommate. She is much prettier than I am and I know you would be bedding her before I was out of sight."

Smiling I looked at her and said, "Tell me more."

Our conversation was interrupted by the arrival of our meal. We ate in silence for awhile. The thought of Sarah leaving had suppressed my appetite. I was thinking it was only a three- or four-hour drive up to the university, but she would be around a lot of other men. Well, I didn't have any strings attached to her so couldn't do much about it.

I finally asked her if she had to move up there to finish her education. She said, "Mike, it is the only place I can get the courses I need and still stay in the state. I really don't want to be away from you again. I can come home some weekends and you can come up anytime after I get settled. You can probably find a job in Columbia--it's a fairly large city."

This started me thinking about what kind of work I could do. I had been raised on a farm and that's about all I knew except being a soldier and there isn't much demand for them in civilian life.

"Maybe I will come up and go to school with you--that way I might be able to keep all of those college guys away from you."

"Yeah, sure," she said. "I bet they will be after me before I get settled."

Smiling, I said, "If you find some good-looking guy that you want to be with, and really care for, just let me know. I'll come up and kick his ass until he changes his mind. Don't let him be too big though as my shoulder still doesn't work like it used to."

She laughed and I thought how pretty she was and how much I liked being with her. Maybe going back to school wouldn't be such a bad idea, but down deep I knew that the first person I ran into who was protesting the war, I would be in trouble.

We sat and talked for another hour after our meal was finished, then she suggested we go see my folks. Now why didn't I think of that? A man needs a woman around to remind him of the things he should do. And of some of the things he shouldn't.

Mom and Dad had just finished their dinner when we arrived so we had to have cake and ice cream as Mom had just baked. Dad said, "It's about time we were hearing from you. Thought maybe you done re-upped and was sent back to Nam."

"Not me," I said. "I have had enough of that hellhole to last me a lifetime. The only thing I ever lost over there was about twenty pounds and a lot of good friends."

This got me to thinking about Tex. I should go see his folks and talk to them about him. Sarah saw my mood change and asked me what I was thinking. I said, "Oh, I was just back in Nam for a few minutes, can't seem to get that place off my mind."

Dad spoke up and asked when I was coming home. He said, "I could sure use some help with the plowing and milking. I have been thinking about quitting the milking business, there isn't much money in it anyway. Believe I will just raise a few Angus and sell the calves in the fall. That way I won't have to feed so much. These winters seem to be getting colder or else I am getting older."

We all laughed at him. Dad was only in his fifties and still in pretty good health.

Sarah helped Mom with the dishes while Dad and I took a walk outside. I started through the gate into the hay field. "Hey, son, I wouldn't go out there if I was you. The damn seed ticks and chiggers are so bad this year they suck the fluid out of the tractor tires." So we walked over and sat on the picnic table.

He finally asked me how I was doing and how much longer I would be in the hospital. I didn't tell him I had been discharged and sure hoped Sarah didn't say anything to Mom. I just said, "I still have some pretty weird dreams, but they don't seem to be as bad or else I am getting used to them. The VA gave me a prescription called Thorazine that helps a lot."

Dad said, "Son, you have a home here as long as you want. You can even stay here and go back to school. Hell, boy, I won't work you too hard." He laughed and put his hand on my shoulder. "You never did tell me about those Purple Hearts you won. Where were you hit and how did it happen?"

I waited along time not saying anything, thinking about what had happened. "Well, if you don't want to talk about it, I understand."

Finally, I said, "I was carrying a wounded Marine to an aid station during a firefight and I took a round in the back of my shoulder. The others were only scratches. Hell, they give those things away for a bloody nose."

Looking up at him, I said, "Dad, it's these damn nightmares I keep having about that place. Once I have one I am traumatized for hours. Sometimes I will go for days thinking about them. I can't seem to get what happened over there off my mind. I saw so many young men get killed and blown all to hell that I have a hard time handling it. I don't trust myself around anyone yet. Hell, Dad, I have scared the shit out of doctors and nurses that are supposed to be used to such trauma."

Mom stepped out on the porch and stood there drying her hands on her apron, saying, "You two can come back in now. All the dishes are washed and it's a lot cooler in here. Besides, the bugs will be feeding on you pretty soon."

I followed Dad into the house. We sat in the kitchen and Mom poured us both a cup of coffee. I sat there trying to think of things to say. It was strange that I found it hard to talk with my parents.

Mom kept asking when I was coming home and when I was getting released from the hospital and getting out of the army. I kept looking at Sarah hoping she wouldn't say anything. I just told her it shouldn't be very long now, and that I had better figure out what I wanted to do with my life.

Sarah could see my uneasiness, so she stood up and said, "Hate to cut things short, but I have an early class tomorrow."

Mom and Dad walked us out to the car. I told them I would be back out in a couple of days. I let Sarah drive; she was used to the roads and knew shortcuts I couldn't remember.

At the motel she parked in front of my room, leaned over and kissed me. "Aren't you coming in?" I asked.

"No," she said, "I've got a pretty hectic schedule tomorrow, so I better get some sleep."

"What about dessert?"

She smiled and said, "We had that at your Mom's, don't you remember?"

"That's not what I had in mind and you know it."

Giving me a quick kiss, she leaned over and opened my door. Pushing me, she said, "Get out of here, Mike, before I call your bluff."

This didn't fit in at all with what I had planned, but I thought, what the hell, there will be another day.

I got out, walked around and kissed her through the window. "You don't know what you're missing."

She put the car in gear and backed away. Watching her drive away I thought that was a damn waste. Sometimes women don't have any idea the pain they leave a man in. It was still too hot to go into that room--maybe that was what changed her mind.

Going down to a little grocery store on the corner, I bought a six-pack, walked over to a little park and sat down on a bench. I opened up a beer. Noticing a couple of guys sitting over by the playground, I picked up the six-pack and walked over and offered them a cold one.

As it turned out, they were both Vietnam vets, so we got to talking about the war. The six-pack didn't last long so I walked up to the store and got a twelve-pack. The men were glad to see me when I got back. We sat there in the grass sweating from the damn humidity as the bugs began to eat on us. One of them slapped a mosquito and said, "I sure wish I had some of that damn skeeter shit we had in Nam." I told him to pour some beer on it, that once they got drunk they couldn't bite.

Dude, as one of them called himself, spoke up and said, "Well, at least here we don't have to worry about the damn leeches crawling up the end of our peckers. Ever have one of those slimy little bastards pulled out of your dick with a pair of those damn sharp tweezers? It sure is hell to get screwed by a damn leech. It's worse than getting chewed on by one of those old snaggletooth gals in Saigon."

I laughed and said, "I wouldn't know much about that. I always tried to pick one that had all her teeth."

Jim, the other guy, spoke up and said, "Old Dude there, he liked them skinny gals, especially the toothless ones. They reminded him of the folks back home in Tennessee."

The night was starting to cool off some so the mosquitoes left us. We soon finished off the twelve-pack and really had a buzz on. Old Dude broke out a bottle of wine they had been hiding. We sat and sipped the vinegar- tasting stuff until my stomach couldn't handle any more. Jim said, "I sure wish I had a joint, a little tote on one right now would just finish off the evening."

Dude told him, "It ain't evening anymore, Jim-boy. Hell, it's nearly daylight."

I didn't care. As I lay back on the cool wet grass, I asked them where dew comes from. I can't remember getting an answer.

As the sun was beating down, I woke up. Some big, ugly cop was standing looking down and kicking me with his boot. I sat up and noticed that Dude and Jim were nowhere around. There were beer cans and an empty wine bottle lying next to me.

"Have yourself a little party, did you, son?" the cop asked.

I tried to get up as the whole damn world spiraled around me. The more it spun, the sicker I got. The officer gave me plenty of room as I stood up and puked out all the fun I had just had.

After I finally got to where I could breathe, he told me to pick up all the cans and the bottle and carry them over to a trash can. I had to make a lot of trips and I nearly fell over each time I bent down to pick one up. After running a record check, the cop came back and asked me if I had been slapping anymore war protesters around lately.

"No," I said, "I just haven't run into any."

"I should run your ass in for being drunk, but looks like you are going to suffer enough today." Giving me back my identification, the cop said, "Don't let me catch you out here again like this."

Smiling, I thanked him and said, "I will try and hide better next time."

He gave me a disgusted look and drove off, leaving me standing there sick, suffering, and confused.

Chapter Eighteen

The walk back to my room was a real bitch. My head was spinning and the damn sun was getting really hot. Wishing I had a hat and a cold beer, I thought, man, how could anyone drink all night and be this thirsty? I'd left the room unlocked so I just opened the door and dove for the bed.

It was late in the afternoon when I awoke. The room was sweltering hot--it must have been a hundred and ten with the humidity twice that. I had beads of sweat on me big as a quarter. Stripping off my clothes, I headed for the shower and stood in the cold water for as long as I could stand it. My head was throbbing like a sick bird's ass, and my stomach was churning like I had swallowed a cat. So, like a damn fool, I took a couple of Thorazine.

It wasn't long before I knew I had to eat something or the damn pills were going to burn a hole in my stomach. Walking up to the corner store, I got a pound of bologna and some crackers along with a couple of six-packs. Back at the motel, I sat at a little table under a shade tree out front. Cracking open a cold beer, I guzzled half of it before setting it down. I noticed an old man sitting in a doorway watching me. I pulled another beer from the six-pack, held it up and motioned him to join me. Giving me a big, toothless smile, he came walking over and sat down. Handing him a beer, I said, "I'm Mike." He reached out a rough brown hand full of crooked fingers as he grasped my hand and said, "Thanks, they call me Old Jim." Offering him some bologna, he just shook his head and grinned, saying, "Don't like to eat when I'm a drinking."

We sat and talked until the beer was gone. By then the damn pills and the alcohol had me feeling like a zombie. I excused myself and headed back to the room. Turning on the fan, I stripped down to my boxers and lay on the bed.

The dreams didn't take long to come. It was dark and the jungles were full of screeching, howling monkeys. The hot, stifling fog closed in, making me gasp for each breath I took.

I lay there in the jungle watching the tiny leeches crawl over my skin. It seemed the more I brushed them away, the more they appeared. The noise of the jungle animals was getting louder and louder as I crawled along the ground. I was soon near a pile of dead soldiers with the old Vietnamese woman sitting on top of them, laughing at me. Her brown, stained teeth made an eerie clicking sound as she laughed.

Tex was there telling me to get up and run, but my legs wouldn't work. He reached down to help me, only it was no longer Tex but the old man I had killed. He was dragging me along the ground holding onto my feet. I tried to kick free, screaming for Tex to help me as the old man dragged me down into a spider hole where it was so dark there was nothing, nothing but darkness. A cold damp blackness enveloped me like I had never felt before. The sides of the tunnels had my arms pinned so tightly that I could no longer move. I quit fighting and just lay there taking long, deep breaths, hearing voices echoing back and forth like they were coming from deep inside the tunnel. Bright swirling lights began to streak through my mind, only to be followed by the sheer darkness of the night.

The stillness was shattered by the wailing sound of a siren. As I opened my eyes to the blinding glare of flashing lights, a crowd of people were gathered around as they moved me along the ground. I tried to get up but something was holding me down as I was lifted up into the compartment of some vehicle. Someone was holding my shoulders, talking to me, asking me things I didn't understand.

Fear hit me as I remembered the old man dragging me. I wanted up but I couldn't get loose. Voices were talking to me, telling me to lay still.

Through a dizzy haze I was aware of riding along in something. People were all around me, talking to me, asking my name. I tried to answer but could only mumble words that didn't make any sense.

The room was dark when I awoke; except for a small night-light over in the corner that let off enough light that I could tell I was in a hospital room. How and why I didn't know. I started checking all my arms and legs, sitting up and moving around. Nothing hurt so I must not have been injured. The last thing I remembered was sitting with the old man and drinking beer.

I got up and walked around the bed into the bathroom. When I came out a nurse was standing at the door. She asked me how I felt. I just said, "I'm fine. Why am I here?"

"Well, Mr. Malloy, it appears that you overdosed on your medication.

Just how many pills did you take?"

I couldn't remember, no matter how hard I tried. I couldn't remember ever taking a pill, but guess I did. So I just smiled and told her that it wasn't the recommended dosage, that's for sure. She frowned and said, "That stuff isn't supposed to be used with alcohol. Do you need a sleeping pill?"

"No, thanks. I believe I have had enough pills for one day."

She turned and walked back out to her desk. I walked around the room for awhile and then out to the nurse's station. I felt naked as a picked bird's ass with my butt hanging out of that damn backless gown.

"Do I have any clothes?" I asked.

"Only what you're wearing," she smiled.

"How in hell am I going to leave here with my ass hanging out in the wind? "You're not going anywhere, Mr. Malloy, until the doctor releases you. Then we will find something for you to wear. He will be in at ten to see you."

Bullshit, I thought. I'm not staying around this damn place just to get my ass chewed out buy some damn quack who probably takes more of his own pills than I did.

Asking if it was okay for me to walk around the halls and get some exercise, she said, "I would keep my back toward the walls when I meet people if I were you. And Mr. Malloy, don't bend over and pick things up."

"You're funny," I said as I walked off down the hall holding the back of my gown shut with one hand. I was bound and determined to find some clothes and exit this place. I looked into each room as I walked by figuring there had to be clothes in one of them. Only thing was the damn nurses could see every door.

Walking back and forth until the nurse left her station, I stepped into the nearest room and opened the closet. Nothing but a few dust bunnies and they sure as hell wouldn't cover much. I could wrap a sheet around me like a toga, but once I hit the street the damn cops would be on me like ugly on an ape. I tried a couple more rooms and bingo! There were pants, a shirt and shoes, all neat as a pin.

Slipping into the closet as quietly as I could, I put on the pants, which were about four sizes too big. The shirt fit me like a man's shirt on a little kid, and the shoes were about three sizes too large. But I put them on without socks and tied them. I sure hoped the big bastard who owned these clothes didn't wake up. I must have been an awful-looking sight. I tucked the shirttail in and slipped out of the closet. Peeking around the corner, I saw that the nurse was still gone so I headed for the elevator, pushed the button and stepped into freedom as the doors opened.

Once on the street I hailed a cab. He pulled over, took one look at me and drove off like he knew I couldn't pay him. Hell, I didn't look that bad, and I had money back at the motel. So I walked on down the street until I reached the main part of town. Seeing a cab parked by the curb, I just opened the back door, got in and told the driver where I wanted to go.

Once I was back at the motel I got enough money to pay the cabbie and even gave him a dollar tip. As I turned to go back into my room, the manager came out and hollered at me. Walking over to him, he said, "Mr. Malloy, we are going to have to ask you to leave. We can't have disturbances like you created going on here. Many of the other tenants were complaining. I don't know what your problem was, but you scared hell out of a lot of these old people who stay here. If you will come by the office in the morning, I will refund any money you have coming, but I want you out of here tomorrow."

He turned and walked off before I could even tell him to kiss my ass. Now what the hell was I going to do? I was really pissed off by the time I got to my room. I felt like tearing the whole damn place apart, but knew better. I just grabbed my bag out of the closet, stuffed everything I owned into it and hit the street. The damn manager could keep what money I had coming. I knew if I went back to the office I would probably kick his ass and go to jail for it.

I walked down to the little roadside park and sat on a bench thinking about what I should do. I sure didn't want to go back to my folk's house; I just couldn't see working for Dad on that damn farm. My money is running out and the little I get from the VA isn't enough to rent a room full-time, let alone enough to eat on.

I lay back on the table, put my bag under my head for a pillow and tried to sleep. The damn buzzing mosquitoes wouldn't leave me alone so I just sat there wondering what was going to happen next. It was like one of those hot sweaty nights in Nam, just sitting in the bush listening and hoping you wouldn't hear anything. I remembered the many times I had rested my head on the barrel of the 16 and thought how simple it would be to reach down and push the trigger.

I can feel the depression creeping back over me; I don't know how much longer I can take the loneliness. Sarah has been gone only for a couple of weeks and I miss her. I need someone to hold and to talk to, someone to love and for someone to love me. God, how did I ever get so messed up?

Light was starting to show in the eastern sky as I stashed my bag in a small culvert and started the walk into Springfield. I still had on the damn sloppy-fitting clothes and shoes I had stolen from the hospital. Going back, I changed into my own clothes and shoved the stolen garments back into the pipe. I laughed to myself as I thought about some poor bastard standing there with his ass hanging out of one of those gowns, wondering where in the hell they put his clothes.

I was hungry and thought where the nearest café would be. It was about a mile to the truckstop on the interstate, so I headed that way, not really caring about what I ate just as long as it was filling.

I must have hit it at rush hour because the place was full. Walking to a table in a back corner I sat down and waited for the gal with the coffee to come by. Looking around, I noticed a large coffee pot and service bar, so I got up and poured myself a cup. It took a long time for the waitress to get to my table. She gave me a smile and took my order. I watched as she walked away.

Just looking at her stirred up a want in me. Why in the hell did Sarah have to go upstate? I went without for months at a time in Nam, so I guess another week or two won't kill me. When a big black man came in, I got to thinking about Tex and the fun we had in Saigon. I'm beginning to see why he kept going back--at least life over there wasn't nearly as boring as what this has turned out to be.

Breakfast wasn't much and I wished I had ordered something else. I finished the cup of coffee that was cold, picked up the check and paid my bill, leaving the cute thing a couple bucks extra.

Going back to where I stashed my clothes, I retrieved the bag and headed toward the river. The sky was filling with dark clouds and I knew a storm was coming. I needed to find a dry place or I was going to get my butt awfully wet. I headed for the bridge that crossed over the river and got there just as the storm hit with all its fury. The lightning and thunder was deafening.

Crawling up under the bridge, I got back far enough so the wind couldn't blow the rain on me. I jumped several times as the lightning cracked, but I felt warm and secure in my little space. Pulling my old fatigue jacket out of my bag, I lay down, covered up with it and went to sleep.

Chapter Nineteen

The storm roared on all night and through the next day. It was getting cold under the bridge even with my coat on, and the damn ground was getting mighty hard. The rain had settled into a steady downpour, and I was cold and hungry. The closest place to eat was at least a three-mile walk. I wasn't hungry enough to walk that far in the rain.

I had been watching this farmhouse across the river. There didn't seem to be much activity going on for a farm. A woman came out and got into a car and drove away. I watched and didn't see anyone else. After the rain slacked up I walked across the bridge and up to the house, where I was greeted by a somewhat friendly big black dog. I knocked on the door and no one answered. Walking around to the back of the house I saw a pen full of chickens. Not seeing anyone, I slipped into the chicken coop and filled my pockets with several eggs, even giving one to the dog to keep him quiet. The stupid mutt just looked at it, so I broke it open and gave it to him. After a lick or two, he decided he liked it. Hope I wasn't teaching him any bad habits.

Taking an empty coffee can that was on the gatepost, I walked back over to the river with the dog following me. I gathered up a few dry limbs and leaves from under the edge of the bridge and lit a small fire. After I got it burning, I walked down to the river and filled the coffee can about half full and set it in the coals close to the flames.

When it started to steam, I carefully put the eggs I had stolen into the water, letting them boil until one of the shells cracked open. I poured the water off and tried to peel one. The hot egg burned my fingers as I juggled it back and forth in my hands. This wasn't going to work so I lay the egg on a rock close by.

That stupid mutt grabbed it and bit into the hot egg, shell and all. He let out a loud yelp and headed for the river. I said, "Serves you right, you damn egg thief! I hope they catch you in the henhouse," as I kicked what he had left of the egg after him. I still had six eggs to eat, and they wouldn't have been half bad if I had some salt and pepper along with something to wash them down. Did you ever try to eat six boiled eggs without anything to drink? They just hang up about halfway down.

I was afraid to drink from the river, but I did sip a little rainwater that was running out of a drain pipe on the bridge, hoped it wasn't running off some roadkill possum laying up there that I hadn't seen.

Stashing my gear up under the bridge behind a couple of rocks, I started the long walk to town. The air felt good after the rain and everything smelled fresh. Not like the damp moldy smell of Nam during the wet season. In this country the air always smells so clean after a storm. The ditches were filled with run-off water and I needed something to drink. My boiled-egg breakfast was fighting back; I would drink anything to wash those damn things down a little. I should have taken another swig of that possum water from the bridge drain.

I was afraid to drink from the ditch so I trudged on toward town, not having anywhere in mind to go except to get a cup of coffee and something to settle my stomach. I didn't make it. The eggs came back up before I got to town. I sat there in the roadside ditch as sick as I had ever been, hoping that old black dog felt just as bad. Why, I don't know. I guess it's like they say: misery loves company.

I lay back in the wet grass running my hands through it and wiped the cool moisture over my face. This made me feel better. As I watched a big puffy cloud float by, I wondered if it would be possible to ride one. I knew better; it was just a thought.

I don't know how that farmer got those hens to lay poison eggs, but I don't believe I will borrow anymore from him. Maybe it was the rainwater. I was feeling weak as I got up and started toward town. My stomach was still turning flip-flops and my brow was wet with sweat.

The truck stop was busy. Since I still wasn't feeling up to par, I just walked on toward town. My money was running short. I could either eat or rent another place to live. To do both was totally out of the question. I figured I could always find a place to sleep as long as the nights were warm. The thought of working an eight-to-five job just didn't appeal to me, even though the small amount I got from the VA never seemed to last very long.

I could see the little motel where I had stayed. I thought about walking over and telling the owner to kiss my ass, but figured all that would accomplish would be to get my butt thrown in jail. So I walked on up to the little park. Dude and Jim were still hanging out; seems they had a tent stashed back in the brush. They started laughing about how they watched as the cop made me pick up all the beer cans. Jim said he would have helped, but that his head hurt every time he bent over.

I asked if they knew a good place to eat. Dude said, "We're headed to the mission. Why don't you come with us? They make a good bowl of soup and you can always get some kind of sandwich to go with it."

It was about a three-mile walk, and they hadn't told me about the Jesus lecture I had to listen to before I got fed. My stomach was really gnawing on my backbone by the time I got that bowl of soup. I ate it so fast I didn't even know what kind it was until I went back for a second bowl. Bob, the guy who ran the mission, introduced himself and welcomed me there.

I ate three bologna sandwiches. Dude asked if I was really hungry or did I just always eat like that? I told them about stealing the eggs and how they made me so sick. Jim said it was probably the water I drank. He said, "One thing you got to watch living on the street is the water. Get yourself a clean jug and always carry it with you full of good water. I've seen men end up in the hospital and nearly die from drinking out of these streams; most of them are about half sewage. Old Dude here won't drink nothing but beer. He tells me fish screw and crap in water and he could never get thirsty enough to drink it."

We sat around in front of the mission all afternoon talking with a bunch of other men. A bottle of cheap wine was soon brought out and they each took a swig. I never did like wine but took a drink of the vile vinegar- tasting stuff.

For lack of anything better to do, we loafed around until the evening meal and attended the night service. Bob told us he had empty cots if we needed a place to sleep. Jim and Dude begged off, but I took him up on it. I helped clean up the kitchen and swept the place out. Bob and I sat up past midnight talking about life and all it has to offer.

He was a really interesting person and dedicated to what he was doing. He grew up on a farm in southern Missouri, and attended bible college here in Springfield until his money ran out. The churches and the community paid him a small wage for running the mission and also gave him a place to live.

He said, "I can do the Lord's work here just as good as if I had a church. If I can help one person find God and get back on his feet, my work has been good for something."

I told him about my bad dreams and the trouble I had sleeping. Bob assured me that he had seen people with all kinds of problems and for me not to worry, that he would pray for me. And he wanted to know if I had ever asked God for help. I'm not a very religious person, but I wonder if God lets something happen to someone, what good is it to ask him for help?

Bob threw me a blanket and told me to sleep on it. I lay there on the cot listening to the sounds of the night. I could hear cars on the street and the motors on the cooling system making a clicking sound each time they turned off and on. Guess it will take me awhile to get used to civilization again.

Bob kicked my cot and told me to get up and help him with breakfast. He showed me how to make the coffee and mix up the hotcake batter. Soon I was frying eggs and flipping pancakes.

The day turned out to be beautiful and I bid Bob goodbye. Walking over to the bank, I drew out three hundred dollars of the meager pension the military blessed me with. I started walking uptown, then sat on a bench and watched the people pass by as I thought about Sarah. I wanted to call her but didn't know where she could be reached. I could call my folks and find out, but there would be a hundred questions that I just wasn't in the mood to answer.

I headed back over toward the college, why I don't really know. I sure as hell didn't want another run-in with a bunch of war protesters. It gets lonely on the street, so I guess I was hoping that Sarah would still be there. The streets around the college were calm, just the usual activity of students headed to class.

The little bar where I smacked the loud-mouth was just down the street. Thinking that no one would remember me, I walked over and bought a beer. I took a table in the back, sat down and checked out all the young college chicks. No one in the place even looked at me so I downed the beer and got the hell out of there. The afternoon had turned into one of those miserable humid days that you get in Missouri. The dark clouds were building in the southwest and I knew another storm was imminent.

It wasn't long before the rain was coming down in sheets with blinding bursts of jagged lightning followed by loud claps of thunder. Running along the street, I stopped in the doorway of an empty building. The rain continued so I sat down and pulled my knees up under my chin. I was wishing I had brought my coat--the rain had cooled the air and I began to shiver. The storm continued and the day got darker. I didn't want to spend the night here but it was better than getting soaked.

I sat and watched the rain splatter on the street and sprayed out from the car wheels as darkness closed in around me. My mind went back to the many nights I sat in the jungle of Nam and listened to the rain hitting my poncho. Tex loved those rainy nights. I remember him saying they were "killing nights," when every predator stalks the darkness looking for a victim. Man was a prey animal after dark; he didn't have the vision to see danger coming. All man has is the superior knowledge to deal with situations. We can think and act quickly on our thoughts. An animal has to react on instinct and what it has learned in killing. They can't think out a way to kill and then plot how to do it. Only man has this evil quality--it's what makes us superior in the animal world. Tex would laugh and say, "That's why we're sitting out here in the night getting our asses soaked while the tigers are curled up in a nice warm den someplace."

I tried to sleep but rest came only in short naps. I would jump each time I awoke, trying to figure out where I was. It was dark on the side street. There was no traffic now, just the pattering of the rain to break the silence of the night. Chills kept shaking my body as I sat with my arms resting on my knees.

As I drifted off into a deep sleep the dampness of the night air pulled me back to when the fog was so thick. All we could do was dig in and wait. I kept seeing movement and wanted to fire on it. Tex held my barrel down and asked, "What if that is our own men out there?" This shook me clear through my soul. I was awake now and listening, footsteps were coming toward me. Maybe I wouldn't be seen and pulled my knees up to my chest as a large figure stopped in front of me.

Chapter Twenty

I sat there frozen, afraid to look up at the dark-clad figure. Maybe he hadn't noticed me there in the darkness of the doorway. I watched as he turned. My head flew back as I was struck in the face. I could taste blood in my mouth as I tried to rise. Someone kicked me, there are more people kicking me now. I can hear their voices as they encouraged each other. They dragged me out into the rain, beating me, searching through my pockets. Giving up I just curled up in a ball and took the blows.

How long I had been laying there I didn't know. I could feel the rain on my skin as I tried to get up, but my arms and chest hurt so badly I just lay back, letting the rain hit me in the face. My eyes were so swollen I could hardly see. Time seemed to drag on as I lay there trying to take deep breaths through the pain in my chest. My lips felt cut and my teeth were loose. It all happened so fast I can't recall what took place.

Then someone was shining a light in my face talking to me, asking how I am and what happened to me. I tried to answer but my jaw must be broken as I couldn't form words and the pain was unbearable. I screamed out in agony as someone lay their hand on my chest and told me to rest easy, that an ambulance was on its way.

Hearing a siren wailing in the far-off distance, I slowly faded into darkness. People were shaking me and lights probed my eyes as I tried to regain consciousness. They were still asking me my name and what has happened. Each breath and movement of my body sent searing pain through me; I couldn't speak.

Again I tried to sit up but hands pushed me back down and told me to lie still. They were here to help me. The rain felt cool on my face and helped to keep me awake. I know I have been beaten, but why?

I screamed in pain as my body is lifted up and put in an ambulance. Gentle voices reassure me that I will be taken good care of. I want to talk but the words come out garbled through torn and swollen lips.

My mind keeps telling me that this isn't real, that it is just another bad dream. I try to wake up but can't come back to reality. I fight the darkness that is trying to overcome me. Have I finally succumbed to a dream so horrible that I can't come back from it? Is this the deep dark pain and depression of insanity?

I awoke lying in a bed and felt heavy bandages on my face; my ribs are bound so tightly I can hardly breathe. Through badly swollen eyes I could make out the form of someone standing by my bed. Gentle hands touched my shoulder as a soft voice asked me how I am doing. I try to speak but the pain is overbearing. A woman's voice tells me not to talk, that my jaw has been broken and my mouth is wired shut. She tells me to rest easy, that she will be back later.

Sleep was slow in coming and brought a lot of pain with it. Every time I moved, I would wake up to the throbbing of my chest and arms. A nurse came in and told me she was giving me something to help me sleep. It wasn't long before I was in a half-mummified state. I couldn't sleep and I couldn't wake up. Weird dreams kept coming to me about cave-dwelling creatures that couldn't see. They gave off a high whistling sound that hurt my ears.

When I awoke, someone was cleaning my room with a screaming vacuum cleaner. I guessed that was where the high-pitched noise emanated. I tried to sit up but my chest hurt so badly that all I could do was turn over and grit my teeth.

I needed to pee so badly I could hardly hold it. There was one of those plastic urinals on the table. It hurt like hell, but I reached over for it and was able to relieve myself. I noticed a nurse watching me from a desk in the lobby. She got up and came into the room and asked how I was feeling. I tried to answer her but could only mumble a few words until the pain stopped me.

The nurse walked back to her desk and got a notepad and pen. She gave this to me and asked me my name. Even though I could hardly see, I wrote down Sgt. Mike Malloy, U.S. Army. Why I don't know; this is just what came to me. She kept asking me what had happened to me, did I know why I was beaten, and if I had any identification. I just wrote down the word, "robbed." She took the notepad and walked back out to the nursing station. I lay there thinking, well, hell, they at least know who I am and why I got the shit kicked out of me. I would have given up my money without taking such a beating. I think being robbed was more of an afterthought.

Those punks were looking for someone to kick around and I happened to be handy.

The more I thought about the beating the madder I got. They didn't call me "Mad Mike Malloy" for no reason. By God, if I ever get out of here some bastard is going to pay. I'll cut the nuts off of some son of a bitch and carry them in my pocket until they rot. We collected ears in Nam and carried them on a string until they stunk so badly you couldn't stand them. They never did dry like they would have back here.

My anger gave me a reason and a cause to live. I lay back and plotted my revenge. I had to get up and get strong again. I gritted my teeth and, through cold sweat and burning pain, I made myself sit up. I was a little dizzy at first but I sat there and held on to the edge of the bed until the world quit spinning. The nurse saw me, ran in and said, "Mr. Malloy, you shouldn't be up yet." I asked her to help me to my feet. She protested, but grabbed my arm as I stood up.

The first few steps were a bit shaky, but with the nurse holding onto me I walked over to the door and back while she kept telling me to get back in bed. After I lay back down, I knew that was a stupid thing to do, but by God I was going to get up and get out of here as soon as I could.

Sleep came quickly; that little exertion seemed to tire me out. I slept for hours, but it was dark in my room when I awoke. I made myself sit up even though I could scream with the pain in my chest. I rested on the side of the bed for several minutes before standing. I made it to the john under my own power, but the nurse was waiting when I came out the door. She told me not to get up without help, that if I fell I could really injure myself, that I didn't need to shove one of those broken ribs through my lung.

This got me to thinking about how badly I had been beaten. With this thought came the anger again. The swelling in my eyes was starting to go down, but the blue bruises around them and the other marks on my face were a real mess. Someone had really used my face as a football. Thinking of this just made me want to get revenge that much more. I would find the people who did this to me; when I get done it won't be a pretty sight.

I drifted off to sleep with the thought of hurting someone still on my mind. Morning came quickly. I had slept good and had no dreams. Maybe anger is what I need to cure me. It has been awhile since I had any nightmares about Nam.

The nurse came in and asked me if I was ready to go for a ride. They were transferring me over to the VA hospital. I just gave her a painful smile and a look that conveyed I knew that I couldn't do anything about it anyway.

She patted my arm and walked out to the lobby. When she returned, she had a glass of juice and a straw. She said, "We can't let you leave here without feeding you." Funny thing is I just realized how hungry I was, and then I realized I couldn't eat if they brought in a whole tray of food. The juice was good and really stimulated my appetite. I wondered if I could sip a hamburger through that straw.

The ambulance from the VA arrived about four in the afternoon. I was really getting hungry and asked the medic for something to write on. I wrote a note telling them I was starving and asked them to get me a milkshake. The driver looked at me like I was crazy, but he didn't seem to have any problem going through a drive-through window. God, that milkshake was good. I drank it so fast it gave me a brain freeze.

The doctor at the VA started asking me questions. Couldn't he see that my damn jaw was broken and I couldn't talk? I finally motioned for something to write on.

He just took it all in stride and kept asking things as I wrote the answers. Like what happened to me? Did I know my attackers? And how bad was I injured? Hell, he had my charts from the other hospital. He must hate to read as much as I do. When I told him I had been here before his eyes lit up a little, and he asked a nurse to get my records.

They put me in a room and left me alone. I was sleepy and tried to yawn (did you ever try that with a broken jaw?). The pain was so bad I woke up and forgot about sleeping. I am having hunger pains, don't know what they are giving me through these drip tubes, but it sure as hell isn't filling my stomach. I sip water, but it is warm and hard to swallow.

God, I hate being in these damn hospitals. I never did like depending on someone to do things for me.

Days dragged by as I lay there thinking of food, but just sipping water and juice through a damn straw.

The doctor came in one morning and talked about releasing me as an outpatient. Fear ran through me as I thought about being on the street alone, not able to talk or chew. He left the room before I could write anything down. I didn't know what to do if they released me. I couldn't go home, not looking like this. I couldn't take my problems back to my parents; I would starve on the street first.

That afternoon they moved me to another ward of the hospital and into a room with someone else. He told me his name was Danny Watts. He, too, had been living on the streets and had gotten the hell beat out of him by a bunch of punks. Dan looked a lot worse than I did. His nose was broken, one eye was swelled shut and the whole side of his face was beaten in.

I wrote him a note telling him who I was and asked what happened to him. He said, "I got a lot of this in Nam when a shell exploded in my face and burned me." We talked for several hours--him talking and me writing. One or both of us gradually drifted off to sleep. The room was dark and quiet when I awoke; I just lay there and stared into the darkness for awhile.

My ribs were healing to the extent that I could get up and move around without much pain. I still had the drip tube in my arm. I guess it was to feed me, but the needle was starting to really hurt and make my arm sore.

I grabbed the post that held the bottle and my notepad and went out to meet the new nurse. She looked up and smiled as I walked up, asking me if she could help me. I scribbled "How long do I have to keep this needle in my arm?" She smiled and said, "Sir; you are going to get awfully weak and hungry without it." I wrote back that I already was! "Can't you put some steak and potatoes in this damn thing?"

She laughed. "Hang in there, soldier, you will get well enough to chew in a week or two."

My arm is getting sore and hurting. The nurse looked at my chart and said she could fix that. She got up and walked me back to my bed, telling me to lie down. I was starting to get excited, wondering what she had in mind.

My evil thoughts were soon shattered when she tore open another package, removed the needle from my left arm and put a new one in my right. I thought, damn, don't these VA hospitals ever do anything good for a man?

The days soon dragged into weeks. I had worn out a dozen pencils and that many notepads. I had written so much I was getting writer's cramp.

The doctor came in one morning and told me they were going to fix me so I could talk and eat again. I was wheeled me into another room with a bunch of trays full of tools, and a lot of lights and what looked like mirrors.

The next thing I knew I was back in my bed and my jaw hurt like someone had pried my mouth open and stuck my foot in it. I moved my mouth and pain shot up through both ears. A cold sweat broke out on my face and I thought for a moment I was going to lose it. I slowly opened my mouth in spite of the pain, then I just lay there and kept opening and shutting my mouth a little at a time.

Like an idiot, I finally bit down too hard. Pain shot out both ears and bounced off the pillow and hit me again. I swore at myself and half screamed at the same time. The nurse must have heard me--she was in there immediately.

She asked if I was okay. I was hurting so badly that I was afraid to answer. Finally I squeaked out, "No." She asked if I wanted a pain pill. I nodded my head "yes." When she gave me the pill I put it in my mouth and took a sip of water. I was almost afraid to swallow, but it went down all right.

I finally got up enough nerve to try to talk to Dan. It didn't hurt too badly if I mumbled my words. He laughed at first and told me to shout a little, that he couldn't hear very well as one of his ears was damaged. I thought, great, here I am I can hardly talk and the guy I am trying to talk to is half deaf.

I got up and walked over and sat in a chair on the other side of his bed. We talked so long that I finally forgot that my jaw hurt until they brought us lunch. I was glad what little food I got was soft. I had some broth, a little scoop of mashed potatoes and some applesauce. Man, I had forgotten how good food tasted. I didn't chew much, just sort of mixed it all up with my tongue against the roof of my mouth and swallowed.

It was the first solid food I had eaten in a couple of months and made my stomach feel funny. I thought for awhile I was going to chuck it all back up. I guess it takes awhile for the belly juices to get things working again after a liquid diet. It wasn't long before I was hungry again and I asked the nurse if I could have something else to eat. She left and brought us both back a dish of Jell-O. It wasn't what I had in mind but it tasted pretty good. I tried to chew it, moving my mouth slowly. The pain was there but as long as I didn't bite down hard it wasn't bad.

Dan and I got to talking about the beatings we took. He told me that this is the second time he has been beaten up by the same bunch of punks since he got back from Nam. That he didn't have enough money to rent a place to live so he had been on the streets ever since he returned. He told me about his wife rejecting him because of his wounds, and about a little girl he had never seen.

The more I heard, the madder I got. Here we fought for this country and they won't help us. The streets are full of men whose lives were ruined by that damn war. Most of us didn't ask to go over there. They took us from our jobs, our schools, our homes, and the least they can do is help us get back to where we were.

Our conversation finally turned back to Nam and where we were stationed and the battles in which we fought. We were both at Da Nang at the same time. I told Dan about shooting the old papa-san and the dreams I have been having about it.

"Hell," he said, "don't let it bother you. The old bastard was probably guilty of something."

Most of those people didn't want us over there, and wouldn't try to help; they just wanted us to keep the Viet Cong off of their asses.

Chapter Twenty-One

I talked to Dan until he fell asleep. Going back to my bed I lay down, picked up a paper and started to read. The next thing I knew it was night and everything was quiet. I lay there staring into a hole though the blackness. I could hear the nurses moving about as they made their rounds, an occasional moan from someone or a cough in another room. Dan was sleeping soundly so I didn't turn on the television.

Time clicked by as I lay there thinking about my life and what had happened to me. I thought of Sarah for the first time in weeks. Sure wish she was here with me. I guess I loved her, but what did I have to offer? All I would need to do was to have one of my wild dreams and it would all be over. I have got to whip this demon that is chasing me. Sometimes I wish to hell that I had been left for dead out there in the jungle or blown across some rice paddy.

The road to self-pity lasted until I fell asleep. Morning brought with it a new day and a new set of problems. The doctor told me I was going to be released on an outpatient status. My mouth was still sore and I had trouble chewing, but I could talk okay and I was getting better each day.

After showering I gathered up what few possessions I had and bid Dan goodbye, telling him I'd see him on the street. He shook my hand and told me to keep my head down and my sights on the enemy.

The nurse had some papers for me to sign and then I could go home. I gave her my best smile and said, "If I had one to go to." She gave me a puzzled look and asked, "Where are you going?"

"Back to the cold, lonely streets."

She then said, "You can go to the mission, Mike, and they will help you get settled."

"I'll be okay," I said and walked out.

The air was cold as I hit the street. It must be September. I can't keep track of time anymore. Not knowing where I am headed I walk toward the center of town. I have no money so decide I better get to the bank. I make the ten-block journey over while enjoying the fresh, cool air. Filling out a withdrawal slip, I go to the open window but I was unable to remember my account number. The teller asked for my identification. I tell her I was robbed and don't have any. She said, "Sir, I can't help you without your identification or an account number."

Anger started to dwell deep within. I asked to talk to someone who could help. A nice-looking lady comes over and tells me to follow her. We went to a large open desk with nothing but a pen set and writing pad on it. She motioned to a chair and told me to have a seat. Fear overcame my anger as I explained what had happened. Taking my name she goes through a file and comes out with a packet of papers.

"Are you Mr. Malloy?" she asked. I nod my head.

"What is your social security number?"

I gave her my number. She looked over the paper and told me that there is no money in my account; that it had all been withdrawn.

Frustration made me fight for words. "There has to be money. My VA check comes here every month. I just got out of the hospital where I have been for the last ten weeks. I haven't made but one withdrawal since I got released from the army. I should have two or three thousand dollars in my account."

She closed the folder and with a smirk said, "Mr. Malloy, if that is who you really are, I can't help you any further until you get some identification."

"And where do I get that?"

Standing up she said, "Try the Veterans Administration, if you really are a veteran."

This pissed me off. I mumbled, "Screw you, bitch," as I got up and left. With no money and no place to go, the street is a cold, desolate place. I didn't have proper clothing to spend a night out in the open and the mission was clear across town.

I told myself, Mike, you dumb bastard, you better start hoofing it over to the mission or your ass is going to freeze tonight. It took me a couple of hours to make the long walk. There were several men hanging around outside when I got there. I went in and grabbed a cup of free coffee. Now, I like weak coffee but this shit's helpless. Well, beggars can't be choosers.

I found an empty chair and sat down to rest, sipping the damn weak, half-cold coffee and wishing I had something to eat.

More men showed up and we were all asked to come into a larger room that was full of chairs. The guy I remembered as Bob came in and greeted all of us. He started reading from a passage in the Bible, one I had heard many times but couldn't remember what book it's from. I sat there trying to stay awake as he told everyone about Jesus. After the brief sermon, we were asked to come in and have soup and sandwiches. I was first in line and the first to go back for seconds. My jaw hurt but I was so hungry I forced it to work.

After I finished eating I helped the others clean up the place. I asked Bob if he had a cot I could sleep on tonight. Giving me a blanket, he led me to another room that had about twenty bunk beds. "Take your pick," he said. "There is a shower with soap and towels in the other room." I grabbed a quick shower and hit the nearest bunk. I was asleep in minutes.

The dreams came. First it was just the lonely jungle with the bird and animal sounds, then the faces of Tex, Georgia Boy and some of the others. They were all laughing at me as I struggled to get out of a rice bog as the mud sucked at my boots. The harder I pulled, the deeper I sank. The old man I killed was standing on the dike aiming an AK-47 at me. I screamed as the orange flames shot from the barrel and bullets splashed the water and ripped at the stands of rice. The old wrinkle-faced woman stood beside him laughing at me as I struggled to get free.

The lights were on as I sat up on the bunk. Someone I didn't know was there, telling me I was all right, that I just had a bad dream. Others made comments about sleeping in the same room with some crazy bastard. The lights were turned off and I lay down afraid to go back to sleep, wondering what time it was. I could hear men talking about their bad times in Nam and the effect the war had on them.

I fought sleep but would gradually doze off for short periods of time, not allowing myself to get into a deep, restful sleep where I might have another dream.

Come morning, the others were all looking at me like I was something from their past, something that should be hidden or put away, never to remind them again of the hell they once lived through. Most of them sat and ate their toast and oatmeal away from me. I really didn't care, but I was embarrassed by my outburst that had awakened them during the night.

After we got the place cleaned up, I bummed a heavy coat from Bob and hit the street. Putting my hand in the pockets I pulled out a five-dollar bill. The coats are donated, but they don't come with money in the pockets. I don't know how the mission helps people like they do, but I am thankful for it.

I headed back over to the VA hospital to try and get some kind of identification, and then I will deal with that bitch at the bank. They are not going to steal my money.

I was told that I had to wait for an hour at the hospital to see someone. They always tell you this and it always ends up being three hours. I guess they hope you will get tired of waiting and just go away. I walked over to the ward and saw Dan. He was healing up but expected to be there for another week or two.

We got to talking about the beatings we both took. He said that he knew of two other men who had been assaulted. I told him, "Don't you think it's time we rounded up some of the boys and taught those little bastards a lesson? The streets are full of combat veterans and more of us are going to get jumped until they kill one of us. The damn police don't care; they would love it if the whole homeless crowd was exterminated."

Dan had experienced a couple of run-ins with the local law enforcement so was pretty well-known by most of them. We sat and talked until they called for me.

One of the staff at the hospital was able to give me a copy of my medical records. Luckily for me they had copied my service card with my picture, so now I at last had something to show Miss Snooty at the bank.

Going back up to the ward, I went with Dan to the cafeteria. By giving them my old room number, they let me eat. My jaw was still sore but it was getting better with each chew--if I don't bite down too hard.

After leaving the hospital I walked the streets, not planning to go to the bank until tomorrow. As the day drew late I started to feel uneasiness in my stomach. I had felt a lot of fear in Nam, but this was almost a panic. I didn't want to spend another dark night alone on the street. I was afraid, afraid that I would be jumped and beaten again.

I quickened my pace and headed for the little park outside of town, hoping that Dude and Jim would still be there. No one was around when I arrived and it was starting to get dark. I was overcome with panic and wanted to run. My heart was beating hard in my chest. I felt weak all over.

I heard a voice holler, "Hey, man." I stopped, turned and readied to run or fight. Jim came walking from the brush and told me to come on over. "We had to move the camp," he said. "The damn cops wouldn't leave us alone."

"Man, am I glad to see you guys. Wish I had a beer or two for you."

Jim smiled and said, "We got some beans on the cooker if you care to join us."

I took them up on the offer and, as we sat and ate by their little fire, I told them about getting beaten.

Dude said he had talked to a couple of men at the mission that had really gotten the hell kicked out of them. "Someone is going to get killed by these punks unless we put a stop to it. There are enough of us out here that if we can get some guys together we could really whip some ass."

I asked if I could spend the night. I didn't have any place to go and didn't want to get caught back out on the street tonight. I didn't think my busted jaw could take another hit for a few weeks. Jim asked if I had a fart sack. He said they had only a couple of bags, but they did have a blanket they could loan me. We crawled into the little sleeping tent and the three of us really filled it up. We talked until sleep overtook us.

When the dreams began, they were just dreams about Nam. I was with Tex and we were back on a ridge where we had spent so much time. He was giving me a hard time about being white and how I had been born a sugar baby with a silver spoon in my mouth. He kept telling me how rough it was to be black, that he had to work twice as hard as I did. He grabbed me and tried to push me off the hill, only it was the old man who was pushing me. I must have hollered or screamed--when I awoke Jim was shoving me and telling me to get off him.

Dude said, "What in the hell is going on? If you two are going to screw each other, get out of the tent first."

Jim laughed and said, "Old Mike here thinks he's back in some Saigon bar. Hell, he thought I was one of them little B-girls with the split skirt. Glad I woke up when I did--I would have gotten screwed for sure."

"I'm sorry," I said and crawled from the tent, taking my blanket with me. Going over by a big tree I sat and wrapped it around myself and tried to sleep. I couldn't remember much about the dream, but I was embarrassed that it had happened and knew I was going to catch hell when morning came.

As it grew light in the east, I threw the blanket aside, looked at the two men sleeping in the tent, got up and headed for the city. I still had the five dollars. I would eat and get things straight at the bank.

Chapter Twenty-Two

It was a cold, crisp morning as I headed for town, knowing the bank wouldn't open for a couple of hours. I walked over to a little café where I knew I could get a good breakfast for a couple of dollars.

Some cute, young girl working there gave me a big smile as I walked in. She looked like she had more energy than brains. She talked all the time she was taking my order. I never did understand what she was saying, but she sure had a nice way of saying it. Pouring me a cup of coffee, she took my order and pranced away.

I sat there sipping coffee and thought about the night before. I knew now I have got to stay alone until I can get these demons out of my mind. I have good nights and bad ones, I just can't figure out what triggers the bad ones. I have a fear of harming someone during one of my dreams. I could have struck Jim instead of just jumping on him.

The waitress brought me back to reality with my breakfast. She was a nice-looking girl and really stirred the want in me. Hell, I probably smelled so bad she couldn't stand to get too close.

The bacon and eggs were good, and I took another cup of coffee, holding it between both hands to feel the warmth of it as the steam floated from the brew. Blowing softly across it, I took another sip and planned my day.

It was still more than an hour before the bank opened so I walked over by the mission. Dude and Jim were hanging around out front; I stopped to talk with them. As I approached, Jim turned and walked off a few steps, saying, "You horny bastard, I'm not getting close to you." Everyone laughed.

Dude said, "Some guy we call "Patch-eye Dan" showed up asking about you. He wants to get some of the boys together to do some serious ass-kicking and teach a lesson to that gang of boys that have been beating up the homeless."

I hung around the mission for over an hour, but Dan didn't show. I told Dude to tell him to count me in with whatever he had planned; I owe some bastard a busted jaw. Dude laughed and said, "It's time we had a little more excitement around here."

I told Jim to watch his ass and left them hanging out there on the sidewalk. I headed over to the bank to do battle with the bitch from hell. At least I had something to show her that would verify who I am.

At the bank I was waited on by a very polite young lady who seemed eager to help me. The mean bitch glared at me over her glasses, like she thought I was there to steal something. I explained to the young lady what had happened and gave her my identification. She looked up my records and told me that my account had been closed. I could reopen a new one and deposit a couple of checks from the VA that had been sent to the old account and that they were holding. They would start an investigation into how the account was closed.

She said, "It will take a couple of weeks to get this straightened out. If someone stole your identity and closed out your account, the bank is insured and you will get all of your money back."

I signed the two checks and opened a new account, drawing out three hundred dollars.

I needed to get off the street for awhile. I walked back over to the old part of town and rented a room for a week in some dive. The room was old but clean. Whoever had been living here must have been a smoker-- everything reeked of tobacco.

Noticing a small grocery store across the street, I walked over and bought a six-pack, a razor and a toothbrush, plus some junk food to snack on.

Back at the room I left the door open to let the place air out, ripped the top off a bag of chips and, grabbing a handful, opened a beer and sat down. At least I was going to have a roof over my head for a few days, which put me at ease for a while.

Fear has overcome me when I am alone on the street. The beating really has made me leery of people. It is the same old gut-wrenching fear I had in Vietnam of not knowing where danger is coming from next. I never thought I would ever be this afraid in my own country. I now see what Tex was saying when he used to tell me he felt safer over there than he did on the streets at home. At least over there we had a weapon to fight with. I sat in the doorway thinking of Tex and watched the traffic as I got lost in my thoughts.

As the day drew on, I kicked the door shut, stripped off my clothes and headed for the shower. The hot water felt good on my skin. My hair was dirty and matted and I washed it with the little bar of soap, wishing I had shampoo. It was good to feel clean again. Looking in the mirror I noticed that I'd lost a lot of weight since getting out of the hospital. My eyes looked dark and sunken, and I had aged a lot.

After the shower I realized I didn't have any clean clothes to put on. So I ran the tub half-full of water and threw everything into it to soak while I ate some more junk food and polished off another beer.

Using what was left of the bar of soap, I scrubbed everything clean, rinsing them a couple of times. I wrung out as much water as I could and hung my clothes all over the bathroom to dry. There was a heat lamp in the ceiling so I left it on to speed up the process.

Lathering up my face with the hand soap, I dug out my new razor and went to work on the beard. It was a slow process as the little safety razor kept plugging up. After a few scrapes and a nick or two, I looked halfway human. I found an extra blanket on a shelf and wrapped it around my waist. Then I opened the door and moved my chair over in front of it, grabbed another beer and sat down.

Some lady who lived in one of the other units walked by. I said "Hi," and she stopped to talk. I told her I would offer her a beer but I was on the last one and couldn't go to the store until my clothes dried. She laughed and said, "I was wondering why you had a blanket wrapped around you."

"I'm headed to the store; want me to get it for you?"

"That would be great." I gave her the money and asked her to get me some deodorant and aftershave along with a couple six-packs.

"What kind?" she asked. "Whatever you like," I said.

She smiled and said, "I don't use men's deodorant or aftershave," and walked across the street.

Something stirred in me as I watched her walk away. Maybe this wasn't going to be such a bad room after all. I finished the beer and a half bag of chips before she got back. I looked her over good. She was a little older than me but still a nice-looking woman. I invited her in and gave her a beer, leaving the door open so things would be proper.

Pulling the blanket up over my shoulders, I walked over to the sink, opened the aftershave and splashed some on my face, almost losing the blanket in the process. As I grabbed for it, she laughed and said, "You don't have to wear that for my benefit."

I said, "Well, the door is open and I don't want to get arrested."

She reached out with her foot and kicked it shut, saying, "Now what's your excuse?"

"I don't even know your name, if that matters, and you don't know mine."

"What's in a name?" she asked.

I turned toward her with the blanket open. "I'm Mike! Mike Malloy."

She stood up, walked over and put her arms around my neck, gave me a big kiss and said, "I'm Millie. It's good to meet you, Mike."

She finished the beer and excused herself, telling me to save her one, that she would be back in a little while.

I lay back on the bed and before I knew it, everything was dark and quiet. Millie never came back--she must have seen something that scared her off. I got up to brush my teeth and went back to bed. Hell, I wasn't in the mood anyway.

It was raining when I woke up. My clothes were stiff but clean and didn't smell too bad. I got dressed and had a beer for breakfast. I moved a chair over and opened the door so I could watch it rain. It was cold and lonely sitting there. Reminded me of all the wet days and nights I spent in the jungle sitting under a large leaf plant we called an umbrella tree. We would be wet for days. The skin on our feet would peel off and get infected to the point some guys couldn't walk. Choppers had to be called in to evacuate them to a field hospital. I would change my socks often and carry the wet ones next to my bare skin to dry them. It was cold and miserable, but better than being crippled. We would rub insect repellent all over us to try to keep the leeches off, and the repellent would get in our eyes and burn like fire. But it was better than having those slimy little bastards hanging onto you.

I didn't see Millie all day and didn't know what unit she lived in. She probably had a boyfriend or husband, and I wasn't about to go looking for trouble. One busted jaw is enough to last me a lifetime.

It was afternoon when I finally got up and shut the door. After getting rid of the beer I was hungry, so I grabbed my coat and walked in the rain over to a little café a couple of blocks away. The place wasn't too crowded so I took a table back in a corner and sat down. I hadn't had a decent meal in days so when the waitress came over I ordered a steak with all the trimmings. The meal was great and the coffee was even better. I sat and sipped it until I had killed a couple of hours.

On the walk back to my room I met a group of four boys walking toward me. I was gripped with fear. I wanted to run but had too much pride to do that. I just stepped off the sidewalk and let them pass. Much to my surprise they all said "Thank you" and went about their way.

My heart was still pounding when I got back to my room. Why had I been so scared? Whatever happened to tough Mad Mike Malloy? Was he left lying on the sidewalk the night he got the shit kicked out of him?

I didn't like being afraid and I wasn't going to stay that way. If I get killed, so be it. Come morning I am going to find Dan and get revenge on those little bastards who did this to me. Mike Malloy may be down, but by God he isn't out.

Chapter Twenty-Three

The rain continued throughout the day. As it got dark I left the lights off in my room and sat by the open door watching the rain fall by the lights of the passing cars.

I remembered the rains in Vietnam and Tex telling me that rainy nights were killing nights. The predator animals could move more quietly and the rain covered their scent, while the prey animals sat in warm, dry places sleeping. I guess that is the way it is with man. It seemed the enemy would always move more when it was raining.

I hated the darkness and the pattering of the rain that covered every sound. I remembered the night the Vietnamese soldier stood so close to me, yet I couldn't make him out except for a faint, dark outline. It was his movement that caught my eye due to the difference in darkness against the jungle sky. If I had been standing I would never have seen him. I was supposed to be the predator that night, but once I quit moving I became the prey.

My thoughts turned to Sarah. Had she ever tried to find me? Was she still in college? I had lost all track of time. It seemed like years since we were together. Bob at the mission told me my father keeps looking for me so he must know I am still around Springfield. I should go home and try to work things out, but I don't have the answers to all the questions they would ask. I can't explain why I am out here, except that the damn war really messed with my head. Every dream seems to end up dealing with that old man I killed or the old woman who beat on me while the water turned blood red and swirled around us. I can still smell the fresh blood and the burning powder from the gun.

I wish Tex was here--maybe he could explain things and help get rid of this madness that keeps haunting me. I should go see his family. It's been a long time and maybe I can handle talking to them now. If the bank ever gets my money back I will buy a car, drive to Austin and try to find them. I remember his father's name is Theodore Lincoln Johnson and they lived on Johnson Drive. That shouldn't be too hard to find.

The bright lights of a car turning into the motel brought me out of my haze. I watched as Millie got out of the cab and walked to her room. The air was getting colder so I shut the door and lay down on the bed. I was almost asleep when there was a faint knock on my door. It was Millie. She asked if I still had the beer for her as she came into the room shaking the rain from her hair.

I said, "No, but I can sure get one in a hurry."

"Forget it," she said. "I just want to explain about the other night. When I got back to the room, my sister was waiting for me. Our mother was very sick and I went with her to the hospital thinking I would be right back, but we ended up staying all night."

"It's okay. I suffered but survived."

"I'm sorry," she said as she ran her hand through my hair and bent over to kiss me. It was then I realized she didn't have a lot of clothes on under her coat. Hell, she didn't have any. I reached out and pulled her close to me, sliding my hands inside the coat, holding her by the waist, feeling the curvature of her body and the softness of her skin. She let the coat fall to the floor as I pushed my face against her breasts, smelling the sweetness of her perfume. She was a well-developed woman, not a schoolgirl like Sarah. I sat there holding her against me for a long time--not talking, just enjoying the aroma of her skin and the softness of her body.

Gently she pushed me onto the bed. As we lay there holding each other, I thought this better not be another dream. If she turns out to be that old Vietnamese woman, she's going to get laid anyway.

I was awakened by the sound of running water. As I lay there and listened to Millie in the shower I thought that was a damn quick night, but one of the best of my life. I got up and walked into the bath. Tapping on the shower door, I asked if she wanted me to wash her back. "Come on in if you're up to it," she said. The hot water felt good on my skin and the excitement of a naked woman rubbing her wet soapy body against me added to the enjoyment.

Flesh and blood needs flesh and blood, and I had needed a woman for a long time. I dreaded going back out onto the street. I wanted someone to hold, to talk to. I held onto Millie as long as I could, not wanting her to leave. She told me that she lived with an older man who drove a truck for a living and was on the road a lot. She didn't love him but he paid the rent for her. With her small income she didn't know what she would do without him. I got the message and told her I would never interfere. She kissed me and told me she would see me later as she slipped out the door.

I sat there in the stillness of my room. It is the loneliness that hurts, and the thought of going back out onto the streets brings on a depressed mood. Ever since the beating I've had a fear of being attacked again. I guess I should carry a weapon; that way I could defend myself. But I would probably go to jail for cutting or shooting some bastard that needed it.

I have two more days of rent paid on the room so I will worry about it then. Getting dressed, I walked over to the little café and had breakfast. The rain had stopped and the sun was trying to shine.

I walked over to the other side of town to the mission. Several men I knew were hanging around out front. Patch-eye Dan showed up and started telling us about his plan to get even with the street punks who were beating up the homeless.

We weren't supposed to really hurt anyone, just teach them a lesson. About twenty of us were to meet at the Grant Street Park. Dan told us to come in one or two at a time so as not to draw suspicion, and to stay out of sight until it got dark. We were each to bring a club with us so that we could bust some ass. He would get someone to go with him and sit on a bench out front until the punks showed up. When the punks tried to cause trouble, Jim and Dan would get the punks to follow them to the rest of us.

We stayed around the mission until after the evening meal, then everyone quickly made their way toward the park. Jim and Dan walked the main street over, taking their time. They sat at the park entrance pretending to be drinking. I went with Dude. We picked up a couple of flat boards from an old pallet behind the feed mill and made our way through the back of the park. I could see men hanging around in small groups where they couldn't be seen from the street. If the cops didn't get word of this, we should have some fun.

We could hear some kids cussing Dan and Jim before it ever got dark, so we knew that we would have some action pretty quickly. It wasn't long after dark that we heard a couple of carloads of kids harassing the men out front. I heard Jim tell someone to get his punk ass out of that damn car and come on back where the cops couldn't see them. We moved up as two men came into the park followed by seven young boys who looked pretty tough. I thought, I hope we have enough to take these guys.

Men came from behind every bush and shrub. There must have been thirty of us; some of these guys I had never seen before. The punks were in deep shit before they knew what was happening. A couple of men grabbed each of them so they couldn't run. A few of them tried to fight but got that taken out of them fast. Some of the boys were in tears and one was shaking so badly I thought he would faint.

One by one we took their pants down, bent them over a picnic table and beat their bare asses with one of the flat boards, making all the others watch while waiting their turn. Someone hollered, "Castrate the little bastards," and handed me a knife. "That's what we do with a young stallion when he gets mean."

Dan grabbed my arm and said, "Don't do it, Mike. If you do, the cops will never stop looking for us."

I said, "One of these little bastards kicked me in the face and broke my jaw. Hell, I had to suck soup through a damn straw for weeks."

I grabbed the kid by his scrotum and pulled it down cutting the end of it off. As I looked up I could see the terror in the kid's eyes along with the pain. It was the look that was in the face of the old Vietnamese man I shot. I dropped the knife in disbelief of what I had just done. I said, "I'm out of here," and everyone split, leaving the poor kids whimpering and wondering what in the hell they had just gotten themselves into.

I was sick as I made my way along back streets and alleys to my room. God, what had I done? Those boys needed a good ass-beating, but no one deserved to be put through that kind of trauma.

At the time I wanted revenge badly enough to have castrated the whole bunch. I'm glad Dan was there--it could have gotten a lot worse. Some of those kids took a pretty good beating and I bet they'll think about it before they jump anyone else.

Once back at my room I took a quick shower and hit the bed. Every time I shut my eyes I could see the terror in that poor kid's face.

I needed a beer in the worst way. Getting up I slipped on my clothes and walked over to the little store. I could hear police sirens screaming all over town. As I came from the store a patrol car pulled up and called me over. The officer started questioning me about where I lived and where I had been.

I asked him what he was looking for. He said, "I'll ask the questions." He wanted to see some identification. I told him mine was in my room across the street. They followed me over and I invited them in. Grabbing my wallet I showed them what I had. They wanted to know where I had been all evening. I told them I had been here in my room asleep for the last four hours. I had been here all day except for when I went over to the café for breakfast.

I popped open a beer and said, "I would offer you guys one except I know you are on duty."

I kept asking them what they were looking for. They told me a bunch of guys just beat hell out of some high-school kids over at one of the parks and I sort of fit the description of one of them.

"Wasn't me, I said. I started to mention that I had gotten the hell beat out of me a couple months ago but thought better of it. So I just said, "I don't go out at night for that reason."

They told me to have a good evening as they left. It was then I noticed blood on my jeans. Had they noticed it? I took off my clothes and threw them in the tub. It was time to do laundry again anyway. I even went so far as to cut my finger with the razor in case they came back.

After scrubbing my jeans several times to make sure there wasn't any blood stains on them, I hung everything up to dry and went to work on the beer.

I had a pretty good buzz on when I hit the sack. The bed was spinning a little and for awhile I thought I would be sick. But sleep came quickly, with the beer putting me into a deep coma-like sleep. Dreams kept coming and going. All had strange faces and characters. One minute I would be in Nam, then back on the street. Nothing seemed to make any sense, just weird shit that I couldn't grasp.

Someone once said that a dream is a wish your heart makes while you are asleep. If this is the case then I'm a sick person. I keep seeing the young boy I cut and the face of the old man, then faces I don't know. I think they are Red and Georgia Boy or the men I saw killed in Nam. I am looking at a skeleton draped in army fatigues walking along dragging another person. A huge tiger keeps biting at the body, only the tiger has my face. I holler and am now awake. I lay there shaking and covered with sweat.

Everything is dark and quiet. The only sounds are the cars passing on the street. It takes me awhile to figure out where I am. The tiger with my face puzzled me--I lay there thinking what it could mean and why I would dream of such a thing. Turning on a light I look at the clock. I have been asleep for only a couple of hours.

A car drives up and someone gets out and knocks on my door. It's the same two police officers that questioned me before. I invite them in and offer them a place to sit. All I have is one chair and a stool so I sat on the bed. They again ask me where I went tonight. I told them I have been here all evening except when I walked over to the store for the beer. "Do you know a Danny Watts?" one of them asks.

"I know a guy called Patch-eye Dan." I lied and said that I couldn't recall his last name.

"Is he one of you?"

"What do you mean, 'one of you'? He is a veteran who got shot all to hell in Nam if that is what you're asking."

"Where does he stay?"

"Hell, I don't know. The last I heard of him he was in the VA hospital."

"The boys who got beat tonight, were they some of the gang that beat and robbed you?"

"I never saw any of the people who beat me and I don't have any idea who you're talking about."

"Come on, Malloy! We have a perfect description of you. Where are the clothes you had on at the store?"

"In the bathroom."

"May we check them?" he asked.

"Sure, but don't get them dirty. I just washed them." "Why would you be washing your clothes late at night?"

"They are the only ones I have. I wash them at night so I can have clean, dry clothes the next day."

This seemed to really piss the officers off. One of them stood up and started toward the bath. He said, "It couldn't be that you had blood on them, could it? Say like from the young boy who got cut tonight?"

"Mr. Malloy, do you have a knife?" the other one asked.

"No, I don't own a weapon of any kind. I saw enough blood and carnage in Nam to last me a lifetime, and I promised God that if he let me survive over there I would never harm another living thing as long as I live. I don't have any idea what took place tonight wherever it was. If it didn't happen here, I wasn't involved."

"Mike?" one of them asked. "Is it okay to call you Mike?" "Call me anything you want--you're wearing the badge." "Do you resent the police?" he asked.

"No, but I do resent being woken up at night and accused of something I wasn't even close to being involved in. As you know, myself and several other men have been beaten up by the punks in this town only because we are poor and have no place to live. It's no fun living on the damn street being cold and hungry and afraid all the time, afraid someone is going to kick your head in while you're asleep or that some cop is going to arrest you and throw you in the tank with every lousy drunk pervert they pick up. Do you run around questioning people every time one of us gets the hell kicked out of us, or do you figure we had it coming?

"No, I don't resent the police but I do think you could serve us as well as you serve other people. After all, most of the homeless men are veterans who can't cope with society. They served their country and are still paying for it. War affects each of us differently; some men come back with demons they can't shake."

"What about you, Malloy? Do you have demons you can't shake?"

"Yes," I said. "I've killed people. Some were enemy soldiers trying to kill me. One was an innocent old man I killed accidentally. His face and spirit haunt me constantly, especially when I try to sleep."

Chapter Twenty-Four

After the officers left, I sat there with the door open staring into the darkness. I couldn't sleep thinking about what we had done. Were we wrong? The young men needed to be taught a lesson. I know I should never have cut that punk--he will live in fear of that the rest of his life, but maybe it will make a better man of him. The wound will soon heal, but what about the one in his mind? Will he have traumatic dreams like I do? It's strange how things in life can trigger other reactions in your body.

I can't undo what I have done so I will have to live with it. Maybe it will help me cope with my life.

My thoughts meander to tomorrow when I will have to move out of here and back onto the street. If the bank has found my money, I will buy a car. I don't want to sleep out in the cold anymore. I could go home, but what would I tell my folks about where I have been for the last couple of years? Dad would never understand and Mom would pretend she does just to protect my feelings.

What about Sarah? I'm sure she has found someone else by now. It would be plain foolish to think she has waited to hear from me. I'm afraid any love she had for me is gone. I should have stuck by her and let her help me through all this madness. I need someone to hold, to talk to. God, it would feel good to hug someone and have them hug me back. Loneliness can be the worst torture known to man; it haunts your soul and kills your spirit, draining your mind of all resources.

I wish Millie would come back over, but after seeing the police she is probably scared that I am involved in something.

I shut the door and went to bed. Sleep came quickly and it was well into the morning before I awoke, having slept the whole night through without any dreams.

My stomach has a sick feeling just thinking about hitting the street again. It is Sunday and the banks aren't open. I've got to find a place to spend the night. There are still a few dollars left in my pocket, but not enough for the room and to eat. I shook the pillow out of one of the cases, stuffing what few belongings I have into the empty case, and threw the pillow up on the shelf in the closet. Maybe they won't notice. Hell, I don't care if they do--they will never find me on the streets and I doubt if I will ever come back here. I hung around the room until the last minute, then stepped out into the cold. Where was I going? The mission was clear across town and there isn't much room inside. I will have to spend the day standing around out front.

I've never felt so alone and lost as I do at this moment. It would be nice to have a family, someone to come home to when the day ends. I've got to get off the street; it's going on three years now since I returned from Nam. I've let that damn war ruin my life.

I walked several blocks before my mind returned to where I was and what I needed to do. Walking by the hospital I turned and went inside. The lobby had a lot of chairs and a couch or two so I just grabbed a paper and sat down. It was warm in there and I was among other people. Some even talked to me, asking if I was visiting someone. I told them I was waiting on my friend who was visiting his mother.

I ate a couple meals in the cafeteria and stayed on different floors and waiting rooms. No one ever seemed to bother me and it was a lot better than sleeping under the damn bridges. I wondered how long I could get by staying here.

There was free coffee available so I grabbed a cup and put lots of sugar in it. I really don't like the stuff but I need the calories to stay warm. Taking the coffee with me I rode the elevator up a couple of floors and sat down in another waiting room with a large window facing the street. Here I sat and read a magazine until I fell asleep. It was dark when I awoke; there was no one around so I just sat there and napped as I pretended to read. It was warm and comfortable here and I figured on staying the night unless someone ran me out.

A couple of nurses walked by and spoke to me but no one seemed to care so I just stretched out in the chair and went to sleep. It was early in the morning when I awoke to the sounds of people coming and going. Grabbing my pillowcase with my gear in it, I went into the restroom, shaved and washed up as best I could.

As I walked through the lobby on my way out, I noticed a box of donuts sitting by the coffee so I grabbed one, got a cup and sat down to read the paper that was lying nearby. I had made a promise to myself that I would get off the streets somehow. I turned to the help-wanted section to see if there were any jobs I could handle.

There were several listed that I thought I could do. One firm wanted security officers, which was a job I was trained for. The place wasn't very far away so I tucked the paper under my arm and walked over. Going in I asked a girl at the desk for an application. She gave me the paperwork and told me I could sit at a nearby table and fill it out.

Everything went fine until I got to the first question: What was my name and address? It was at that moment that I knew Mom and Dad were going to see their long-lost son whether they wanted to or not. I couldn't remember their number so asked for a phone book. It felt strange seeing their name and address. It was like looking back in time. My life was going to change the moment I wrote down their number on the application. I knew I would never live on the streets again.

I felt like a new person as I gave the girl the application. She smiled and told me they would call me for an interview.

As I walked down the street knowing I had to call home, I wondered what I would say. My hands shook as I put money in the phone and dialed the number. When Mom answered I stood there speechless as my mind searched for the right words. I just said, "Mom, this is Mike." She started crying and asked where I was. I told her I was in Springfield. She said, "I've been praying for you, son, praying that you would come home to us. Where have you been?"

That was the hard part. I just said, "I've been around, Mom. I will try to explain later."

She told me to please stay on the line while she got my father. Dad sounded old and out of breath when he answered.

"Is that really you, son? Where have you been? We have searched everywhere for you."

"Dad, I'm sorry. I had a lot of things I had to work out. Would it be okay if I come home? I need to get off the street and get my life back in order. I promise I won't become a problem for you."

"Good Lord, son, don't talk like that. You know you are always welcome here. Hell, boy, this is your home. Where are you? Can I come and get you?"

"That would be great, Dad. I'm at the Woodshed Café over on the old bypass."

He said, "I know where that is, boy. Just grab a cup of coffee and we will be there shortly."

I felt a lot of remorse as I hung up and went inside. When my coffee came I was shaking so badly I could hardly hold the cup. Sadness and a feeling of relief washed over me as I sat there staring out the window and thinking about my life.

The last five years seemed like a bad dream. Had I really been through all of that? Most soldiers return from war to a hero's welcome. For me, it has been a long road home. Most of us just drifted back one at a time to a country that seemed too busy to care, or else to a bunch of protesters that seemed to hate us.

What will my folks think when they see me with my dirty clothes, long hair and everything I own stuck in a pillow case? I thought about getting up and leaving, but knew I couldn't do that to them. Part of me wished I had never called and the other part is so anxious to see them I can no longer sit still. I paid for my coffee and walked out to the parking lot.

I was afraid to look when a car turned into the lot. I took a deep breath as I realized it wasn't them. At least I had a few more minutes to get myself together. Then someone called my name and I turned to see my folks coming toward me. Mom was half running, half walking and Dad had a look on his face like he was seeing me for the first time. I wanted to run to them and to run away at the same time, so like a dumb idiot I just stood there with a smirk on my face.

Mom almost knocked me down as she grabbed and hugged me with both arms, all the while trying to talk through trembling lips. Dad just took hold of my arm and looked into my eyes, saying, "It's good to see you again, son." Mom kept crying and asking where I had been and why I didn't come home.

Tears ran down my face as I held her tight and said, "I wanted to, Mom, but it's a long story. War does things to you, things that are hard to live with and to explain."

Dad put his arm around my shoulder, squeezed my arm and pulled us with him. "Come on, son, let's go home. We can talk about all this later."

He held the keys out to me when we got to the car asking if I wanted to drive. I said, "No thanks, I'm a little out of practice. I would probably wreck it before we got out of the lot."

"Any place you want to go?" Dad asked.

"I need a change of clothes unless you still have my old ones."

Mom spoke up and said, "Everything you had is still in your room just as you left it."

"Well, let's go home then. I need a good meal, a hot shower and about a week's sleep."

Chapter Twenty-Five

The ride home was quiet as the car bounced along the country roads. We each sat staring at the landscape, lost in our own thoughts. I knew both Mom and Dad had a million questions to ask, but they just tried to make small talk. I was happy to be headed home, yet I wanted to distance myself from these people. It was like I was in a car with strangers. Here I was with my own mother and father, but I didn't feel the love for them that I once had.

The farm still looked the same as we drove up the lane. My old shepherd dog Sparky came out to meet us as we pulled into the yard. I got out of the back seat and opened Mom's door. The dog just stood there and looked at me. He stepped back as I reached out to rub his head and walked over to dad.

Mom asked if I was hungry.

"I could eat something; you don't eat too often living on the street."

I realized I shouldn't have said anything about that, but figured the best way was to get everything out in the open. She said, "I will fix us a sandwich and then we can talk."

Dad said, "Come on, boy, and I'll show you what I have done with the farm while we were waiting."

As we walked toward the barn, he said, "You'll be glad to know I got rid of all them dang milk cows. All I have now is beef, and I raise a little grain and hay to feed them. It doesn't pay as much, but we get by and it's a lot less work."

We walked around the place until Mom came out on the porch wiping her hands on her apron and hollered that our sandwiches were ready.

I followed Dad into the house and waited for him to wash up. When I walked into the bath, one look at myself in the mirror made me jump. I didn't realize I looked that bad. My hair was stringy and needed combing, and my eyes looked dark and sunken. I had lost a lot of weight, and my clothes were a wrinkled mess. No wonder the folks looked at me the way they did.

I washed my hands, splashed some water on my face and ran my wet hands through my hair, pushing it back as best as I could. There was a comb and brush but I wouldn't use it until I have time to clean up. Mom motioned toward the table as I came in, told me to sit wherever I liked and to help myself.

Dad passed me a sandwich as Mom filled my glass with tea. As we sat enjoying our food, I was waiting for the first question.

Dad asked, "So where have you been hiding? We have looked all over Springfield for you."

I took a sip of tea and said, "I've lived under about every bridge in Greene County for the last couple of years. It has been cold and lonely, even scary at times."

Mom asked, "Mike, why would you live like that when you have a home right here?"

"It's hard to explain, Mom. I didn't have money for a place to live, and I have problems caused from the war."

"Well, surely the veteran's hospital would have helped you."

"They tried, Mom, but there are things I just had to work out on my own.

I still have a long way to go, but think I can do it."

Dad said, "Well, by god boy, you're home now and you're going to stay home no matter what problems you got. Your Mom and I can help you put that damn war behind you."

Mom said, "It seems like you boys who come back from Vietnam have a lot more problems than other soldiers did. Why is that?"

I thought for a moment and said, "When other soldiers came home they were welcomed by a ticker-tape parade with politicians giving speeches thanking them for what they had done. We were snuck in the back door, one at a time, told not to even wear our uniforms because of the war protesters at the airports. They treated us like we were criminals; it seemed our country was ashamed of us. We were called murderers and baby-killers.

It was like we never had been in a war, the people didn't give a damn if we came home or not.

"Men died there, Mom. Young men like me were crippled for life, both physically and mentally, yet people treated them like dirt. Most of us didn't volunteer to go over there; we went because our country sent us.

"I killed people over there, Mom, people who were trying to kill me. But people got killed who were innocent, too. I can shut my eyes and still see their faces, yet I can't remember the names of my buddies who were killed. We gave new men nicknames so we never knew who they really were. You didn't want to make friends with someone because it hurt so much when they got wasted.

"I have a hard time sleeping, Mom, and I have some horrible dreams. So if I am asleep, don't touch me to wake me up. Just holler at me. I awake pretty violently sometimes and I might hurt you."

Dad spoke up and said, "This is enough of that for awhile. You clean up and get some rest. We can talk more later. It's good to have you home, son."

Mom said, "The towels and washcloths are still in the same place in the cupboards so use what you want. There is shampoo on the shelf by the shower."

I laughed and ran my hand through my hair as I stood up. "I think I need to wash this, do you? I've got to get it cut."

Mom reached out and grabbed me, hugging me close as tears ran down her face. "Mike, I'm so glad you're home. I prayed for you every night, wondering where you were and what you were doing. And, Mike, you have got to call Sarah. She has something to tell you, and she is always asking where you are."

I just gave her a tight squeeze and said, "Okay, Mom, but first I am going to see if I can find some clean clothes that still fit me and take a long hot shower."

The shower felt great. My old clothes were a little loose on me, but they fit. Three of Mom's home-cooked meals every day will soon take care of that. I wondered what Sarah has to tell me. Surely she hasn't waited for me all this time. She probably wants to tell me she has found someone else, and I can't blame her, even though I still have strong feelings for her. Anyway, I don't have any intention to call. She has probably forgotten that I exist and was just trying to be nice to Mom.

After the shower I would have loved to lie down and sleep for a few hours, but knew I had to visit with Mom and Dad.

Going into the living room where Dad was watching the news, I sat down and tried to read a magazine, something I hadn't done in years. Dad turned the television off and asked if I wanted to talk. Mom asked if I wanted some coffee. I said, "Sounds good to me, just make it black." I hadn't drunk much coffee living on the street. She brought both Dad and me a cup, then sat down beside me and said, "So, Mike, tell us about living on the street."

"Well, Mom, I got the hell beat out of me by a bunch of boys one night, which put me in the hospital for several weeks with a broken jaw."

Dad said, "I read in the paper awhile back where some boys were jumped and beaten pretty severely by a bunch of street people. One of them was even cut with a knife. It seems like it isn't safe to walk the streets anymore."

"Dad, it isn't safe to live on them anymore, either. I know several homeless people who have been hurt pretty badly by some of those punks. If they got slapped around a little then they got what they asked for."

Dad looked at me and asked, "You didn't have anything to do with that beating, did you?"

I just smiled and said, "Dad, you know I wouldn't do anything like that."

Mom just sat there and sipped her coffee saying, "I can't believe you actually slept on the ground under bridges when you had a warm comfortable bed here at home. Mike, it just doesn't make any sense. We're your parents and we could have gotten you any help that you would have needed."

"I know that, Mom, but at the time my mind wasn't working right. I didn't want you and Dad to see the trouble I was going through."

"Well, what changed your mind and made you want to come home?"

"After my last beating I got scared and fed up with living like that. I wanted to get a job and change my life. I was filling out a job application and needed an address to put down for a residence, and I didn't think any bridge in Greene County would look good on the application.

"It's that simple, Mom. I decided to put in for a job one day when I was reading the want ads, and that is why I'm here. I wish I could say it was out of love for you and Dad, or because I was homesick. Truth is, I missed you guys and wanted to come home, but the nightmares I kept having made me afraid to be around people. I hope I never have one while I'm here. If I do, just give me time to wake up and I will be okay."

"What do you think causes them?"

"Mom, I was questioning an old Vietnamese man in a rice paddy because one of our men had stepped on a land mine and I thought he had planted it. So I was threatening him with my weapon and it went off just as this old woman came up over the dike. I killed this old man and the woman screamed and beat on me as the water turned blood-red all around us.

"We walked off leaving her there alone, holding onto his body. I can still see it all every time I lie down and try to close my eyes. We were there to help those people and I killed an innocent old man. I hope this explains some of it for you, Mom, because I don't want to talk about it ever again."

Dad sat there looking at me and said, "Son, in war innocent people get killed. It is part of war. God knows you didn't shoot that man on purpose--it was an accident. People get killed accidentally every day and it's just a fact of life we have to live with."

Mom said, "Sarah should be here while are talking about this, then she would understand why you were gone so long. I should call her; she lives only a couple miles from here."

"Mom, Sarah doesn't care about me anymore. She is probably married or at least engaged and out of college by now and working somewhere. I don't think she will be interested in me anymore, Mom."

"Mike, she calls here at least twice a week asking if we have heard from you. She really wants to talk to you and has something very important to tell you."

"Yeah, I bet she does--like she has met someone else and doesn't want anything to do with me ever again."

"She lives close by and is working for one of the colleges. I promised her I wouldn't tell you this, but I have to. Mike, you have a two-year-old son and he looks just like you did at that age."

Dad looked at me and smiled, saying, "Yes, boy, you now have something else to think about besides that damn war."

I just sat there too stunned to say anything. Mom was looking at me with this strange expression on her face, like you have really done it this time, son.

I said, "Please don't call her tonight. Give me a little time to think about all of this. I need to sleep on it, but doubt if I will get much rest tonight."

Chapter Twenty-Six

My bed felt good. I lay there staring into the darkness thinking about Sarah and of being a father. Never in my most vivid thoughts did it ever cross my mind that I had fathered a child.

Maybe this is what I need. Like Dad said, I now have something else to think about besides that damn war. What will I say to Sarah, that I'm sorry I ran out on her and she couldn't find me? How can I tell her I just lost myself on the streets for the last couple of years? Somehow I don't think she is going to buy my story no matter what I say.

Looking at a picture of me and Dad when I was about five, I try to picture what my son will look like. I like the idea of being a father and having a son to teach how to do things. I wonder what she has told the boy about me.

God, I hate to see morning come. I have faced a lot of bad things in my life but this is one I would like to skip. I want to see my son and be with Sarah, to hold her and tell her I love her. But how can I do that after what I have done? Will she believe me or just think I am telling her that because of the boy? I have always loved her but never wanted to admit it.

I fell asleep thinking about all of this. It was almost ten in the morning before Mom called and asked if I was going to sleep all day.

I got up and showered and shaved. After getting dressed I walked into the kitchen to face Mom and the day. Dad was reading the paper and sipping on a cup of coffee. He laid the paper down and looked up over his glasses at me. "What have you got planned for today? Looks like you slept okay last night."

"I need to go to the bank, get a haircut and renew my driver license if you have time to chauffer me around."

Dad laughed and said, "I'll take you anyplace you want to go, even by Sarah's workplace if you like."

Mom jumped in and said, "I don't think that is such a good idea to spring Mike on her where she works."

Dad just laughed again and said, "I was only joking with the boy, Mother, don't get your drawers in a twist."

"Well, he should call her today. And I am sure she will be over here with Michael as soon as she finds out you're home."

After breakfast Dad drove me into Springfield to the bank. They had gotten my account straightened out and replaced my money that had been taken. I drew out five-hundred dollars and left the rest in a checking account. Then we drove to the motor vehicle department where we waited a couple hours to get my license renewed.

Dad was pretty quiet through most of this. He finally asked what I was going to do about Sarah and my son.

"Well, Dad, I am going to marry her if she will have me. The boy needs a father and I do love her."

"Then don't forget to tell her that before you ask her to marry you. Women are funny about things." He laughed and said, "Let's have lunch before you get that haircut. I'll try to remember some other things to tell you about women that will keep your ass out of trouble."

After lunch we drove over to a little town called Willard where Dad always gets his hair cut. The barber wasn't very busy so we didn't have to wait long. He had cut my hair when I was a kid and pretended to remember me. I doubt if he really did.

Dad asked if there was anything else I needed to get before we went home. I said; "Yeah, some courage. I would rather have my ass kicked than call Sarah."

Dad chuckled and said, "You're on your own there, boy. You should have thought about that while you were having fun making babies."

"I guess I didn't realize how easy it was to make one; I sort of got carried away in the process."

"Well, son, one thing for sure--you're going to have the rest of your life to remember and a son to remind you every time you look at him. And, if you're lucky, a good wife to see that you don't forget."

"I know I have to call her, but think I will wait until she gets off work. Will you take Mom out to dinner or someplace so I can be alone when I call? I don't have any idea how she is going to react, and something tells me it isn't going to be good."

The more I think about it, the sicker I get. Damn, doesn't the world ever get done kicking you?

Dad looked over at me as he pulled into the yard. "You look a little peaked, son, are you all right?"

"I guess, other than having a bad case of fear."

"You'll make out okay, just tell her the truth and about the problems you've been having. And by all means, don't forget to tell her how much you love her and how happy you are to have a child. The important thing is let her know you want her and the boy, that you will work and make a good home for both of them."

Mom came out to the porch, gave us each a hug and asked if we got all our problems solved while we were out.

I just smiled and said, "Mom, I believe my problems are about to begin."

She asked if we wanted a cold drink. I sat at the table, grabbed a cookie and nibbled on it as Mom poured the tea. Dad looked at me half- smiling as he took a drink. Is he trying to cheer me up or is he having fun watching me sweat? I think he is just happy that I am home.

The phone rings and I almost spill my tea. I can tell by the expression on Mom's face that it has to be Sarah. She talks a minute then holds her hand over the mouthpiece and tells me it's Sarah. Mom tells her to hold on, that someone wants to talk to her. That surely was an overstatement--I did not want to talk.

I took the phone as Dad grabbed Mom by the hand and dragged her out the back door. I said, "Hello." Everything was quiet for a moment, then she said, "Who is this?" I knew all hell was about to break loose as I said, "This is Mike."

She took a deep breath and let out a big sigh as she loaded up.

"Mike Malloy, where in the fucking hell have you been? You bastard, I have been looking for your ass for more than two years now. You son of a bitch, you knock me up then run and hide like some damned coward.

"How many other little bastards have you fathered and run out on? I'm coming over and your ass had better be there. I've got a million damn questions for your sorry ass and you better be working on some answers."

She slammed the phone down so hard it hurt my ear.

I looked out and Mom was still trying to pull away from Dad. I know they both would like to hear what's going on. I wish they could and I couldn't. I walked out and told them Sarah is on her way over and could we be alone for awhile?

"I don't know how much screaming and cussing is going to take place, but I would just as soon you two don't have to hear it."

Mom smiled at me and went to get her purse, telling me to be gentle and not to lose my temper. They drove off without asking any questions.

I stood there in the yard watching the dust from their car make a long trail up the road. Walking over to the picnic table, I sat down and stared across the field. Something touched my leg. I looked down as Sparky sniffed me. I scratched his ears, telling him at least you are finally making up to me.

I sat there with a knot in my stomach that grew bigger as I saw a car coming down our lane. I wanted to get up and run, to go hide and never be seen. This fear was worse than what I had faced in Nam. Over there I didn't know what was coming. Here I did, and I knew I didn't have a weapon to fight with. I didn't have a plan or words thought out to use. Hell, I doubt if I can even talk.

I walked out to meet the car as Sarah drove into the yard. She was crying when she got out of her vehicle. Even through the tears I thought, God, what a beautiful woman she had become.

She pulled away from me as I reached out. She stood there looking at me as tears streamed down her face. I thought about how pretty she was and the love I felt for her. I grabbed her and held her so tight she couldn't get loose. Finally she quit fighting and released great body-shaking sobs as she rested her head on my chest and cried.

"Damn you, Mike Malloy."

"Sarah, I'm so sorry. I just didn't believe you cared for me anymore. I never had any idea that we had a child. I would have been with you all the way had I known."

She pulled away and stood there dabbing at her tears.

"Well, you sure as hell didn't check with anybody to try and find out, did you? Where in the damn hell have you been for the last two years? No one knew where you were, not even your parents. They came to my college graduation, where I stood with a belly so big my gown wouldn't hide it. They were there when I gave birth to their grandson. Where was the father? God only knew. I heard he was hiding under some damn bridge someplace, sucking on a bottle of cheap wine. You ought to be sorry, you rotten bastard. I don't see how in hell you EVER had nerve enough to show your face around here again after what you have put me and your parents through."

I placed my hands on each side of her face and kissed her. She pulled away saying, "I suppose you think that makes everything okay. You want to go make another baby and go hide again? That's about all you're good for."

That one hurt.

"Please, Sarah, don't say things like that. I would like to make you my wife and have lots of babies with you, but I would never run out on you again and you know that."

She stood there trembling as she searched for words. "Mike, I have built up so much hate and resentment for you over the last two years. You don't know how hard your parents and I have searched for you. I cursed you every time we couldn't find you. We knew you were in Springfield. The VA didn't have any idea where you were, and the guy who runs the mission said you showed up there only a few times. Would it have been so hard to have picked up a phone and called one of us? I know you have problems caused from that damn war, but wouldn't it have been easier to let the people who love you help solve those problems?"

"Sarah, I'm sorry, I know I messed up. Please give me another chance. I was so screwed up from that war, I just went with what my mind told me to do. I love you so much, I thought of you every day wondering where you were and what you were doing. I just couldn't seem to break the hold the streets had on me. I wanted to call you, to come looking for you. I walked by the college many times hoping you had come back. There is nothing I want more than for us to be together and raise our son as a family."

"Yeah, and how do I know that tomorrow you won't be gone again? Gone someplace where even God can't find you. Or that you won't crawl into another bottle and numb your mind to the world and everyone who cares. No! Mike, I need a lot more than that. I have embarrassed my family, your family and all our friends, plus I have been humiliated beyond belief. That little boy you call your son is classified as a bastard child, do you think you can change all of that with just a few sweet words?"

"I'm back now, Sarah, and I don't care how tough it gets. I'm going to get a job and support my son and you, if you'll let me."

"Mike, I want to believe you."

Facing her, I spread my arms and pleaded.

"Then help me, don't turn me away. I know I've been wrong, but when your mind plays games with you it's a hard thing to fight. Living on the streets gets to be a way of life, it grips hold of you. It is a cold, lonely, miserable way to survive, even scary and dangerous at times. It's just you against the elements, no one to tell you what to do, where to go. All you do is try to find a warm place to sleep and something to eat.

"I have slept in open sheds, in unlocked trucks and cars, under people's houses. I've even gone in and eaten food out of their refrigerators when they left the house open. I didn't see it as stealing--it was surviving. There are a lot of men and a few women out there who need help, but they don't realize it. The street has gripped them and become a way of life. A way of life I will never go back to."

I took her by the hand and we walked out back to the picnic table. I held her close, trying to say how much I loved her, and how I wanted us to spend the rest of our lives together. She pushed me away and sat down.

"Mike, when I came over here I intended to tear you apart, to let you know how much I hated you for what you have done, to take our son and leave, never speaking to you again. I sure didn't expect you to say you loved me and wanted to marry me. Are you sure it's not just because of our son?"

"I always planned on asking you to marry me, long before I ever knew we had a kid. Only I figured that by now you had fallen for some college dude and was happily married living in a little cottage someplace. That's one of the reasons I never bothered to call. Where is our son? I would like to see him."

"He is with your parents. I met them on the way over here and he wanted to go with his grandma and grandpa, which I figured was a good idea. He didn't need to hear all the cuss words I had planned for you. And now I'm so damned mad because I'm not mad enough to say some of the ones I had planned."

She looked up at me and smiled. "Down deep I still care for you, Mike Malloy, you rotten son of a bitch."

She walked around the table, grabbed me by the hair, pulled my head back and kissed me long and hard, yanking some hair out in the process. Pushing my head sideways she said, "Your folks and our son are going to be back here in a few moments, and damn you, don't embarrass me by trying to be all lovey-dovey. If you do, I'm going to slap the hell out of you. You've got a long way to go and a lot to prove to me before I'll ever be with you again."

We sat at the table across from each other not talking, just looking at one another. I could see the hurt and frustration in her beautiful blue eyes. Reaching out, I took hold of her hand and gently rubbed it, all the time watching for a change of expression, anything that would tell me she cared or that she still loved me. All I could see was a cold, hard stare that penetrated clear through my body. Her blue eyes never blinked. She just sat there and looked a hole through me, like she was searching for something, maybe a soft spot, or a chink in my already battered armor.

There was no softness in her look, but a hard warning that told me I might have one chance and one chance only, that if I screwed this one up I would never get another.

Chapter Twenty-Seven

We were brought back to reality by the sound of a car coming up the lane. I helped Sarah up and took hold of her hand as we walked out toward the front of the house. She pulled loose from my grip as my parents got out of the vehicle.

Adrenalin shot through my body as I saw my son for the first time. Sarah walked over and took him from my mother. Carrying the boy toward me, she said, "Michael, here is someone I want you to say hi to. This is your father. Can you say 'Hi Daddy'?" The words sounded strange, as the boy squirmed in his mother's arms looking at me.

Reaching out I took his small hand in mine and said, "Hi son." The boy pulled away from me as I looked at him. I couldn't find the words to say anything more. Finally Mom spoke up and said, "Let's all go inside before the mosquitoes start to bite."

Sarah put little Michael down and we each held his hand and helped him up the steps onto the porch.

She took him with her into the kitchen where Mom was fixing us a cold drink. Dad and I sat in the front room with neither of us saying anything. I thought how nice it would be to have my own home and a family. I did have a family of sorts, and it would be for real if I don't mess this up.

Dad said, "Well, what do you think of your son?"

"I believe he is a little bigger than I was at that age. He does look a lot like I did, according to all the pictures I have seen of me as a boy."

"How did things go between you two? I didn't see any blood."

"Well, Dad, you haven't looked in my shorts. I never got such an ass- chewing in all my life, and the swear words she used she must have been saving up for a long time. I sure as heck don't want to make that woman mad ever again."

"Well, you were gone for more than two years, and she saw that as running out on her. What do you plan on doing?"

"I asked her to marry me but she said I had a lot to prove first. I guess I will take it slow and see if I can earn some respect and forgiveness. First I have got to get a job and earn some money. I get a little disability from the military but they will probably take that as soon as I can make a living."

Mom and Sarah brought the refreshments in where Dad and I were. I couldn't keep my eyes off Sarah or my son. Every time our eyes met she would look away. This hurt but I guess I can see why. I tried to get my son to come to me but he held tight to his mom.

I was getting stressed out by the situation so I got up and went outside. I sat on the porch steps hoping Sarah would come out. As I sat there tears started to run down my cheeks. I couldn't figure out what was happening to me. I didn't want to cry in front of anyone so I got up and walked out to the gate and took a walk through the field down to the pond where I had fished as a kid.

The old willow log was still lying there. It had decayed some but was still solid enough to sit on. I sat down and was overcome with emotions. Tears streamed down my face and my whole body shook. I couldn't stop crying so I just sat there staring through tears at the wind-blown riffles on the water, reliving my whole life. How long I had sat there I don't know.

Hearing something, I turned and there stood Sarah, not saying a word. I didn't know what to say or do so I just sat and continued to stare at the water.

After what seemed like and eternity, she lay her hand on my shoulder and said, "Mike I'm sorry."

This brought forth a flood of tears that I couldn't stop. I stood up and hugged her tightly, wetting her blouse, saying, "Please forgive me, Sarah. I never meant to ever hurt you or cause you pain. I got so wrapped up in my own problems I forgot about the people who mean the most to me. God, I love you more than life itself. Give me a chance to prove that to you."

Slowly she pushed me away and held me at arm's length. Looking into my eyes she said, "I still care a lot for you, Mike, but there is a lot of hurt I have to get over. I'm not about to rush into anything that is likely to cause me that much pain again. Let's just take it one day at a time. Michael needs his father and I want to give him the chance to grow up with you. But you have a lot to prove to both of us and I'm not about to let you come into his life and hurt him like you did me by disappearing again."

I turned, squatted down and dipped my hands into the cold pond water and washed my face. Wiping my wet hands through my hair, I took hold of her hand and we walked back toward the house. I kept looking at her, thinking what a fool I have been. Can I ever make it right?

She never spoke a word as I led her down the path through the tall grass. It was as if she was lost in a deep thought and didn't want to be disturbed.

When we got to the gate, she pulled loose from my hand and went into the house alone. I stopped and looked at my own reflection in the glass of the back door. I didn't want to go in looking too bad. I have caused enough trouble for the people I love without upsetting them again.

Sarah was getting Michael ready to leave when I came in. I asked her to stay awhile longer but she said she had a lot to do and had to go to work tomorrow. "I have a job, Mike. Something you ought to be getting."

I forced a smile and told her I was waiting for an interview with a security firm driving an armored car.

"Well, you should be trained for that, especially if you have to shoot someone."

I didn't like that remark but let it go. It did get me thinking about what I might be getting myself into.

I walked with her and the boy to her car, opened the door and picked up my son. I held him for a moment before putting him in the vehicle. Sarah got in, shut the door and rolled down the window as she started the motor. I stood there with my hand resting on the door looking at her. She never met my gaze, just patted my hand and said, "Take care, Mike. Call me," as she put the car in reverse and backed away.

I watched her drive out of sight and prayed that she wasn't driving out of my life for good. I have never felt so sad and lonely since the loss of my friend Tex Johnson. I made a vow to myself that I would get her back no matter what it takes.

After Sarah and my son left I walked back out to the pond. I wanted to be alone, to sort out my thoughts and think about the life I had ahead of me. The bad dreams I had been having were the least of my worries now. I have got to get a job and start building a life for myself and my family. It angered me to think I have wasted more than two years living on the streets. I know that I am a better man than to let a few bad situations get me down. Hell, I have always been a fighter and it's time to gear up and start fighting for what I want in life.

I got up and just walked around the farm looking at Dad's cattle. It was almost dark by the time I got back to the house. Mom had a hundred questions to ask and I really didn't want to answer any of them. But I sat and talked with her and Dad until bedtime. I was really tired when I lay down and it wasn't long before I was asleep. Morning came quickly; I had slept well with no bad dreams. Maybe that old army doctor knew what he was talking about when he told me all I needed was to get something else on my mind.

At breakfast I asked Dad if I could borrow the car or pickup, that I needed to make a quick trip to Texas before I get tied down with a job. I explained that I had made a promise to a dead friend that I would go see his parents when I got home. They live in Austin. He was a sergeant I served with and, after three tours in Nam, he got killed in a chopper crash on his way home.

"Take whichever one you want, son."

Mom spoke up and said, "Why don't you ask Sarah to go with you? We could keep Michael, and it would give you two a chance to talk things over a little more."

"I'll ask her, but don't be surprised if she tells me to go there and stay." "Well, at least call and ask--all she can say is 'No'."

"Believe me, Mom, she can say a lot more than that, and not as gentle as you put it. Things are a long way from being good between us. I hurt her and it is going to take some time for that to heal."

I waited a day before calling her. I didn't want to seem too pushy and also wanted to give her some time to think things over. When she answered, I really didn't know what to say, so I just said, "Hi, this is Mike." There was only silence for what seemed like a long time. Finally I said, "If this is a bad time I can call back later."

She said, "Hold on a minute," so like an idiot I stood there holding a phone to my ear listening to the buzzing and crackling of the line. I felt like hanging up.

"I'm sorry," she said when she came back. "I had Michael in the tub giving him his bath, and he loves the water so I have to watch him pretty closely."

She asked if I could call back in about twenty minutes so that she could put him to bed. Putting the phone to his ear, she asked if I wanted to say goodnight to my son. I felt sort of foolish but said goodnight to him. She tried to get him to say something but all he could do was murmur something. I guess I am going to have to get used to this kid thing.

After she hung up, I walked out on the porch and sat down. Sparky came up and I scratched his ears as I told him my tale of woe. He really didn't seem interested but pretended to be a good listener as long as I scratched him.

I thought about how I was going to ask Sarah to go to Austin with me. I should just go by myself and take some time to think things over. I needed to be alone for awhile but I was afraid if I tried that I would never come back. After waiting for what seemed a lot longer than twenty minutes, I called Sarah back.

She seemed to be in a good mood so we just talked about the boy and anything else that came up. I gradually got up nerve enough to ask her if she was interested in taking a trip with me for a few days.

She asked what I had in mind. I explained about Tex and how I had promised to go see his parents. To my surprise she agreed to go, saying, "This will give us a good chance to talk without all the distractions, that is if your mom will keep Michael."

I about fell over and had to fight to keep from showing my excitement.

Sarah needed a couple days to get things arranged at work, so we agreed to go the first of the week.

I spent the rest of the week helping Dad around the farm. Calling Sarah each evening, we would talk for hours. I could tell she was softening up some, but still had moments where she would revert and chew my ass good and proper.

Monday finally arrived and Sarah showed up early with Michael. I had Dad's pick-up ready to go, but she insisted on taking her car and doing the driving, saying, "Mike, you haven't driven in several years and I wouldn't trust you in a big city like Austin."

I put my gear in her car, got the boy settled, and we were on our way.

Chapter Twenty-Eight

Once we were on the interstate, Sarah opened that car up like she was a fighter pilot on a scraping run. I asked her if she was in a hurry. She just gave me a funny look and said, "Mike, you have been out of the mainstream so long you would get your ass run over out here." I agreed and told her I was glad she came along.

I sat back and tried to relax, hoping she didn't get us both killed. I would hate to think I survived Nam just to get my butt scattered all over the interstate.

There was no freeway when I was learning to drive, so I had never driven on one. I'm glad she's driving; I would have pulled off at the first exit and taken a back road to God only knows where. My knuckles were white from gripping the sides of the seat and my mouth was dry as a bone.

All the while she just kept talking and dodging in and out of traffic like we were on some thrill ride at a carnival. I hoped it didn't become bumper cars--at this speed there wouldn't be much left.

I picked up a road map and tried to read it. Sarah said, "I know where I am going." I thought, me, too, but I don't want to get there quite this quickly.

She took an off-ramp as we neared the Arkansas line and pulled into a viewpoint. We got out and looked at the Ozark Mountains stretching out before us. Some of the deep gullies dropped below sea level, winding out as far as you could see. I was overcome by the vastness of the country. All of it was covered with a heavy forest of oak, maple, elm, and hickory.

Putting my arm around Sarah, I squeezed her tightly and asked if she wanted to go for a stroll in the forest. She smiled, gave me a quick kiss and guided me back to the car. "We have a long way to drive today, Mike, so relax and enjoy."

We came into Little Rock after what seemed like five or six agonizing hours. She asked if I was hungry. I said, "No, I've been chewing my tongue for the whole trip, and I think I swallowed it a couple of times." She just looked at me and laughed.

We had to make a stop for gas. There was a little sandwich joint next to the station so we went in and had a burger. I was feeling queasy from the high-speed run we had just made and it felt good to be sitting still again. I looked at Sarah and she wanted to know what the smirk on my face was about. I just grinned and said, "I was thinking what a hell of a fighter pilot you would make."

She said, "I actually once thought about being a pilot but decided it was too much of a career for me. I want a family and a husband, not necessarily in that order. Seems like I already have a start on a family-- know where I can find a husband?"

"Yes, I just happen to know this good-looking man who might be interested. All you need to do is find a preacher."

"You're funny, but shouldn't we think about getting a license first?"

"I have a better idea: let's just find a room and start on the family. We can do all that other stuff later."

"Dream on, Mikey, it ain't going to happen. We might share a room but you can bet your sweet cheeks we're going have separate beds. You might as well forget about what you have in mind. I came with you so we could be together and talk about what we want in life."

I knew I was losing this conversation. As soon as we were back on the road I shut my eyes and went to sleep. It was getting late in the day when I woke up.

"Where are we?"

"We just crossed over into Louisiana. We should spend the night in Vicksburg--there is a civil war museum there I would like to visit."

We found a Western States Motor Inn that we could afford and stopped for the night. The room was nice and clean with two large beds. I said, "You know it's a shame for us to disturb both beds and make all that work for the poor gal who has to clean the rooms."

"Fine, you can sleep on the floor. That way you won't disturb your bed."

She started undressing and said she wanted to take a shower before I bought her dinner. Stripping off all her clothes she walked past naked as a picked bird's ass, hitting me in the face with her towel as she went by.

I just sat there and watched her, thinking what a great body she had and wondering what game she was playing now. Hell, I thought, I will just call her bluff. I took off my clothes, walked in and opened the shower door. She protested at first and tried to push me out. I just squeezed in against her and pulled the door shut. Picking up the soap, I washed her back as I held her close, pressing her firm breasts against my chest. She tried to push me away. Putting the soap back in the holder, I took her head in my hands and kissed her long and hard. After a brief struggle she murmured, "What the hell," and kissed me back. We stood there holding each other while the water streamed off our naked bodies.

Gently I released her and opened the door. Grabbing a towel I wrapped it around my wet body, not wanting to push things too quickly. I shaved while she finished her shower and washed her hair. When she shut the water off and stepped out, I wrapped a towel around her and started drying her. She turned her back as I rubbed it dry, reaching around I cupped a breast in each hand and kissed her on the neck. I could feel a tremble run through her body as I whispered, "I love you, lady. Someday you're going to make some lucky man a good wife, and I hope that man is me."

She turned and pulled me close to her, kissing me for a long time. Pushing away, she said, "Finish your shower and get dressed. I'm hungry."

"Yeah, me too, and all I need is right here." "Take a cold shower, Mike, you'll be okay."

She was dressed and ready to go by the time I got out of the shower. That had put a damper on what I had in mind. Do women get a big thrill out of getting a man worked up, then leaving him cold and wanting?

Well, hell, I have been down that road enough times to be able to read the signs. I got dressed and asked if she was ready to go. There was a café attached to the motel so we walked over and had dinner. It was a clean, quiet little place and the food was good.

There was live music playing in the lounge, so after dinner we went in, had a glass of wine and listened to the band.

I asked Sarah if she would like to dance. She said, "I didn't know you danced."

"I don't, but I like to hold the ladies while they do."

She stood up laughing and told me I could hold her while she tried. I held her close and slowly we moved with the music. It felt good holding her and smelling the aroma of her body.

We stayed on the dance floor swaying to the music in our minds even after the band had stopped playing. I could have held her like this all evening. Taking her hand, I led her past our table, grabbed our things, and walked back toward the motel. The wine and music had relaxed Sarah to the point that she was holding me pretty tightly by the time we got back to the room.

I unlocked the door, picked her up and carried her over to the bed. Closing the door I sat down beside her and slowly unbuttoned her blouse one button at a time. Pulling it off over her shoulders and letting it drop to the floor, she lay there trembling like a schoolgirl doing this for the first time.

Taking hold of my hand, she said, "Mike, I told myself I wouldn't do this, but I love you so damn much."

Pushing me back on the bed, she turned and kissed me until I thought I would smother, all the while I kept rubbing her back, feeling the softness of her skin and fumbling with that damn bra fastener one-handed, wondering why in the hell they don't put a quick release on them.

She got tired of my fumbling and stood up. "I see you haven't had much practice with these," she said as she took it off, threw it at me and walked off into the bathroom.

I undressed, turned the bed down and crawled in between the sheets, wondering all the while if I was doing the right thing.

Vicksburg was a typical southern city with lots of little shops and friendly people. We found the museum and spent a couple hours going through it, looking at all the old photos. Some of them took me back to Vietnam, to all the blood and carnage I had seen and lived through.

It suddenly dawned on me that I hadn't had a bad dream in more than two weeks. Had I done all that to myself by not returning to the people I loved?

Sarah spoke, jarring me out of my dilemma. "We better get moving if we want to get to Austin before dark."

Following a map, we took the back roads through much of Texas, enjoying the farms, ranches and small towns along the way. It was getting late by the time we got close to Austin. Sarah wanted to stop but I wanted to get into the city so we could look up Tex's folks in the phone book and ask if it was okay to visit.

We finally found at a place called Texas's Best Motor Lodge. I grabbed a phone book as soon as we got settled in the room. After going through about five pages of Johnson's with a dozen different spellings; I couldn't find a Theodore Lincoln listed. Sarah told me not to worry, that we could go to the Chamber of Commerce and they would find them if they were still in Austin.

Looking at a map at the front desk we found Johnson Avenue. It wasn't far from where we were. There was a restaurant and coffee shop just down the street so we decided to walk down and have dinner. It was a nice, comfortable little place that was set back from the street farther than the rest of the buildings. There weren't many patrons in the place. Before we had finished eating a couple of police officers came in.

Sarah told me to ask them if they knew Lincoln Johnson. I said, "Yeah, sure. In a city this size I'll bet they will know just where he lives."

Giving me a smug look, she got up and walked over to where they were drinking coffee. When I looked over, she was motioning for me. The officers asked us to sit down and join them. I introduced myself while Sarah and the waitress brought our unfinished meal over to the table. After talking with the two officers, they told me that one of their fellow officers was named Johnson and he was raised over on Johnson Avenue.

I explained to them how I was looking for the parents of a good friend who had been killed in Nam, that I really didn't know his name--we just called him Tex.

"Sounds like our man," said one of the officers. "He spent a couple of tours in Nam. Maybe he is a brother or relative to this guy you're talking about. He's working tonight so we will send him over if you're willing to wait. What did you say your name was?"

"Mike, Mike Malloy."

They got up, said it was good meeting us and walked out to their patrol car.

I told Sarah we couldn't be lucky enough to have a member of Tex's family working for the police.

We waited around for nearly an hour and were just getting ready to leave when another patrol car pulled into the lot. A tall, husky black police officer stepped out of the car. He was a dead ringer for Tex. I told Sarah that guy has to be a brother. Hell, he could be his twin.

My mouth went dry and my knees felt weak as the officer came through the door. He took one look at me and bounded across the restaurant, grabbing me in a bear hug, all the time saying, "Malloy, you son of a bitch, where in the hell did you come from? I figured you were left lying in some damn rice patty or else rotting in a military stockade."

A tear ran down my face as I hugged the man I thought was dead. I had never felt so speechless in my life; all I could do was stand and look at the big guy. He laughed and said, "Hell, Malloy, don't go getting all soft on me now."

"Damn it, Tex, I was told you were killed. We came down here to see your folks and your ugly butt shows up. What did you want me to do? It's like we're looking at a damn ghost. Man, if you had been white, hell, I would have fainted."

"Yeah, I heard about that, messed up my getting-out pay. The damn army wanted to pay my folks the insurance instead of giving me all my back pay. It was some other poor bastard named Johnson. I liked to have never gotten that mess straightened out. I had to go show the dumb idiots that I was still alive. They even ran my prints through the damn FBI files to make sure I was really me."

Asking where we were staying, he said he would be off duty in about an hour and he wanted us to come spend the night. I tried to beg off the best I could as I still had some unfinished business with Sarah. He wouldn't have it, telling me he had a new bride he wanted us to meet and a baby on the way. Sarah said, "I bet she would just love for us to come barging in at this hour of the night. We will wait till morning and you can come get us."

After he left we sat and had another cup of coffee. Sarah said, "You didn't tell me he was black. Not that it makes any difference, he just wasn't who I was looking for. I was expecting some tall Texan with a big white hat."

"Let me tell you he is a red-blooded American and the best damn soldier I ever knew. The police department is lucky to have him. The things he taught me in Nam are why I am still alive. I've never made a better friend. When I heard he was killed I really came apart. I think that is what put me on the downward spiral."

As I walked with Sarah back to the room, I was really jazzed. It had never occurred to me that he might still be alive. I had my speech all ready for his folks and now I can't even remember what I was going to say.

It was hard to sleep. I woke up every hour or so looking at the clock. I couldn't wait to talk to Tex again. I thanked God all night long for keeping him alive. It's strange seeing him again--why does a person accept things that they hear for the truth? It was a real shock seeing him alive after I had thought he was dead. I should have known that it would take more than a helicopter crash to kill him.

The ringing of the phone jarred me out of a sound sleep. Tex wanted to know if we were ready for breakfast. He would meet us at the same café in half an hour. This didn't give us much time as we had been asleep.

Chapter Twenty-Nine

We grabbed a quick shower and hustled out the door, only being a few minutes late. Tex and his wife were waiting. He got up as we came in and walked over to greet us. Leading us over to their table, he introduced us to his wife Pam. She was a beautiful young thing and I could see why Tex chose her.

Pam was one of those people who you feel like you have known your whole life. She was easy to talk to and really made us feel comfortable. We ordered breakfast and talked while we ate.

I knew that Tex would soon ask me what I had been doing, and the thought of having to telling him I had been living on the street was going to be an embarrassment. We finished eating and were having coffee when the subject came up.

"So, Malloy, what have you been up to since you got out of the Army?"

I picked up my cup and took a sip. I looked over it at Sarah who was sitting there with a questioning look on her face. Not knowing what to say, I decided to tell him the truth.

"I've been a bum living on the street until a couple of weeks ago, when I finally decided to get a job and try to put my life back together. When I called my folks and went home, not only did I find out Sarah was still single, but that we had a two-year-old son. Let me tell you, there isn't anything in this world that will bring you back to your senses like finding out you're a father."

"Whatever possessed you to live on the street in the first place?"

Everyone was looking at me like they were eagerly awaiting the answer.

"I kept having these horrible dreams that would wake me up screaming and fighting. It would scare hell out of anyone around me and I was afraid I would hurt someone. So I decided I wanted to be alone. Not having any money or anyplace to live I just started sleeping anywhere I could stay dry. You remember the old man I shot in the rice paddy and the old woman who kept screaming and beating on me? We just walked off and left her sitting there in the bloody water holding onto his body."

"Yeah, I remember you had a few bad memories about that, but I thought the army shrinks cured you and sent you back to the outfit. Hell, man, that old bastard was guilty of planting those mines. We never had another man injured from one after you blew him away. Didn't you read my report?"

"I guess I did, but figured you were just trying to cover my sorry ass. When I got a medal for it, it seemed to make things worse. Man, I came back from that place as screwed up as Hogan's goat."

Pam spoke up and said, "That's enough talk about that damn war. Let's go home where we can visit and I will be a lot more comfortable. The baby is starting to kick and it feels like he's got feet as big as his daddy's."

We all got up and headed out with Tex and me arguing over who was going to pay the check.

Tex had a hundred-acre spread with a big ranch house just outside of Austin. It was fixed up really nice with a corral and barn. He even had a couple of horses.

I said, "You didn't tell me you were a big rancher with lots of land."

He just laughed and said, "Malloy, this is Texas. Most people have backyards bigger than this."

Going in, Pam showed us where to put our things and took us on a quick tour through the house. Tex grabbed us a couple of beers as we went through the kitchen. It was still morning. He smiled and said, "I wonder who it was who said a man can't drink until after five--must have been someone's wife." We all laughed and walked out to their back deck.

He asked if I wanted to go for a ride. I declined, telling him I wasn't a cowboy, but that Sarah would love to go. She had been raised around horses.

Pam and I sat on the deck and watched them saddle up and ride out into the field. She asked me about Tex and how long I knew him.

"I met him in Vietnam and he taught me how to stay alive. He was a great soldier and knew how to train men. He would have made one hell of an officer--his knowledge and leadership kept a lot of men from getting killed."

She said that he won't ever talk about the war; it was like something that had never happened to him. She knew he had a lot of medals but would never say how he came about getting them.

I told her about the time we staged a phony battle that turned out to be real, and how we all got medals for it. She said, "He often talks about you, Mike, wondering whatever happened to you."

"You know, I thought for several years he had gotten killed in a chopper crash on his way home. I about fell over when he walked into the café last night. The reason Sarah and I came down here was to talk with his folks. He's the best friend I ever had, and to know he is still around will make my life a lot better. I spent many lonely nights sleeping under bridges talking to him like he was there with me. People probably thought I was nuts, and maybe I am. He has already told me things that will make what I did over there a lot easier to live with. You've got a good man there, Pam. Take care of him and he will never do you wrong. You just don't find men of his caliber every day; he's that one in a million they talk about, born with more natural qualities than most men ever learn."

She smiled at me and said, "Mike, I believe that you love him as much as I do." "Like I said, they don't come any better."

We watched Sarah and Tex run the horses across the fields. Pam said, "I love to ride, but I don't think junior here would appreciate all that bouncing around."

"I never learned to ride. In fact, I have never been on a horse. To tell you the truth, they scare me. I guess I don't really care for anything that has more legs than I do, except my old dog Sparky."

Tex and Sarah came riding up about that time. Sarah got off and said, "It's your turn now, Mike."

Tex grinned at me and told me to get on. When I admitted I had never been on a horse, he just laughed and climbed down saying, "Well, it's about time you tried it."

Now this was the last thing I wanted to do. Tex let the stirrups out a little, told me how to get on and, at the same time, told me that getting off is easy. "All you have to do is turn loose of everything and fall."

"Yeah, that's what's worrying me."

"Just remember the horse knows what he is doing even if you don't, so just hang on until you get the feel of it."

I put my left foot in the stirrup, grabbed the horn on the saddle and pulled myself up as Tex held the reins. The horse moved sideways, scaring the hell out of me.

Tex mounted his horse and handed me my reins. That dumb horse just stood there.

"How do I get him to go? Better yet, how do I get him to stop?"

"Just lean forward and kick him in the ribs--he'll go. To stop, just lean back and pull back gently on the reins." He showed me with all the skill of a real horseman.

When I leaned forward and kicked the horse, he took off so fast I almost fell off backwards, yanking back on the reins at the same time. The horse stopped so quickly I thought for a minute I was going to go sailing over his head.

Tex laughed and said, "Try it a little more gently next time."

Sarah and Pam were dying of laughter and the poor horse was wondering what was going on.

"Okay, now how do I turn this dumb beast that is smarter than me?" "Just lean the way you want to go and move the opposite side hand over his mane like this," he said as he turned his horse around so easily.

By now my heart is beating in my chest and I am scared to move. Gradually I leaned forward and nudged the horse with my heels. He started off at a walk, jarring the hell out of me with each step.

Tex rode up beside me and told me to stand in the stirrups a little and to rock with the gate of the horse.

I looked at him and asked, "What do we do next for fun, go jump in the cactus?"

He laughed and kneed his horse into a run, knowing damn well that mine would try to keep up.

I was bouncing all over that horse's back trying to stay on as we raced across the field. Once we were at the barn, I managed to get the damn thing stopped. I climbed down and my legs hurt so badly I could hardly stand.

Tex got down laughing and said, "Now wasn't that fun?"

"You always did have a warped sense of humor. No, it wasn't fun. I'll have to go change my shorts after that little venture."

Sarah came out, put her arm around me and said, "Mike, you looked like one of those little bobble-headed dolls in a car window."

"I felt like one, too. I think I would rather walk than ride very far."

Tex pulled the saddles off and hung them on the corral as he turned the horses loose, saying, "We can ride some more this afternoon."

"You and Sarah can. I've had all the cowboy I want for awhile."

We stayed three more days with Tex and Pam, even getting to meet his parents who I had originally come to see. With Tex and Sarah urging me on, I gradually learned to ride a little better, enjoying it and losing my fear of horses.

On the day we left, I gave Tex a big hug and thanked him for all he had done for me. Most of all, I thanked him for being my friend. I told him I am finally home from that damn war, and it's been a long hard road.

Epilogue

Sarah and Mike were married that December with Tex standing as Best Man. They honeymooned in Austin, visiting with Tex and Pam.

Mike Malloy never beat the horrors of war; he was often plagued with bad dreams but, with Sarah's help and understanding, he managed to live with it. Seven years later, he was killed by a drunk driver on one of the back roads he often took to avoid driving the interstate that he feared.

Author's Note

Time has swiftly gone by and forty-some years have passed since I have heard of any of the people mentioned in this story. The names of people and places have been changed to protect those still living.

Some of the events have been dramatized to enhance the story. But the effects of post-traumatic stress disorder (PTSD) are real. Please don't judge the homeless men and women you see on the streets. You never know what events in their lives have put them there.